MURDER AT THE BALLGAME

Because the sides of the bleachers were lined with tarps, it was very dark at first and it took Hannah's eyes a moment or two to adjust to the dimness. When they did, she glimpsed her mother standing a few feet away from her.

"What's wrong?" Hannah asked, moving forward.

"It's . . . it's him!"

Hannah drew her breath in sharply as she saw her mother was standing, with something in her hands, over a bulky figure lying there . . .

Books by Joanne Fluke

Hannah Swensen Mysteries

STRAWBERRY SHORTCAKE MURDER
BLUEBERRY MUFFIN MURDER
LEMON MERINGUE PIE MURDER
FUDGE CUPCAKE MURDER
SUGAR COOKIE MURDER
PEACH COBBLER MURDER
CHERRY CHEESECAKE MURDER
KEY LIME PIE MURDER
CANDY CANE MURDER
CARROT CAKE MURDER
CREAM PUFF MURDER
PLUM PUDDING MURDER
APPLE TURNOVER MURDER
DEVIL'S FOOD CAKE MURDER
GINGERBREAD COOKIE MURDER
CINNAMON ROLL MURDER
RED VELVET CUPCAKE MURDER
BLACKBERRY PIE MURDER
DOUBLE FUDGE BROWNIE MURDER
WEDDING CAKE MURDER
CHRISTMAS CARAMEL MURDER
BANANA CREAM PIE MURDER
RASPBERRY DANISH MURDER
CHRISTMAS CAKE MURDER
CHOCOLATE CREAM PIE MURDER
CHRISTMAS SWEETS
COCONUT LAYER CAKE MURDER
CHRISTMAS CUPCAKE MURDER
TRIPLE CHOCOLATE CHEESECAKE MURDER
CARAMEL PECAN ROLL MURDER
PINK LEMONADE CAKE MURDER
PUMPKIN CHIFFON PIE MURDER
JOANNE FLUKE'S LAKE EDEN COOKBOOK

Suspense Novels

VIDEO KILL
WINTER CHILL
DEAD GIVEAWAY
THE OTHER CHILD
COLD JUDGMENT
FATAL IDENTITY
FINAL APPEAL
VENGEANCE IS MINE
EYES
WICKED
DEADLY MEMORIES
THE STEPCHILD

Published by Kensington Publishing Corp.

PINK LEMONADE CAKE MURDER

JOANNE FLUKE

Kensington Publishing Corp.
www.kensingtonbooks.com

KENSINGTON BOOKS are published by

Kensington Publishing Corp.
900 Third Avenue
New York, NY 10022

First Kensington Hardcover: August 2023

First Paperback Printing: July 2024
ISBN: 978-1-4967-3612-3

ISBN: 978-1-4967-3613-0 (ebook)

10 9 8 7 6 5 4 3 2 1

Printed in the United States of America

This book is dedicated to John J.
I couldn't have done this without you!

Acknowledgments

Grateful thanks to my extended family for putting up with me while I was writing this book.

Hugs to Trudi Nash and her husband, David, for being brave enough to taste many of my recipes and even try them out on their kids.

Love and admiration to the "Girls Afternoon" regulars: Karen, Gina, and Trudi for testing, and approving, the drinks and treats that my son makes for our soirees.

Thank you to my friends and neighbors: Mel & Kurt, Gina, Dee Appleton, Richard Jordan, Laura Levine, the real Nancy and Heiti, Dan, Mark & Mandy at Faux Library, Daryl and her staff at Groves Accountancy, Gene and Ron at the SDSA International, and to all of my friends at HomeStreet Bank.

Hugs to my Minnesota friends: Lois Meister, Bev & Jim, Val, RuthAnn, Dorothy & Sister Sue, and Mary & Jim.

Big hugs to my editor, John Scognamiglio. His patience seems endless and his suggestions are insightful and incredibly helpful.

Hugs for Meg Ruley and the staff at the Jane Rotrosen Agency for their constant support and sage advice.

Thanks to all the wonderful people at Kensington Publishing who keep Hannah sleuthing and baking yummy goodies.

Thank you to Robin in Production, and Larissa in Publicity.
Both of you go above and beyond to support the Hannah books.

Thanks to Hiro Kimura for his delicious Pink Lemonade Cake on the cover.
I wish mine looked exactly like that!

Thank you to Lou Malcangi at Kensington for designing all of Hannah's gorgeous book covers.
They're deliciously wonderful.

Thanks to John at *Placed4Success* for Hannah's movie and TV placements, his presence on Hannah's social media platforms, and for being my son.

Thanks to Tami Chase for designing and managing my website at **JoanneFluke.com** and for giving support to all of Hannah's social media.

Thank you to Kathy Allen for putting the recipes through their final test.

A big hug to JQ for helping Hannah and me for so many happy years.

Kudos to Beth and her phalanx of sewing machines for her gorgeous embroidery on Hannah's hats, visors, aprons, and tote bags.

Thank you to food stylist, friend, and media guide Lois Brown for her expertise with the launch parties at Poisoned Pen in Scottsdale, AZ.

Thanks also to Destry, the lovely, totally unflappable producer and host of *Arizona Midday*.

Hugs to Debbie R. for expert help with social media and thank you to everyone who's joined Team Swensen.

Thank you to Dr. Hirsch, Dr. Rahhal, Dr. and Cathy Line, Dr. Kowalski, Dr. Levy, and Dr. Umali for answering my book-related medical questions.

Hugs to all the Hannah fans who read the books, share their family recipes, post on my Facebook page, **Joanne Fluke Author**, and watch the Hannah movies.

Chapter One

Hannah removed a sheet of cookies from her industrial oven and slid them onto a shelf in her bakers rack. They smelled marvelous and she hoped that they'd taste just as wonderful as they smelled! Just then there was a knock on the kitchen door.

"Coming!" Hannah called out, heading for the back door of her Lake Eden, Minnesota, bakery and coffee shop. Just in time, she remembered to look through the peephole that Mike Kingston and Lonnie Murphy had installed in the door, and she was surprised to see that her early-morning visitor was her sister Andrea.

"Andrea!" she said, pulling open the door. "I thought you weren't coming in until ten this morning."

"I wasn't, but Bill called me from the sheriff's station. Do you have any coffee?"

"Of course I do." Hannah gestured toward the kitchen coffeepot. "Help yourself."

"Thank you!" Andrea said, heading toward the coffee machine immediately. "Will you call Bill at the station? He's got an emergency on his hands."

"Of course." Hannah hurried to the phone on the wall and dialed Bill's number. It took only one ring and Bill answered.

"Winnetka County Sheriff's Station. This is Bill speaking."

"Hi, Bill. It's Hannah. Andrea said you had an emergency?"

"Yes. Mike's here. He was waiting for me when I unlocked the door. He wants out."

Hannah sighed deeply. "I'm sorry, Bill. Perhaps I should have warned you, but I didn't think he'd actually do it."

"He's outside, filling out the paperwork right now. What do you think I should do? Mike's the best detective I have and I can't afford to lose him. He seems to think that Lonnie and Rick Murphy can handle his job, but . . . they can't."

"Are you in your office alone?" she asked.

"Yes. Can you think of some way to help?"

"Maybe. Do you have Mike's personnel file?"

"It's right here in my file cabinet."

"Get it out and tell me if Mike has listed Stella's cell phone number or her home number."

As Hannah listened, she heard a drawer being pulled out, and a moment later she heard papers rustling.

"I've got both numbers," Bill confirmed.

"Give them to me. I want to try to call Stella. She's the one who recommended Mike to Sheriff Graff, and she might be able to help us."

"Good idea!"

Bill read off the numbers, and Hannah scrawled

them down on the shorthand notebook she always kept by the phone. "Okay. Let me see what I can do. There's one other thing, Bill."

"What's that?"

"Do you think that Mike is independently wealthy?"

It took a moment for Bill to answer. "No, at least I don't think so. Why do you want to know?"

"It's just an idea, but can you tell Mike that you'll have to get the permission of the Winnetka County Board before he can get his retirement money?"

"I can say that. It's true, Hannah. If the board doesn't approve Mike's application, he won't get his retirement."

"Good! That should give us a little time. One more thing, Bill."

"What's that?"

"Can you stall Mike a little? And then can you bring him down to The Cookie Jar when he's through with the paperwork?"

"I can do that."

"Good. If I can get in touch with Stella, I'll have her here, waiting for you and Mike."

"Thanks, Hannah!" Bill sounded very relieved. "Are you going to try to talk Mike out of retiring?"

"I'll try, and with any luck, Stella will be here to try, too. All I want you to do is delay Mike as long as you can."

"Will do. Any ideas on how to do that?"

Hannah took a moment to think about that. "Yes. Have Mike write a letter to the Winnetka County Board, in detail, listing his reasons for wanting to retire early."

"Okay. I'll do it. Anything else?"

"Not that I can think of off the top of my head. Just delay bringing him here for as long as you can."

"You got it."

Hannah hung up the phone and turned to Andrea. "I have to call Stella. Pour me a cup of coffee, please, will you?"

"No problem. Do you want me to dish up some of those cookies?"

"Of course! When have you ever seen me turn down cookies?"

Hannah had the urge to cross her fingers as she dialed the phone, but she resisted, half-afraid she'd dial a wrong number. She punched in Stella's home number first, hoping she could contact Stella before she left for work at the Minneapolis Police Station.

"Hello?" a female voice answered after the third ring.

"Stella?" Hannah held her breath, hoping it was Mike's mentor and trainer.

"Who's calling, please?"

"It's Hannah Swensen at The Cookie Jar in Lake Eden."

"Hannah!" The voice suddenly became much friendlier. "What's going on at my favorite bakery and coffee shop?"

"Trouble," Hannah said, getting right to the crux of the matter. "Mike Kingston is in Bill's office right now, filling out the paperwork to resign."

"Oh my gosh! How did this happen? Last I heard, he was happy there in Lake Eden!"

"He was! Then all of a sudden, after the fishing tournament . . . *Boom!*"

"Exactly what do you mean when you say *Boom,* Hannah?" Stella asked.

"Stella, it was like flipping a switch. Mike was fine one minute, and then the next minute he wanted out."

"So there wasn't any lead-up to this? No ominous black skies above, or flashing danger signs before this life-changing proclamation?"

"Not really. Although he did say something to me right after the fishing tournament."

"What?"

"He said he was worried that he was losing his humanity, and that he felt as if he was browbeating the suspects he interviewed into confessing because all he was interested in was closing cases."

"Uh-oh. That sounds like classic cop burnout to me!"

"Do you think that you can talk Mike into staying with the department?"

"I don't know, but I'll certainly try. Tell me one thing, Hannah . . . has Mike ever taken a vacation?"

Hannah thought for a moment. "I don't think so."

"Okay. I'll call Bill and then I'll get on the road. I hope you have cookies because I won't have time to stop for breakfast."

Hannah laughed. "Of course I have cookies! I always have cookies."

"Good. I'll be there soon."

"Thank you, Stella! In the meantime, do you want me to assemble the troops?"

"The troops? What troops?"

"Everyone in Lake Eden who wants Mike to stay here. There's my mother, Norman, Doc Knight,

Grandma Knudson at the church and . . . and a bunch of other people."

"Good idea, but can you fit them all in your kitchen?"

"No, but Lisa will be here in a couple of minutes, and we'll push some tables together. We can all sit in the back of the coffee shop. Maybe, if Mike sees all the people that want him to stay here, he'll change his mind."

"I doubt that, but it can't hurt. Go ahead, Hannah. I'll see you soon."

There was a click on the line, and Hannah reached up to replace the receiver. "Oh, boy!" Hannah sighed. "What a mess."

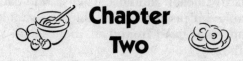

Chapter Two

"Is Stella coming?" Andrea asked, when Hannah came back to the work station.

"Yes, but I'm going to need some help. Stella agreed we should assemble the troops."

"What troops?"

"All the people in Lake Eden who might help us convince Mike to stay here."

Andrea took a moment to digest this. "Okay," she said, accepting the steno pad that Hannah handed her and turning to a blank page. "How about Grandma Knudson?"

"Write down her name in your notebook. Do you think that you can convince her to come down here and help us?"

Andrea laughed. "Of course. You know how Grandma Knudson always wants to be a part of the action. What do you think about asking Reverend Bob and Claire?"

"They'll come and they'll bring Grandma Knudson with them. I'm almost sure of that."

"I'll call Mother and Doc. They'll help us." Andrea looked pleased. "Do you think we should invite Aunt Nancy and Heiti?"

"Definitely!"

"Will do! How soon will Stella be here?"

"She said she was going to climb in the car, and drive straight here. She asked me if I had any cookies."

Andrea laughed. "I heard you say that. Do you want me to put some on a plate for Stella?"

"Yes, and for anyone else we can think of that'll help us convince Mike to stay."

"Do you think we should call Sally and Dick?"

Hannah thought about that for a moment. "I'm not sure. I know Mike likes them, but it was right after the fishing tournament that Mike told me he was having a problem. Write down their names, but I'd better ask Stella about that."

"You're going to call Norman, aren't you?"

"Yes. Doc Bennett is filling in for him today so that Norman can do some paperwork, so I know he's free. And he's one of the best friends that Mike has here in Lake Eden."

"Even though they're rivals for your affection?"

"Yes. They both know how I feel about them. I've told them that if they were somehow rolled into one person, I'd be rushing right down the aisle."

Andrea laughed. "I believe you. You've always had a soft spot for both of them. How about asking Earl and Carrie to help us?"

"That's a good idea."

Andrea made her way over to the bakers rack and, using oven mitts, pulled a large cookie sheet off the rack and carried it over to the work station where Hannah was sitting. Placing the cookie sheet down on the surface of the table, Andrea next found a large, round cookie platter and placed it on the work surface as well. Opening one of the large drawers in the work station, she took out a bright metal spatula and began to use it to transfer the cookies from the sheet to the cookie platter.

"What a lovely shade of pink these cookies are. Which ingredient did you use to get them that color? Was it grenadine by any chance?"

"Yes. You know how I feel about using food coloring, especially if there's something natural that I can use as an alternative. Try one, Andrea. I want to know what you think of them."

"I thought you'd never ask," Andrea said with a laugh, as she eagerly reached out for a cookie.

Hannah watched her sister's face. Andrea loved cookies and she was a good judge of what they should taste like.

"Wow!" Andrea began to smile. "They're great! These are some of the best cookies that you've ever made!"

"Thank you." Hannah was pleased at Andrea's reaction. "Do you think that I should sell these cookies at the baseball fields in the Snack Shack?"

"Yes."

Andrea took another bite of her cookie. "I'm pretty sure I heard you say before that grenadine is made of pomegranate juice, and I know that's extracted from pomegranate seeds. But what do pomegranate seeds taste like?"

"They're sweetish, but a bit tart, a little like the cookies."

Andrea glanced at the clock. "I'd better put on another pot of coffee."

"Yes, and both of us had better help Lisa move some tables together in the coffee shop. Then we'll think of anyone else we should call, and we'll do that."

PINK LEMONADE WHIPPERSNAPPER COOKIES

Preheat oven to 350 degrees F., rack in the middle position.

Ingredients:

1 15.25-ounce box lemon cake mix *(I used Duncan Hines Perfectly Moist Lemon Supreme Cake Mix)*

2 cups Cool Whip

1 egg *(beaten)*

½ teaspoon of lemon zest *(use just the yellow part of the lemon rind, be careful not to grind in any of the white part)*

½ cup powdered sugar *(in a separate bowl for rolling the cookies in)*

enough grenadine to color the batter pink *(I used about 1 and ½ ounces)*

Directions:

Prepare a cookie sheet by lining it with parchment paper.

Spray the parchment paper with Pam or another non-stick cooking spray.

Into a large bowl, add the lemon cake mix, Cool Whip, egg, lemon zest, and just enough grenadine to turn the batter pink.

Combine until just mixed through by using an electric or hand mixer.

After it is all mixed, put plastic wrap over the top of your mixing bowl, then set in the refrigerator to chill for 20 minutes.

Remove bowl from the refrigerator after it has chilled for 20 minutes.

Place your powdered sugar next to the mixing bowl (you will only scoop out one teaspoonful of the Whippersnapper mixture at a time into the powdered sugar).

Drop small balls of dough by the teaspoon into the powdered sugar and roll them around until the small balls of Whippersnappers are completely coated in the powdered sugar.

Place each Pink Lemonade Whippersnapper on a cookie sheet, no more than 8-12 cookies to a sheet.

Place cookie sheet in the oven and bake at 350 F. for 10-12 minutes, until cookies are slightly brownish on the top.

Remove to a cold stovetop burner or wire rack to cool for 5 minutes.

Using oven mitts, take the parchment paper (with the Pink Lemonade Whippersnapper Cookies still on it) and remove to the counter-top or another wire rack to finish cooling.

Yield: 2-3 dozen pretty, soft, and moist cookies.

Serve these Pink Lemonade Whippersnapper Cookies with strong, hot coffee or glasses of icy-cold milk for a yummy snack.

Chapter Three

Hannah made a couple of calls on her own, then got up to remove the Pink Lemonade Cakes, which she'd baked earlier, from their pans on the bakers rack to the top of the work station for decorating. Once that was done, she poured herself a fresh mug of coffee and sat down on her favorite stool. "Do you have any ideas about decorating the Pink Lemonade Cakes for the banquet at the community center?" she asked her sister.

"I do," Andrea responded quickly, looking pleased that Hannah had asked her. "I gave some thought to edible flowers, but I decided to try my hand at the pastry bag instead."

"Really?" Hannah was surprised. She knew that Andrea had been experimenting with various frostings in the pastry bag, but she hadn't known that her sister felt that confident about her ability to use those frostings to decorate.

Andrea looked amused. "I think I've got it

nailed. The pastry bag isn't that difficult if you practice. And I've been practicing all week."

Hannah smiled. "That's good. What do you have in mind?"

"Pink roses. I've got the right tip to make those. And then I'm going to write *Summer Solstice* in fancy lettering."

"That sounds wonderful. Anything you can do will be appreciated. You know how hopeless I am at decorating cakes."

Andrea laughed. "I know. I watched you try once. It was . . ."

"Painful?"

"Yes, that's the word. I felt so sorry for you. You're such a great baker, but decorating is . . . or maybe I should say seems to be . . . uh . . ."

"Beyond me?" Hannah supplied the phrase that Andrea seemed to be searching for.

"Exactly!"

"That's why I'm so glad you're here, Andrea. You've always been so much better at things like that."

"And you've always been a better baker than I am," Andrea responded loyally, but Hannah noticed that her sister looked quite proud of her new talent. "Did you get a chance to call Michelle?"

"Not yet, but I'm sure she'll come. She can always get someone to fill in for her this morning."

"I'd better plate some more cookies, just in case," Andrea said, heading for the bakers rack. "I think you've got enough for everyone who's coming."

"Are you sure?"

"Not entirely. I called Mother first and she said

she was going to activate the Lake Eden Gossip Hotline."

"Good heavens!"

"I know. And that means we may have a big crowd. Did you bake any more cookies?"

"I did. I was here early. I've got Molasses Crinkles, Black and Whites, Chocolate Chip Crunch, and Cashew Chips in."

"We should be all right then."

"I think so, but I can always run back here and make more if we need them." Hannah paused and looked slightly worried. "Maybe I'd better do that right now."

"I'll do it. I know how to make Black and White Cookies. I've been practicing at home. Grandma McCann says I'm getting very good at it."

"That's a real compliment, Andrea, especially from someone like Grandma McCann."

Chapter Four

Hannah looked up when she heard a knock on her back kitchen door.

"I'll get it," Andrea volunteered. "Maybe it's Stella."

Hannah watched while her sister went to the door, looked through the peephole, and laughed out loud.

"It's Stella," Andrea reported, "and she's standing there holding out her coffee cup like a beggar asking for a coin. I'll let her in, fill up her cup, and you two can talk strategy. I think I heard Lisa unlock the front door. I'll go help her and Aunt Nancy."

Andrea let Stella in from the back door, and gestured toward a stool at the work station. "Have a seat, Stella. I'll get coffee for you. How about some fresh baked cookies?"

"Thanks. I could use them!"

"Great to see you again, Stella," Hannah said. "I'm so glad you're here."

Andrea delivered Stella's coffee and brought a plate of cookies. "Try these, Stella. I think these are some of Hannah's best yet!"

Stella took a bite of the cookie and smiled. "Wonderful, and they taste delicious."

"I'm glad you like the cookies." Hannah accepted the compliment. "What's our strategy for this morning, Stella?"

"I'm not sure what the final strategy will be. For right now, I think it's a good thing to show Mike that we're all behind him and we want him to stay. Then we'll play it by ear."

"Do you think it'll help if he knows how many people really want him here?"

"It's worth a shot, Hannah. Did Mike say anything more to you about why he wanted to leave?"

"Not really."

"Then it probably is a case of classic cop burnout. It happens, sometimes, even to the best cops."

"You mean it happens to everyone?"

"Not everyone, but it happens to a lot of cops, yes. It's the stress of the job. Even bad cops burn out occasionally."

"But Mike *is* a good cop, isn't he?"

"Of course. No question about it. I think he's just frustrated. Maybe he needs some time away to relax and to think about what he really wants."

"Do you think you can help him?"

"I'm certainly going to do my best. I called Bill, and he said that Mike hasn't had a vacation since he joined the department. I'm going to take him out to my parents' cabin on Long Lake. We can go out on the lake and fish, or just sit in a boat, or paddle a canoe, and watch the sun on the waves.

There's something very soothing about being on the water."

"That's what my mother always says. She still owns my grandparents' cabin and she hauls Doc out there when he gets stressed. She swears that just paddling around in a canoe helps to ease tension."

"I think she's right. I know it works for me. The feeling of water gently rocking the boat has always had a soothing effect. Let's go out in the main room. I think Mike needs to know that everyone here loves and supports him. That could make a real difference. We can figure the rest out later. I've got one idea . . . You can always drive out and bring something in the crockpot for supper. Mike loves your cooking and he's going to miss you a lot. I truly believe one of the great disappointments in Mike's life is that you refused to marry him."

Hannah took a moment to digest that. "You mean, that if I'd said yes, Mike would be all right?"

"No, not at all. Mike's conflicted, Hannah. Norman's his best friend, and Mike could be afraid you might marry Norman someday, and leave him out in the cold."

"But I could never do that, Stella! I love both of them so much. There's just no way I can choose between them."

"I know that and you know that. I'm not sure Mike always does." Stella stood up. "Let's go. Do you think Grandma Knudson will be here?"

"I'm sure she's here already! Grandma Knudson wouldn't miss this for the world. She loves to be in on the action and you can always depend on her to have her finger on the pulse of the community. That means Reverend Bob and Claire will be here, too. Mike will get plenty of support from everyone. You can bet on that!"

"Good! Let's go!"

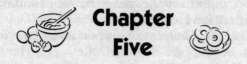

Chapter Five

Stella started to push through the door to the coffee shop, then stopped and turned to look at Hannah. "It looks like you've got quite a few people in the coffee shop already!"

"What we call the Lake Eden Gossip Hotline must be working at warp speed," Hannah explained.

"How does that work?"

"Well . . . Andrea called Mother, Mother called a few of her closest friends . . ."

"And those close friends called a couple of their close friends?"

"Exactly right."

"So it's like a telephone tree?"

"Yes," Hannah said as she and Stella walked into a scene that would have been perfect for a Hollywood sitcom. Seated at the tables, enjoying what seemed like half of the baked goods that The Cookie Jar had to offer, were Grandma Knudson, Reverend Bob and Claire, Dick and Sally, Delores and Doc, and what appeared to be about half of all the residents of Lake Eden.

As if on cue, Grandma Knudson rose to her feet. "Here they are!" she declared. "Let's give Hannah and Stella a round of applause." She swiveled to face Stella. "We're prepared to do anything you want us to do."

"Good." Stella smiled at her. "We just want everyone to tell Mike how much we need him here in Lake Eden . . . and how much we want him to stay."

"Should we go up and talk to Mike in person?" Irma York asked.

"Absolutely," Hannah replied. "He needs to know how we feel about him and how much we depend on him."

"Do you think you can talk him into staying here?" Claire asked.

"I don't know, but I'll do my best," Stella replied.

"But will it do any good?" Aunt Nancy asked.

"I don't know, but it'll certainly be good for his ego." Stella gave a little smile. "I'm going to help out by taking Mike on a little vacation. Bill told me that Mike hasn't taken one day of vacation since he's been here, and that could be one of the reasons he's so discouraged."

"You've dealt with this type of thing before?" Lisa asked, delivering coffee to both Hannah and Stella.

"Many times. Mike's a good cop. I trained him myself, so I know he takes his responsibilities seriously. I think part of the problem is that he's just plain exhausted and that makes him feel depressed . . . and maybe uncertain about his job and even about his life here."

"Where are you taking Mike on vacation?" Reverend Bob wanted to know.

"To Long Lake. My parents had a vacation home out there and I kept it when they died."

"That's just perfect!" Delores declared. "I know when Doc gets stressed out, it always helps when we go out on the lake and just watch the waves lap up against the boat. It's very peaceful on the water."

"Something else that helps is chocolate," Doc suggested. "I always keep a little box of chocolate truffles hidden in my file cabinet for Lori."

Delores laughed. "And I know it, too, so I usually eat them all before he even gets around to offering them to me."

"I think you should have married Mike, Hannah." Irma York spoke up. "Then he'd want to stay here in Lake Eden."

Hannah shook her head. "That wouldn't have made any difference in his staying. We are not sure he's even leaving . . . but isn't that why we are all here? We are here to talk him out of it? Besides, I couldn't marry Mike, and you all know why."

"Because you can't choose between Mike and Norman?" Dick asked.

"Well . . . yes. That's certainly one reason!"

Sally laughed. "Then there's also the fact that marrying both Mike and Norman would be illegal and immoral."

"Right!" Hannah gave a quick nod.

"Not to mention the fact that there are only seven days in a week," Reverend Bob spoke up. "It could very well have led to a scheduling nightmare!"

Grandma Knudson laughed so hard, she almost choked. "Bobby!" she chided him.

"Well . . . it could have! That's an odd number of days!" Reverend Bob defended himself. "Sorry, Hannah. I probably shouldn't have said that."

"Besides, it's really only six days a week, Bob, and that's an even number!" Grandma Knudson said with a grin. "Even our good Lord rested on the seventh day!"

Everyone laughed at Grandma Knudson's comment.

Just then Norman walked into the room. "I'm here," he said to Hannah. "Where do you want me?"

"Hi, Norman, we were just talking about you. Sit right here," Stella answered him, patting the seat next to her. "Since you're Mike's best friend in Lake Eden, I want you to sit between Hannah and me."

Norman took a seat, then Lisa gave out a whoop of excitement . . .

"Here they come!" Lisa warned, pointing to the sheriff's car that had just pulled into the reserved parking spot out front. "Let's all applaud when Mike walks in. We have to let him know that we love having him with us here in Lake Eden and we want him to stay."

Bill opened the door to the coffee shop and he and Mike walked inside. There was a round of applause, and Mike looked puzzled.

"Is it someone's birthday?" he asked.

"No, the applause is for you," Grandma Knudson told him.

Mike glanced at Bill. "Is this an intervention?"

"Well, you *could* call it that, if you wanted to."

Grandma Knudson got to her feet. "You know, Mike, people say I'm outspoken. But this time I think I'm *right-spoken*. We all want you to stay here in Lake Eden with us!"

"She's absolutely right, Mike!" Sally said. "We are all here to tell you that we love you, and we want you to stay!"

Dick chimed in. "True. You make us feel safe."

Grandma Knudson said, "You make *everyone* feel safer, Mike."

"I think everyone here today feels that way, too!" Hannah declared emphatically.

There were sounds of agreement from every corner of the room until Reverend Bob stood up from his chair and spoke. "Mike, we know it is ultimately your decision to make, whether you stay with us or not, but I hope the love and support shown for you today, given from all the folks assembled here, might persuade you to change your mind about leaving. There is a common saying, *Act in haste, repent at leisure,* that I think might apply. Mike, there are so many people whose lives have been enriched by you working and living among us in Lake Eden. Won't you reconsider?"

Mike thought about it for a moment, then nodded. "I do love Lake Eden, both the town and the people who live in it. Reverend, I'm not saying yes quite yet, but I will think about it, I really will."

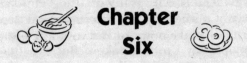

Chapter Six

There was a lovely, cooling tropical breeze on her face and Hannah smiled in her sleep. She took a deep breath, expecting to inhale the perfume of exotic tropical flowers, but, instead, she smelled the scent of . . .

"Fish?" Hannah said aloud, startling the two cats who were lying on either side of her feather pillow.

It took a moment for Hannah to realize what was happening. When she did, she laughed out loud, startling the two cats so much, they hopped off their comfortable perch and landed with twin thumps on the floor.

"I guess you're hungry," Hannah told them, glancing at the clock on her bedside table. It took another moment for her to register the numbers and, when she did, she sat up with alarm. "Uh-oh!" she said to the two cats. "I overslept! And that means you're hungry . . . right?"

"Rrrrow!" Moishe responded.

"Roww!" Cuddles echoed, in a much softer tone.

"Okay. I'm awake now. You did your job. Just stay here while I take a quick shower and get dressed."

It didn't take much coaxing for the two cats to return to their respective sides of Hannah's pillow. Hannah petted them both, slipped her feet into the moccasins she used as slippers, and padded off to the bathroom.

Hannah showered quickly and dressed in clean jeans and a long-sleeved tee shirt. Once she'd brushed her teeth and run a comb through her hair, she exited the bathroom and came out to find her two sentinels now sleeping on her feather pillow.

"Okay. Let's go," she said, heading for the bedroom door with the two cats following in her wake.

As she passed the door to the guest room, Hannah heard the shower running. Norman was up. She hurried down the stairs, turned on the kitchen light, and activated the coffeepot she'd set up the previous evening.

"You sound like you're starving. Are you ready to eat?" she asked.

Both cats turned to stare at her, and Hannah laughed. "Do you want salmon? Or tuna?"

The two cats stared at her but didn't respond. "Okay," Hannah told them. "I'll choose this morning. You're going to have a little of both on top of your kitty crunchies."

Hannah was almost certain both Moishe and Cuddles looked pleased at her decision.

It didn't take long for Hannah to arrange the

two cans of cat food on top of the kitty crunchies that both cats loved. Once the resident felines were contentedly crunching their food, Hannah poured herself a cup of morning coffee, inhaled the bracing scent, and took her first scalding sip.

"Oh, great! You've got the coffee on!" Norman greeted her. "Thanks, Hannah. It's so good having you here with me."

Hannah smiled. "Thank you, Norman." And then she thought, *Norman's wonderful and he's always so appreciative every time I do something for him.*

For a moment or two, Hannah and Norman sat at the breakfast table, sipping their coffee. Then Hannah asked, "What would you like for breakfast? I've got some Caramel Pecan Rolls left if you'd like a couple of those."

"That sounds really good. You know . . . you don't have to make breakfast for me every morning. We could always go out to The Corner Tavern, or to Hal and Rose's Café in town."

"I know, but I enjoy fixing your breakfast. After all, you're letting Moishe and me stay here."

"And I'm very glad to have you both," Norman responded immediately. "We designed this house together. Half of it's yours."

"Thanks, Norman. But you gave me the master bedroom already."

"That's true. I did it on purpose. And I guess I should admit that I had an ulterior motive. I was hoping the fireplace in the bedroom would entice you to stay here with me."

Hannah smiled. "It's really tempting. I love that fireplace."

"So do I. Maybe I should convert the guest room next door to another master suite. I could probably find someone to make a fireplace that could be seen from both rooms. Then we could share it."

"Would it be a see-through fireplace?"

"Yes. I've seen pictures of them in magazines. It might not be that difficult to do."

Hannah's mind started pondering a question she really didn't want to ask. If they both had master suites and the fireplace was a see-through fireplace, could they watch each other?

Just then Hannah's cell phone rang. "Uh-oh! I hope I remembered to put my phone in the charger."

"You didn't, but I did it for you, Hannah. Go ahead and answer. It should be fully charged by now."

"Hello?" Hannah answered. "Hi, Stella! How's everything going?"

"It's going fine, but I think Mike's going to get pretty tired of my culinary achievements."

"Oh?"

"Yes. I only have one thing I make really well and that's bacon and eggs. I'm sure he'd appreciate something different, especially if you made it. Do you think you can put something in the crockpot and bring it out to us?"

"Of course I can! Would you like something in particular? If not, I could always make Lakeside Stew."

"That sounds great! What is it?"

"It's a bratwurst stew with carrots and cut-up potatoes."

"That sounds perfect. If I give you directions, can you bring it out here for supper?"

"Sure. Where are you . . . exactly?"

"My parents' cabin is on Long Lake, the one by Long Prairie."

"I've been there!" Hannah said quickly. "I'm not very good with directions, though. If I put Norman on, can you give him all the details?"

"I'd be happy to. There's no way I want us to miss out on something called Lakeside Stew."

Hannah motioned to Norman, and he got up to take the phone. "Let me get some paper. Hold on a minute."

Hannah listened while Norman grabbed a pen and paper and wrote down Stella's directions. "Thanks, Stella," he said. "I won't have any trouble driving out to you. My parents used to go out to a little place on Long Lake called the Rock Tavern. They loved the hamburgers there, and I was fascinated by the colored bottles that were set into the walls."

"They're still there, along with the macramé bottle cap curtains, and the view of the lake is still gorgeous. It's good to know that some things don't change very much. And that reminds me. If you and Hannah feel like staying overnight, it's a three-bedroom cabin and the sofa in the living room makes into a hide-a-bed."

"Thanks, but I think I'd better leave that up to Hannah. The baseball tournament starts the day after tomorrow and tomorrow night is the dinner and dance at the community center. We almost have to be back for that because Hannah is going to serve her special Pink Lemonade Cake for dessert after the dinner."

"How about those luscious cookies I had for breakfast yesterday? Is she going to serve those, too?"

"Yes, at the Snack Shack." Norman turned to wink at Hannah. "Just between you and me, Stella, they won't let Hannah watch the tournament in person."

"Why not?"

"Hannah gets just a bit too involved. The last time she went to a town baseball game, she told the home plate umpire that he needed glasses."

Hannah made a face at Norman, and he laughed. "She's not real happy with me right now, Stella. I guess I shouldn't have told you that. The ladies usually relegate Hannah to the Snack Shack and don't let her watch when the Lake Eden Gulls are playing. Hang on, I'll give you back to Hannah."

"I'm not *that* bad!" Hannah yelped, as Norman passed the phone back to her. She gave Norman a bit of a frown and quickly spoke into the phone. "At least . . . I don't think I am, Stella. All right, I admit I get a little hot under the collar, but only when the umpire is wrong."

"What else are you selling at the Snack Shack for the tournament?" Stella asked, changing the subject.

"Cinnamon Toast Popcorn Balls, and Curveball Cookies."

"That sounds interesting. And you're serving your Pink Lemonade Cake at the banquet?"

"Yes. Are you bringing Mike to the Summer Solstice Parade or the banquet?"

"I don't think so. It may well be time for reverse psychology."

"What do you mean?"

"Yesterday, at The Cookie Jar, Mike got a nice ego massage. Everyone who was there told him how much they loved him and that they wanted him to stay in Lake Eden. He knows that, but now I think he should get a dose of reality."

"You're the expert. Just tell me what you want us to do, and we'll do it." Hannah glanced over at Norman and he nodded in agreement.

"I want you to tell Mike that you and Norman have everything under control. I think Mike needs to hear that he's not indispensable."

"But . . . he is!"

"I know that, and you know that. I need Mike to think about exactly what might happen if he actually left Lake Eden."

It took Hannah a moment, but then she connected the dots. "Okay, I think I see what you're doing. Do you want me to remind Mike that Bill is a detective, and so are Rick and Lonnie, and that they can take care of anything that comes up?"

"Exactly! And don't forget to add you and Norman to the mix. Say that you're also willing to help."

"I got it," Hannah agreed.

"Oops! I just heard the shower go off. I'll tell Mike that you and Norman are coming out for supper tonight and you're bringing one of your meals in the crockpot. He's going to like that."

"One other question," Hannah said. "Do you have soup bowls, spoons, and kitchen supplies?"

"Of course. My parents lived out here year-round. My mother loved to cook, and there's a fully equipped kitchen."

"Then we're all set," Hannah said, smiling as Norman gave her a thumbs-up. "We'll see you and Mike later. And please tell him that Norman and I just want him to relax and enjoy his vacation at the lake with you."

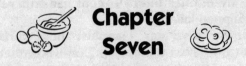

Chapter Seven

Hannah removed the last two cake pans from her industrial oven and placed them on shelves in the bakers rack. She was heading for the kitchen coffeepot next, to check on the fresh pot of coffee she'd just finished brewing, when there was a knock on The Cookie Jar's back kitchen door.

It was Andrea's knock. Hannah recognized it and she opened the door. "Good morning, Andrea."

"Hannah! You didn't look through the peephole! I was watching to make sure."

Hannah sighed. "I know. I should have done that, but I recognized your knock."

"Anybody could duplicate my knock," Andrea said with a frown. "Really, Hannah! You just have to be more careful."

"You're right," Hannah agreed quickly. "You're here early. Is something wrong?"

"Not really. It's just that I needed coffee. Bill's

already gone, and I didn't want to put on a whole pot just for myself."

"Well, you're in luck. I was just about to check on the fresh brewed pot now. Help yourself, and I'll tell you the latest in the Stella-Mike story."

Andrea hurried to the kitchen coffeepot and poured a cup for herself. "Okay. Come and sit down. I *do* want to know what's going on with Mike and Stella at the cabin."

Hannah walked to her favorite stool at the work station and sat down. "Truthfully, there's not too much to tell except that Norman and I are going out to Stella's cabin tonight for dinner."

"Then you're going to see Mike?"

"Yes. Stella asked me to bring something in the crockpot, so I'm going to make my Lakeside Stew."

"Lakeside Stew?" Andrea looked puzzled. "What's that?"

"It's just a stew with potatoes, and carrots, and meat. It's made in the crockpot. Stella said she was afraid that Mike would get tired of her making bacon and eggs for every meal."

"Stella's not a good cook?"

"That's what she said."

"I know how she feels. The only things I make well are peanut butter and jelly sandwiches. And . . . actually . . . I'm not too sure about those."

Somehow, through a supreme effort, Hannah managed not to say anything about Andrea's peanut butter sandwiches with mint jelly. Hannah had been the recipient of those particular sandwiches more times than she wanted to count, but she'd keep quiet about those! She wouldn't hurt her sister's feelings for the world.

"So, tell me more about Lakeside Stew?" Andrea asked.

"It's just a stew with bratwurst, carrots, mushrooms, potatoes, and celery."

"That sounds good."

"It always is. And the best part is, it's really easy to make. Do you have time to go shopping for me this morning?"

"Sure. What do you need?"

"I'll dictate a list to you. I want you to buy everything double for me."

"Double? Why?"

"I have extra crockpots down here, and I thought that once I teach you how to make it, you could make another pot of Lakeside Stew for you, Bill, and the kids tonight."

"Wonderful!" Andrea looked very excited at the prospect. "I'll need pen and paper."

Hannah walked over to the phone and picked up the stenographer's pad that sat there. "Here," she said, handing the pad to Andrea. "Let's start with small red potatoes. And remember, everything's doubled."

Andrea wrote that down. "Okay. How many do you need?"

"Two pounds for each slow cooker. So that's four pounds in total. We're going to wash them and cut them into quarters. We'll also need two cans of chicken broth."

"All right. What else?"

"Onions. Get a big package of Florence's chopped onions. They're in the produce section, and they're already pre-cut for us."

"Got it. What else?"

"Carrot sticks. You can get the kind Florence

stocks for kids' lunch boxes. Then all we have to do is cut them up into half-inch sticks. Oh, and get a bunch of celery."

"Anything else?"

"Yes, two cans of sweet corn. And this is the hardest part. We'll need four pounds of brat-wurst."

"You mean . . . like hot dogs?"

"No, not exactly. Ask Florence what she has on hand, and she'll tell you. She usually carries a lot of different kinds of bratwurst. Just ask and she'll explain the different kinds to you."

"Okay, but what kind shall I get?"

"That's up to you. I know that I want the Polish sausage type and the knockwurst, but you can get some different kinds if you'd rather. Florence will explain each of them to you, and you can choose which types you want to use in your crockpot for tonight."

"Wonderful!" Andrea looked delighted at the thought.

"That's right. And remember, if you taste your Lakeside Stew and think it's too bland for your family, you can just add some Slap Ya Mama hot sauce to perk it right up."

"Right!" Andrea finished her coffee in one swig. "Florence is probably open by now. I can go down there and get what we need."

"Perfect. And once we put the Lakeside Stew together, maybe we can bake more Pink Lemonade Cake layers. We'll need to bake quite a few of those for the banquet."

"Right, Hannah! I'll be right back."

"Wait a second," Hannah said, as Andrea stood up. "I almost forgot. Write down two cans of Campbell's Cream of Mushroom soup, two cans of Campbell's Cream of Celery soup, and two cans of Campbell's Creamy Tomato soup. And we also need four small cans of sliced mushrooms or mushroom pieces."

"What are those for?"

"We're going to make our own version of Golden Mushroom soup. Campbell's already makes a canned Golden Mushroom soup, but sometimes Florence's distributor doesn't carry it, or it's sold out."

"You mean . . . some of the soup that I'm going to buy, when mixed together, will make our own Golden Mushroom soup?"

"That's right. The only reason I know this trick is because Grandma Knudson taught me how to do it a couple of years ago."

Andrea smiled. "Grandma Knudson knows everything, doesn't she?"

"Yes, at least it seems like it. She's been cooking and baking for years and she's discovered all the shortcuts."

"I think she should teach cooking classes on KCOW television," Andrea said. "I'll shop now and bring everything back here. And thank you for helping me make something new for Bill and the kids."

"Not a problem. In fact, it's my pleasure. Hey, before you leave, remind me later that I have something else you can make for Bill and the girls!"

"Really? What's that?"

"It's called Tropical Pie and it's got a pear, apricot, and pineapple filling."

TROPICAL PIE

Preheat oven to 375 degrees F., rack in the middle position.

Ingredients:

    1 frozen deep-dish premade pie crust *(I used Marie Callender's)*

    1 15-ounce can apricot halves *(cut into slices as you would for an apple pie)*

    2 15.25-ounce cans pear halves *(cut into slices as you would for an apple pie)*

    1 20-ounce can pineapple slices *(cut each ring into 8 chunks)*

French Crumble:

    1 cup all-purpose flour

    ½ cup *(1 stick, 8 tablespoons, ¼ pound)* cold, salted butter *(cut into half-inch chunks)*

    ½ cup brown sugar

Directions:

Remove the deep-dish pie crust from package and thaw according to package directions.

In the bowl of your food processor combine the flour, salted butter, and brown sugar.

Process with the steel blade in an on-and-off motion until the resulting mixture is in uniform small pieces.

In a medium-sized bowl combine the apricot slices, pear slices, and pineapple chunks with ½ of the French Crumble mixture.

Arrange this mixture in the deep-dish pie shell.

Sprinkle the rest of the crumbled mixture over the top of your pie.

Pat the top down with your impeccably clean hands and cut several slits in the top to vent.

Place your pie on a baking sheet lined with aluminum foil and bake at 375 degrees F. for 45–55 minutes or until the top is golden brown.

Remove from the oven and let your pie cool on a cold stovetop burner or wire rack.

Yield: 8 pie-shaped servings of tropical delight.

Serve with strong, hot coffee or glasses of icy-cold milk.

Hannah's Note: This yummy dessert can be topped with a scoop of vanilla ice cream, a slice of cheddar cheese, or both!

Chapter Eight

"I'm back!" Andrea came in the back door of The Cookie Jar, carrying two large sacks of groceries. "I got everything on your list, plus a couple of extra things for me."

"Good." Hannah removed the last pan of cookies from her industrial oven and slipped them on the shelf of her bakers rack. "Just put them down on the work station and we'll unload everything."

"Will do," Andrea said, setting the sacks of groceries on the stainless steel surface.

Hannah walked over and sat down on her favorite stool. "What did you get?"

"Everything you wanted for both of us and a couple more things for me."

"Like what?"

"Like . . . this!" Andrea pulled out a paper-wrapped package to show Hannah. "Florence had lots of different types of sausages, and she explained them all. Not only that, she actually cooked a couple of them in her little toaster oven and let me taste them."

"Florence is very helpful. Especially when it comes to explaining the products in her meat case."

"Yes, she is."

"What kinds of sausage did Florence help you find for us?"

"Apple and celery sausage, Polish sausage, the sausage that looks like fat hot dogs, and something that looked like white sausage."

"Weisswurst?"

"Yes! If it's okay with you, I want to put the apple and celery sausage in my Lakeside Stew."

"Good idea. I know how crazy Bethie is about apples."

Andrea laughed. "Sometimes she's a little too crazy about apples."

"What do you mean?" Hannah asked, knowing full well that her youngest niece could be both funny and charming on occasion.

"Bethie got worried the other day because she ate an apple star."

"A what?"

"An apple star. Sometimes I don't peel the apples. I just cut them into slices with the seeds in the center."

"I get it," Hannah responded. "When you do that, the seeds make little stars in the center."

"Exactly! Bethie loves apples cut that way, and the other day, she forgot, took a big bite of the apple slice, and before she knew it, she'd swallowed a couple of apple seeds by mistake."

Hannah chuckled. "Did Bethie think she was going to grow an apple tree in her stomach?"

"That's exactly what she thought! She worried so much, I had to feel her stomach every morning this week and convince her that no apple trees were growing inside her tummy."

"Tracey didn't tell her that?" Hannah asked, mentioning her older niece.

"Tracey told her, but Bethie didn't believe Tracey. She wanted me to tell her, just to make sure Tracey was right."

"I'm glad you got it all straightened out," Hannah said. "You said you bought a couple of extra things. What else did you buy?"

"Instant mashed potatoes. Those are for me, and I paid for them. Florence gave me a tip, Hannah. She said that I could use instant mashed potatoes to practice my frosting techniques."

"Okay. She did explain that instant mashed potatoes wouldn't taste like frosting, didn't she?"

Andrea laughed. "Of course she did. She said she'd read about that in an article, and they used instant potatoes all the time to double for ice cream and powdered sugar frosting on photo shoots and on television. The article said that the lights were so hot, they tended to melt the frosting or the ice cream."

"So you decided to practice with the pastry bag using instant mashed potatoes?"

"Yes! I really think I can learn to frost your Pink Lemonade Cakes for the banquet. Florence showed me all the little decorating tips she had to fit on top of the pastry bag. There's one for rose petals, and another one for making little stars, and another one for writing names and things like *Happy Birthday* and *Congratulations*. I'm sure I can do it if I practice."

"I'm sure you can. You're very artistic."

"That's what Bill says. Do you want me to go home and get my crockpot? I've got one."

"That's not necessary," Hannah said, reaching down to open the sliding door built into the work station. "Look under here, Andrea."

Andrea glanced down at the sliding door that Hannah had opened. "You have a whole battalion of slow cookers!"

"Yes, I do. We use them for quite a few things around here."

"Like what?"

"Like keeping melted chocolate hot. Sometimes Lisa dips cookies in melted chocolate or in white chocolate. Other times, we dip some cookies in melted peanut butter chips."

"That makes sense."

"It saves on time." Hannah stood up and took out two slow cookers. "Let's start the stew, Andrea. You can begin your Lakeside Stew here, and then take it home with you when you go."

"Perfect!" Andrea looked delighted. "Thanks, Hannah. Bill is going to be so excited that I learned how to cook something different, not to mention tasty! He was such a good sport about the peanut butter and mint jelly sandwiches I used to make."

"Then you don't make those anymore?"

"Heavens, no! They were horrible and I didn't like them either. I just didn't know how to make anything else. You've taught me a lot, Hannah."

Chapter Nice

Once Andrea had left to take her slow cooker home and plug it in, Hannah finished baking yet another batch of cookies. She was just getting ready to sit down, when there was a knock on the back kitchen door. She hurried to answer it and stopped, her hand on the knob.

"Who is it?" she asked, knowing that Andrea would complain if she didn't look through the peephole.

"It's Norman," the voice on the other side answered, and Hannah opened the door.

"Great timing, Norman," she greeted him with a smile. "I was just about to take a coffee break."

"Great timing? Maybe yes, maybe no," Norman said, looking slightly concerned. "Do you have time to go down to the hardware store with me? There's something I want to show you."

"I don't see why not. I just finished baking Watermelon Kool-Aid Cookies and I was due for a little break anyway. Just have some coffee while I check with Lisa and Aunt Nancy to see if they can cover for me," Hannah told him.

"Sounds good," Norman said, pouring himself a cup and sitting down. "I'll finish this cup of coffee while you ask them."

When Hannah came back, Norman asked, "Is everything okay with Aunt Nancy and Lisa? Can they cover for you for a few minutes?"

"Sure, as long as I'm back within an hour. We can go now. I could use a breath of fresh air. But I must confess you've got me curious about what you and Cliff have cooked up for me to see over at the hardware store."

Chapter
Ten

Norman got out in front of the hardware store and came around the car to open Hannah's door.

Hannah waited until he'd opened it for her and then she smiled at him. "Thank you," she said as he closed the door, took her arm, and escorted her into what had been her father's hardware store.

"Hey, Hannah! Hi, Norman!" Cliff greeted them. "Come into the back room with me. I want to show Hannah what we came up with and ask her whether she thinks it'll work or not."

Cliff escorted them into the back room and motioned to a large cage made of hardware cloth that was sitting on the old desk, near the back of the room. "Here it is." He gestured toward the cage. "What do you think?"

Hannah walked over to look at the cage and was surprised to see that it had two handles, one on one end and the other on the opposite end. "Is this for the cats?"

"Yes. I consulted with Sue and Bob Haggaman and they had an idea which just might work. If Moishe gets nervous going up the stairs to your condo, Cuddles can slide over and . . . well, you know."

"Hmm . . . that's interesting," Hannah said, resorting to an age-old Minnesota phrase that meant she wasn't sure what Cliff was attempting to accomplish.

"We thought it might be worth trying." Norman took over Cliff's partial explanation. "Moishe gets more and more scared the closer he gets to the condo. So we are hoping if he starts to get too frightened, Cuddles will go over to Moishe's side of the carrying case and calm him down."

It took Hannah a moment to formulate her answer. "Well . . . at least we can give it a shot. Who knows? It might work out really well." She turned to Norman. "When were you thinking about a trial run?"

"I thought that I would leave that up to you. After all, you are the only one who will know when you are ready to visit the condo again."

Hannah was truly moved by Norman's efforts to be understanding about her feelings, even if it did look as though Norman couldn't wait to try out the new kitty carrier that he and Cliff had dreamed up.

"Thank you for not rushing me, Norman," she said to him gently. "Moishe was so traumatized when Ross, the man I thought was my husband, was killed in the living room, I'm not sure when he'll be able to go back. I'll never forget how terrified Moishe was when I found him cowering under the outside staircase. Moishe loved Ross. I did, too, until I realized the kind of snake he really was. I wish Ross had been more like you, Norman. It seems to me that right when I least expect it . . . that's the time you do something that shows me just how thoughtful and understanding you are."

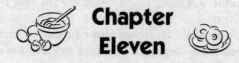

Chapter Eleven

Hannah returned from the hardware store, hung her sweater on the hook by the back door, and walked through the kitchen and into the coffee shop. "Everything okay, Lisa?"

"We are fine, Hannah," her partner answered. "Except we are running out of Chocolate Chip Crunch Cookies."

"I'll bake more right now," Hannah promised, heading for the walk-in cooler.

In less than five minutes, her cookies were in the oven and Hannah had just refilled the kitchen coffeepot, when there was a knock on her back kitchen door. "Coming!" she shouted. "Who is it?" Hannah asked, actually glancing through the peephole.

"It's me! Do you have coffee?"

"Hello, Mother." Hannah pulled open the door. "I'm surprised to see you today."

"Well, I thought since Doc had an early call at

the hospital, I'd stop by to see you. Do you have coffee?"

"Of course I do. Sit down and I'll get you some."

Delores hung her light summer sweater on one of the hooks by the back door and took a seat at the work station. "What smells so good?"

"It's either the Pink Lemonade Cakes I just baked, or the Pink Lemonade Whippersnapper Cookies that I made earlier."

"Heavenly!" Delores pronounced, taking a sip of the coffee that Hannah had just delivered. "Could I have a couple of cookies? I didn't have time to eat anything yet, and I didn't feel like stopping at Hal and Rose's Café."

"Of course, Mother." Hannah walked to the cooling rack and filled a plate with cookies.

"I love the color," Delores said, reaching for a cookie and smiling as she took a bite. "They're good, Hannah!"

"Thank you, Mother. I'm glad you like them," Hannah responded, sitting down across from her mother with her own cup of coffee.

"Hannah!" Lisa burst through the swinging door that divided the kitchen from the coffee shop. "You've got to come out here! Wait until you see what's happening outside!"

"I've never seen Lisa so excited," Delores said, getting up from her stool. "I wonder what's going on."

"Let's find out." Hannah led the way into the coffee shop and both women hurried to the window to look.

"Look at that, Hannah!" Delores exclaimed. "It's Bernie 'No-No' Fulton, and he's holding his very own parade!"

Hannah stared at the gold Cadillac that was driving slowly past the coffee shop window. Delores was right! There was No-No, his long, sandy blond hair flowing in the breeze, acting as if he had not a care in the world. "Look at him! He's got three of our high school girls riding up on the back ledge!"

Delores harrumphed. "What a show-off! What is he doing with our high school girls in the first place? He's a grown man. Why, he's almost in his thirties! That's a scandal in the making." She turned to Lisa. "You know, Lisa, I think Herb should give him a ticket for holding up traffic. He has two cars and a tractor behind him. And that's practically a traffic jam for Lake Eden."

Lisa laughed. "He may be six foot four and good-looking, but that doesn't give him the right to break the law! And it is true. He *is* holding up traffic. I'll call Herb and get him right on it!"

Delores and Hannah waited while Lisa dialed her phone. "Do you see him, Herb?" she asked. "He's just turned at the lumberyard, coming back this way with three of our local high school girls riding up on the back ledge of his car. Isn't that dangerous? And illegal?"

There was a moment of silence and then Lisa laughed. "Yes, I think you should do that. You bet we'll watch! Hannah and Delores are right here with me and there are six or seven customers lined up to watch."

"Herb's going to do it?" Hannah guessed, when Lisa got off the phone.

"Yes! He said he'd be happy to. No-No's going to get pulled over for reckless endangerment and impeding traffic!"

Hannah, Delores, and the other customers watched as Herb pulled up behind No-No's convertible in his squad car. A short second later, Herb's red light came on from the top of the cruiser, followed by the whoop of the siren. "Pull over to the curb," Herb said, using his loudspeaker. "Ladies? Get down onto the rear seat. Riding up on the back ledge is dangerous."

Everyone in the coffee shop laughed as Herb, looking every inch the traffic officer, got out of his cruiser, wrote out a ticket, ripped it out of his ticket book, and handed it to No-No.

"Herb looks very official!" Delores commented.

"That was just a perfect slap down for Mr. Big Shot," Irma York commented. "Good for Herb!"

Lisa smiled proudly. "Herb knows the law, and Lake Eden has an ordinance against causing reckless endangerment."

"What's that guy doing here anyway?" Hattie Johnson asked. "I thought he was a pitcher in the big leagues for the Twins."

"Not anymore," Delores told her. "He only pitched for one season in the majors. He was sent down and played in the farm leagues for part of a season, called back up to the majors, and the next thing you know, he was out of baseball completely! Now, I don't know if it's true or not, but I heard that there were rumors about No-No and some kind of illegal betting. It was all kept very hush-hush, but he was released from the majors, then a while later he got banned from organized baseball entirely."

"Is he pitching in the baseball tournament?" Hattie asked.

"Yes," Lisa said, answering her question. "After

the Twins sent him down, it seems as though he brought his *troubles* with him down to the farm leagues, too, but they got wise to No-No quickly in Iowa. But, due to the way the Winnetka County All-Star Tournament regulations were written, and because he's been completely out of organized baseball for over a year, No-No is now eligible to pitch in our baseball tournament."

"Well, I hope he loses!" Irma said, going over to pat Delores's arm. "He never should have dunked you like that!"

"Thank you," Delores said, giving a little sigh. "He dunked me three times in a row, three years ago at the Winnetka County Fair, and I was ready to kill him when I came out of that tank! He ruined one of my favorite dresses!"

"I just got in a new shipment," Claire said. "Come over to Beau Monde and take a look. We have a couple there that look almost like the one that No-No ruined for you in the dunk tank."

Delores perked up immediately. "Really? What time will you open this morning, Claire?"

"Just as soon as I finish my coffee. I'm almost positive you're going to find something you'll love."

"Hello, ladies," Herb greeted them as he opened the front door of The Cookie Jar and came in.

"You looked very official, giving No-No that ticket," Hannah praised him.

"Yes, you did." Several of the women nodded in agreement.

"Did you see what happened to No-No?" Norman's mother, Carrie, asked, rushing through the front door. She stopped when she spotted Herb and went over to pat him on the shoulder. "Good work, Herb! I hope you gave him an expensive ticket!"

Herb smiled. "I did. Lake Eden can use the money." He looked over at Delores. "I hope that ticket makes you feel a little better."

"Thank you, Herb." Delores smiled back. "That man is a cad and a bounder!"

"You sound like one of your Regency romance novels, Delores."

"You're right. I do. They had a real talent for describing people like him back then. I know one thing for sure . . . I'm never going to forgive him for embarrassing me that day! I'm going to get even, just you watch. I'm not sure how, but I can tell you one thing for certain. It's not going to be pretty!"

Chapter Twelve

"**D**o you know that there are over one hundred and fifty different lakes named *Long Lake* in Minnesota?" Norman asked Hannah, pulling out of the Lake Eden city limits and onto the highway.

"I knew it was a common name for a lake, but didn't know there were that many!"

"I guess we're lucky that this particular Long Lake is fairly close," Norman commented, speeding up a bit. "Your Lakeside Stew smells really good, but I don't smell any fish. I expected salmon or cod, or even walleye."

"You don't smell fish, because there isn't any," Hannah told him. "This Lakeside Stew is a bratwurst stew, without any fish at all in it."

Norman laughed. "Leave it to you to do something unexpected!"

"Are you disappointed that I didn't use any fish?"

"Not at all. What did you use?"

"Mostly I used Polish sausage and brats. I put several different kinds of bratwurst into the Lakeside Stew."

"I didn't know that there were more than a couple types," Norman said, sounding surprised.

"There are a lot more than most people think, and Florence seems to carry them all. She made some up in her toaster oven for Andrea, and Andrea was totally amazed with how good they were."

"What else is in your stew?" Norman asked.

"Campbell's Cream of Celery soup, mushroom pieces, potatoes, carrots, Campbell's Cream of Mushroom soup, and quite a few other ingredients."

"That all sounds good to me. Look at this cute little place." He pointed to a small restaurant that they were slowly passing.

"That's The Hub," Hannah stated.

"That's what it says on the bench in front. Have you been there?"

"Yes, several times with my parents when I was little. They had great steaks there, and Mother knew the woman who owned it. Her name was Doris. I don't really remember, but I think her husband's name was Hank. Anyway, Doris was always very nice to me, and she used to give me nickels to play their pinball machine."

"Here's the turnoff for Stella's cabin," Norman said, turning off the highway and onto a gravel road. "When she gave me directions on the phone, she said it was about three miles in. It's a big cabin, Hannah . . . three bedrooms. She said she'd really love it if we'd stay until Mike went to bed for the night."

"That's okay with me, if it's okay with you," Hannah responded.

"It's fine with me. So that's what we'll do then. Stella probably wants to talk to us about Mike after he retires for the night."

They rode on in silence for another couple of minutes and eventually Norman pulled up into a paved driveway.

"Is this it?" Hannah asked.

"Yes. I'll carry in the crockpot, Hannah. You can take the bag with whatever else you brought."

"Okay. All I have are a few finishing touches."

"Like what?"

"Like oyster crackers, Goldfish crackers, some gravy mix, and a couple of bottles of Cold Spring Export for Mike."

"I've got ginger ale and lemonade for me," Norman said, opening the back door and taking out a cooler with lemonade and a couple bottles of ginger ale.

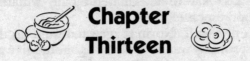

Chapter Thirteen

"This cabin is huge, Stella!" Hannah said once she'd finished plugging in the slow cooker and helping Stella set the table with soup bowls and spoons.

"I know. When my parents retired, they lived here year-round. They even had a monarch garden."

"I know what that is. As a matter of fact, I've got one, too. Did they have help setting theirs up?" Norman asked, putting the lemonade, ginger ale, and beer away in Stella's refrigerator.

"You betcha. They got instructions from the University of Minnesota website telling them exactly what to plant to attract the butterflies. The monarchs that their garden attracted were beautiful . . . bright orange and deep black. My parents used to go to California every year to visit my aunt and uncle and they had a monarch garden, too. Dad said that the California garden had only light yellow monarchs, and that was because the monarchs' colors were determined by the climate and the food they ate."

"Hey, Mike!" Norman greeted him as Mike came into the kitchen. "How's the fishing?"

"Not good. I got totally skunked today."

"Well, sit down and drown your sorrow with one of the Cold Spring Export beers we brought."

"All right!" Mike looked pleased as he sat down at the table and accepted a bottle of beer from Norman. "Something smells really good in here."

"It's Hannah's Lakeside Stew," Stella explained. "She brought everything, including oyster crackers."

"That's good. I'm glad she brought those. Oyster crackers will be the closest thing to fish that I'll eat today. The fish just weren't biting at all!"

"Don't worry, Mike," Hannah said with a grin. "If you really miss fish all that much, I've got you covered. I brought Goldfish with me, too!"

Mike looked confused until Norman spoke up. "She means those little crunchy cheese crackers, Mike."

"Very funny, Hannah," Mike said with a chuckle. "For a second there, you had me going."

Stella poured a glass of white wine for Hannah, and sat down at the table across from her guests. "It's pretty out here, isn't it?"

"It is," Hannah replied. "We drove past a place I recognized from years ago. It was a steak house my parents used to frequent. We went there almost every Friday night. That's the place where I embarrassed my dad."

"How did you do that?" Stella asked.

"He left money on the table for a tip, and I picked it up because I thought he'd forgotten it.

And then, when we got back, I forgot to get the money out of my pocket to give it to him."

"Did you give it to him eventually?" Mike asked her.

"Yes, but it was a couple of months later when I wore that particular little coat again. I remember telling him that he forgot it on the table and I picked it up for him."

"Did he explain about tips?"

"Yes! And I was so embarrassed about my mistake that I didn't want to go there again."

"But you did?" Norman asked.

"Yes, and I apologized to Doris for picking up Dad's money, and I promised never to do that again." Hannah chuckled.

"And she understood what you meant?"

"Yes. As a matter of fact, she laughed and gave me an envelope with some nickels to put in their jukebox. The Hub was my favorite place after that."

Hannah lifted the cover on the crockpot, gave the stew a stir, and reached for the soup ladle. "Dinner's ready," she announced.

"Oh, good!" Mike sounded very grateful. "I thought I was going to starve to death sitting here smelling your stew."

LAKESIDE STEW
(a crockpot recipe)

Ingredients:

2 pounds of red potatoes *(washed and quartered)*

2 large or 3 medium sized carrots *(peeled and roughly chopped in 4 pieces each)*

3 ribs of celery *(chopped into chunks about the size of your little finger)*

1 large yellow or brown onion *(peeled and diced)*

1 15-ounce can of whole kernel sweet corn *(I used Libby's)*

2 cans mushrooms *(I used Green Giant)*

2 pounds of good Bratwurst, Knockwurst, or Polish Sausages *(sliced into 1-inch pieces)*

1 12-ounce can of chicken broth *(I used Swanson)*

2 10.5 ounce cans of cream of mushroom soup *(I used Campbell's)*

2 10.5 ounce cans of cream of celery soup *(I used Campbell's)*

1 teaspoon of dried basil

1 teaspoon of cayenne pepper

1 teaspoon of paprika *(we all love Hungarian paprika, but regular paprika works just fine*
1 and ½ cups of half & half *(or 1 cup of heavy cream)*

Directions:

Place potatoes, carrots, celery, onion, corn, and mushrooms in a 5- or 6-quart slow cooker, stirring to mix all the vegetables together.

Layer your 2 pounds of sausages over the top of the vegetables.

Combine your chicken broth, cream of mushroom soup, cream of celery soup, and seasonings together in a measuring cup, stir everything up, and pour it over the sausages in the slow cooker.

Set the slow cooker to **LOW** and cover it with the lid.

Cook covered for 6 to 7 hours. *(By this time the sausages will be incredibly tender and the vegetables will be "cooked to a turn.")*

Stir the 1 and ½ cups of half & half, *or the 1 cup of heavy cream,* into the stew.

Cover the slow cooker once again and turn it up to **HIGH**, cooking your stew for 30 minutes more.

After 30 minutes have passed, turn the slow cooker down to **WARM**, and you are done!

Serve your Lakeside Stew in either bowls or soup mugs, with a bowl of sour cream, some freshly chopped parsley, and chopped fresh tomatoes to top it all off *(if you want to make it more special for company).*

Heck, if your guests are looking particularly hungry that day, try adding a fresh green salad and good, crusty bread, and create a small feast for them!

Chapter Fourteen

Hannah looked up in surprise as Stella got up from her place at the table and quickly moved toward the kitchen. "Do you need another hand, Stella?" Hannah asked.

"No, that's okay. I just forgot a couple of things," Stella replied. "I've got this well in hand, but thank you for asking."

After a minute or two, Stella came back from the kitchen carrying a serving platter stacked with several small bowls, each one filled with a different item.

"Gosh, Stella," Norman said, leaping to his feet, "let me help you carry that."

"Me, too," Mike said, getting up as well, quickly following Norman's lead in offering to help.

"Okay, boys,"—Hannah laughed out loud—"you're not fooling anyone, you know! Stella and I both know that the reason you two are so anxious to help now, all of a sudden, is that you're both ready to eat *and* you are curious to know what's in the bowls on the platter, right?"

"You've sure got them pegged, Hannah," Stella said, joining Hannah in laughing. She rolled her eyes at the two men as she maneuvered deftly around them, ducking and weaving at their attempts to grab the platter, and continuing on her way to the dining room table. "Just look at the poor waifs, Hannah! Can't you see that they're slowly wasting away with hunger as we speak?"

Hannah got up, helping Stella to unload the bowls from the platter, while still giggling at Stella's description of Mike and Norman as *poor waifs*. "I'm sure you're correct, Stella." She chortled out the words in a way that kept threatening to break into full-blown laughter. "Absolutely anyone could see . . . that the platter is far too heavy for them to lift, even if they weren't so weakened with hunger by the long wait for dinner!"

"Very funny, ladies," Mike said, sitting back into his chair. "I'll have you know, we are not *that* hungry. It's not like we're—" Just then, Mike's stomach gave off a deep growl, and the whole table burst into laughter, including a red-faced Mike.

"Speak for yourself, Mike," Norman said with a straight face. "Oh wait . . . I think your stomach just did it for you!"

"Enough about these wee starving lads, Hannah. I can't wait to try the Lakeside Stew!" Stella announced. "Everyone just grab whatever additions you want from the small bowls in the middle of the table. We've got shredded cheese, oyster crackers, regular crackers, Goldfish crackers, chopped onion, and there is even a bottle of *Slap Ya Mama* hot sauce for Mike."

Mike dipped his spoon in his bowl, took a spoonful, and began to smile. "This is really good, Hannah!" he said, reaching for the Slap Ya Mama hot sauce and shaking a few drops into the Lakeside Stew.

"Thank you," Hannah responded.

"It sure is," Norman agreed, reaching for some Goldfish crackers and adding them to his bowl. "I know that I'll love these Goldfish cheese crackers in it, but it's just wonderful the way that it is!"

"Well, personally, I like oyster crackers in my stew," Stella responded. "Looks like there's something for everybody tonight. And after we finish eating, I'd like to take you all out to the Rock Tavern."

"Where's that?" Hannah asked.

"About five miles from here, around the long side of the lake. It was built over fifty years ago and the grandchildren of the original owners still run it."

"Is it built out of rocks?" Hannah asked, reacting to the name.

"Yes, and the rocks have sawed-off bottles between them. There's a bright light outside at night so you can see the colored bottles glow between the rocks."

"Sounds pretty," Mike said.

"It is. And just in case you're curious, Mike, they've got Cold Spring Export on tap. I called ahead to make sure."

"Even better!" Mike said, taking another spoonful of his stew and smiling. "You really made a great stew, Hannah. I think I just got a piece of Polish sausage."

"You probably did. Florence had Polish sausage, apple and celery sausage, and even Weisswurst."

"Weisswurst?" Mike looked curious. "What's that?"

"White sausage. I sent Andrea to the store and I swear she bought every different kind of sausage that Florence had in her meat case. She also bought corn, mushrooms, and potatoes for the stew."

"So this stew really *does* have everything in it," Norman said with a smile. "It's really good, Hannah."

"Yes, it is," Stella agreed. "Do you have a recipe, Hannah? I could add it to my limited repertoire of bacon and eggs."

"Maybe it's a limited menu, but your bacon and eggs are great!" Mike complimented her.

"Thank you, Mike, but I have a feeling you're going to get pretty tired of them soon." She turned to Hannah. "Can you leave us some stew if there's any left over? We can't go fishing tomorrow because the cable man's coming sometime between eight and two."

"We're getting cable television?" Mike looked excited at the prospect.

"Yes, but don't get too excited," Stella warned him. "He told me on the phone that the only station he thought we could pull in out here was KCOW-TV."

Mike gave a little shrug. "That's better than nothing. I wonder if they'll televise the baseball tournament in Lake Eden."

"They probably will," Hannah answered. "Mother was talking to Mayor Stephanie Bascomb about it the other day, and she thought they'd cover it."

"Great!" Mike looked very pleased at the news. "I love baseball. If the cable gets hooked up in time, we'll probably see you on television, Hannah."

"That's doubtful. I'll be at the parade if you get the cable set up in time for that, but I'm working at one of the Snack Shacks during the game."

Norman started to grin. "Hannah wasn't very nice to the umpire the last time she watched a ball game. Now they keep her in one of the three Snack Shacks so she can't yell at the officials."

Hannah sighed. "I'm afraid so. I turn into a loudmouth when I think they've called the strikes and the balls wrong. I guess I'm just lucky they let me go to baseball games at all in Lake Eden."

Chapter
Fifteen

Hannah sat bolt upright in the bed that Stella had provided. For a moment, she was totally disoriented, but then she remembered that Stella had asked them to spend the night at her parents' cabin. She jumped out of bed, grabbed the robe and slippers that Stella had given her, and hurried out into the living room. "What's happening?" she asked, looking around the room in confusion.

"I forgot to tell the *city boy* about the loons," Stella explained. "Can you help me make us some hot cocoa?"

"Of course. You take care of Mike, and cue Norman in on what's happening. I'll take care of the hot chocolate. Do you happen to have any miniature marshmallows?"

"Right here," Stella said, pulling a bag of minia-ture marshmallows out of the pantry. "They're fresh, so don't worry about that. Hot cocoa with marshmallows will probably calm Mike right down."

It only took a few minutes to prepare the hot chocolate, and Hannah carried out four cups and the saucepan she'd used to make the cocoa. "Is it okay to set these cups here?" she asked Stella.

"That's fine. Just put the pot down on that trivet." She turned to Norman. "Sorry about the rude awakening, Norman. I forgot to tell the *city boy* here that it's mating season for Minnesota loons."

Norman chuckled. "Don't worry about it, Stella. I just about jumped out of my skin the first time that I heard a loon. It's a very eerie cry, especially if you don't know what it is or where it's coming from."

"Right," Stella agreed. "It sounds like an insane woman laughing. I'd better go get Mike before he totally freaks out."

A few moments later, Mike came into the living room, looking a bit embarrassed. "Sorry," he apologized. "I had no idea that loons sounded that way. It was . . ."

"Unnerving." Norman provided the word Mike was looking for. "I felt the same way the first time I heard one."

"Minnesota has a lot of strange things," Hannah said, pouring hot cocoa for each of them. "For example, there's the Pink and White Lady's Slipper. That's the state flower."

"What's so unusual about that?" Mike wanted to know.

"It's poisonous. Isn't that strange?" Norman answered him. "When I moved back to Minnesota, I went to the University of Minnesota website to learn more about the state . . . Did you know that the official Minnesota state drink is milk?"

"Given how many dairy farmers there are here, that makes sense," Stella chimed in. "But I've got one a little harder for you. What is the Minnesota state tree?"

"I know this one . . . it's so easy," Mike said. "It's the Christmas tree, right?"

"Close, but no cookie, Mike," Hannah spoke up as she joined in on the impromptu early-morning Minnesota trivia battle. "It's actually the Norway Pine. I know because Tracey had to do a report on the early days of logging in Minnesota!"

"Very cute, Hannah," Mike said. "I see what you did there with the *close, but no cookie* comment. All right, I've got one for you . . . What is the Minnesota official state bee?"

"What?" Norman frowned at Mike. "There is no such thing as an official Minnesota state bee, unless you're talking about a spelling bee or a quilting bee!"

"Wrong, Norman. There is an official Minnesota state bee. It is, in fact, the Rusty Patched Bumblebee," Mike proclaimed.

"Are you okay, Mike?" Hannah asked, looking concerned at Mike's sudden turn into an apian expert.

"I'm fine," Mike replied. "Why do you ask?"

"No particular reason. I guess that I never knew that you had a secret identity before."

"What do you mean? What secret identity?"

"Detective Mike . . . *the bee whisperer,*" Hannah said.

When the groans from Mike, Norman, and Stella had died down a bit, Hannah continued. "Okay, everyone, I've got one final Minnesota trivia question for you, and then we should all try and get a little more sleep. Ready? What is the Minnesota state perfume?"

"Eau de 10,000 Lakes?" Stella guessed quickly.

"Le parfum de green bean casserole?" Norman asked.

Hannah burst into laughter at their silliness. "No, my friends, not even close . . . it's Deep Woods Off."

Chapter Sixteen

Hannah had just removed the last sheet of Chocolate Lace Cookies from the oven when there was a knock at her back kitchen door. It was a knock she recognized, a knock that was timid at first and then gained volume almost as if her early-morning caller was saying, "Yes, I do belong here. Hurry up!"

"Coming!" Hannah called out, hurrying to open the door. "Come in, Andrea. I just put on a fresh pot of coffee if you want some."

"Great!" Andrea stepped in and went straight to the kitchen coffeepot. "Do you want some?"

"Yes." Hannah walked over to the work station and was about to sit down when her sister did something that surprised Hannah.

Andrea reached out and hugged her. "Thank you, Hannah!"

"Me?" Hannah was surprised. "Thank you, Andrea, but why are you thanking me?"

"Because Bill told me that I was a genius last night. And it's all because of you."

"Me?"

"Yes. It was right after he tasted the stew you taught me how to make. He loved it, Hannah!"

"Well . . . good!" Hannah responded, a bit uncertain exactly what she'd done to deserve this early-morning gratitude.

"I also tested out an alternative recipe for Blue Cheese Meatloaf Mountains."

"Blue Cheese Meatloaf Mountains?" Hannah was thoroughly puzzled. "What are those?"

"It's little individual meatloaves with blue cheese in them, made in muffin tins."

"But . . . I didn't teach you how to make that . . . did I?"

"No. I got the idea from Rose at the café, I just used the recipe for meatloaf that you got from Grandma Swensen as the base, and added blue cheese. Then, after it was baked, I piped a snowy mashed potato top over that, with little parsley trees dotted all around it."

"That was very smart of you. Wait a second . . . you frosted the meatloaf mountain with what?"

"Mashed potatoes! The girls and I practiced using all those decorating tips that Florence sold me. It was easy to use the pastry bag with those. And when Bethie and Tracey went to bed for the night, I practiced some more with real frosting from a can. I'm pretty sure I can frost the Pink Lemonade Cakes you made for the banquet, Hannah. I can do rose petal shapes to make the side of the cake decorations now and then I can put little roses on top to finish."

"With frosting . . . right? Not mashed potatoes?"

"Yes, with frosting," Andrea said with a laugh. "You'll let me try to do it, won't you?"

"Of course I will! Roses would be pretty on top of the cakes. And if things don't turn out the way you think they will, we can always scrape off the frosting and you can do it again."

"Good!" Andrea looked very excited. "I'll get started just as soon as I finish my coffee, but . . . don't watch me, Hannah. You might make me nervous."

"Okay, I won't look," Hannah promised, picking up her coffee cup and taking a sip. "I'll just bake a few more cookies and then you can decorate the cakes."

An hour later, Andrea asked, "What do you think?" gesturing toward the Pink Lemonade Cake that she had just finished frosting.

Hannah came over to look and began to smile. "Perfect!" she said. "All that practice with the pastry bag must have helped. You did a beautiful job on those pink roses. They're a cake decorator's dream! Just wait until Mother sees them. Everyone's going to be very impressed with you."

"Thank you." Andrea looked pleased. "I'll frost the rest of the Pink Lemonade Cakes now."

"Take your time," Hannah told her. "We've got all day to prepare for the banquet tonight."

PINK LEMONADE CAKE

Preheat oven to 350 degrees F., rack in the middle position.

Coat two 8-inch or 9-inch round cake pans with Pam or another non-sticking baking spray (the kind with flour in it) and line with parchment paper.

Ingredients

1 18-ounce box White Cake Mix *(plus any ingredients the instructions on the box call for)*

1 envelope *(0.23 ounce)* Kool-Aid Pink Lemonade Natural Flavor Unsweetened Drink Mix

1 teaspoon finely grated lemon zest *(just the rind, not the bitter white part)*

2 teaspoons vanilla extract

1 ounce grenadine *(find this in the liquor section of your grocery store—but it is non-alcoholic)*

Note: 1 ounce of grenadine = .5 Tablespoons

Directions:

For the cake, in a large bowl, prepare the cake batter according to the package directions.

Mix in the 1 envelope *(0.23 ounce)* Kool-Aid Pink Lemonade Natural Flavor Unsweetened Drink Mix.

Stir 1 teaspoon finely-grated lemon zest *(just the rind, not the bitter white part)* and 2 teaspoons of vanilla into the batter.

Stir in the ounce of grenadine and that completes the batter.

Pour the batter evenly between the 2 prepared cake pans.

Bake at 350 degrees F., for 30 to 35 minutes, or until golden brown and a toothpick inserted into the cakes 1-inch from the center comes out clean.

Using oven mitts, remove the cakes from the oven and let them cool 10 minutes on a cold stovetop burner or wire rack.

After 10 minutes have passed, turn the pans upside-down over a wire rack and let them cool completely while you make the frosting *(recipe follows)*.

PINK LEMONADE CREAM CHEESE FROSTING

Frosting Ingredients:

8 ounces cream cheese, softened to room
temperature

1 cup *(2 sticks, 16 tablespoons)* salted butter, softened to room temperature

1 pinch table salt

2 teaspoons grated lemon zest (just the
yellow zest, not the bitter white pith)

4 cups powdered sugar

4 Tablespoons Frozen Pink Lemonade
Concentrate

1 Tablespoon grenadine (you can find
this in the liquor department of any
grocery store)

**Hannah's 1st Note: This frosting is easier if
you use a stand or hand mixer**

Directions:

Mix the softened cream cheese and softened
butter together in a large bowl.

Add in the salt and grated lemon zest. Mix
until well combined.

Add the powdered sugar, 1 cup at a time, mixing after each addition.

Add the Frozen Pink Lemonade Concentrate and the grenadine.

Mix until everything is well combined

Let your frosting chill in the refrigerator for 30 minutes.

To Frost Your Pink Lemonade Cake:

Take the first of your cake layers off the cooling rack and put the first layer, upside down, on a cake plate.

Using a frosting knife, slather the top of the layer with the Pink Lemonade Cream Cheese Frosting.

Put the second cake layer, right-side up, on top of the frosting you've just spread.

Use your impeccably clean palms to press down a bit on the second layer, to make sure that it is securely in place on top of your frosted layer.

Then, again using a frosting knife, frost the sides of the two-layer cake. Use the edge of the frosting knife to smooth out the frosting.

Slather the rest of the frosting on top of your cake and spread out evenly.

Smooth the frosting you placed on the top of your cake.

That's it *(Unless you want to grate a tiny bit of lemon zest on the top of your comply frosted cake to make it extra fancy)*!

Hannah's 2nd Note: If you have any leftover frosting, spread it on saltine crackers or graham cracker for a snack for kids or grandkids when they get home.

Chapter Seventeen

"Hello, everyone," Delores said, taking a seat at the large, round banquet table where Hannah, Norman, Andrea, and Bill were waiting for her. She looked down at the two-layer Pink Lemonade Cake that was sitting there, as a center-piece, and smiled. "I love those pink frosting roses on our cake, Hannah. They are quite elegant."

"That's Andrea's work," Hannah said quickly. "She frosted all the Pink Lemonade Cakes here for the dinner tonight."

"Well . . . they're just beautiful!" Delores congratulated Andrea. "You've always had an eye for color and detail, Andrea."

"Thank you, Mother," Andrea said, waving at someone who had just come in the door. "There's Michelle. And she's with Lonnie and Rick."

"I'm so pleased they're here! And they're right on time, too," Delores said, waving at them. "We have room for everyone here at the table, don't we?"

"We do," Hannah said, quickly counting the number of chairs. "It's fine, Mother. Everyone can sit with us."

"Stephanie's going to give the welcome speech," Delores informed them. "And she told me that she was going to introduce all of the Summer Solstice Queen candidates first, then some of the notable All-Stars, and finally, the names of the baseball teams that will be playing in our All-Star Baseball Tournament. She said that we even have several players that used to be in the big leagues."

Hannah winced. She really hoped that No-No wasn't among them. She knew how much Delores disliked him, and her mother wouldn't be silent about that fact.

Several girls from the Home Economics classes at Jordan High walked around the tables serving coffee, and then Stephanie Bascomb got up to speak.

"Thank you all for coming tonight," Stephanie said. "Lake Eden is very fortunate to be hosting the Winnetka County All-Star Baseball Tournament and I will mention those teams tonight . . . but first, we have several luminaries that I'd like to introduce."

"I hope Doc gets here in time to hear the rest of Stephanie's introductions," Delores said, giving a little sigh.

"He's still at the hospital?" Hannah guessed.

"That's right. There was a patient that he was very concerned about. He promised me that he'd try to get here, but"—she glanced at her watch—"it doesn't look to me like he's going to make it in time."

"We're here, Mother," Andrea pointed out.

"I know, dear, but I wanted Doc to get a good look at THAT man."

"You're talking about No-No," Hannah guessed.

"Yes. I'll never forget how he embarrassed me at the Winnetka County Fair. That was one of the worst moments of my life!"

"I know, Mother." Hannah reached out to pat her mother on the back.

"We ALL know," Andrea added, looking around the table.

"Thank you, everyone," Stephanie Bascomb said, smiling at the guests. "I'd just like to point out a few things before we start tonight's program. As I said . . . there are several notable luminaries I'd like to introduce, but before that, I'd like you all to look down at the absolutely lovely Pink Lemonade Cakes that Hannah Swensen made for our dessert tonight. And Hannah's sister, Andrea Todd, decorated your lovely cakes. So let's give Hannah and Andrea a round of applause for a dessert fit for a king, or rather, fit for a Summer Solstice Queen!"

There was a round of applause from the audience and Stephanie went on. "Thank you. And now . . . one of our first luminaries . . . a man who made his dream come true by pitching in the big leagues. And since he retired from organized baseball, over a year ago, this means that he is eligible to pitch in our Winnetka County All-Star Baseball Tournament! Here he is, Bernie *No-No* Fulton! Come up here and take a bow, Bernie. And while he's making his way up here, I'll also tell you that No-No pitched a perfect game during the season he was pitching up in the majors, so we are expecting quite a performance from him during our All-Star tournament."

"Show-off!" Delores muttered, as No-No stood up to take a bow. "He's the one who came to the Winnetka County Fair and dunked me three times in that tank of water. I swore I'd get even with him someday, and I still feel the same way I did then!"

"Delores!" A voice spoke up from behind Delores's shoulder. "I see you're wearing a really nice dress tonight. Have you been in any good dunk tanks lately?"

"You . . . cad!" Delores said loudly, and drew back her hand in preparation to slap him. "I'll get even with you for that, No-No! Everyone heard me before, and now I'll say it even louder. I promise you all that I will get my revenge on you!"

No-No just laughed, then walked up the steps to the stage to join Stephanie at the podium. "As you all can see, I'm shaking like a leaf now that Delores has promised to take her revenge on me. All I can say is . . . good luck, Delores. You may very well think about getting your revenge, but it's never going to happen!"

Stephanie winced slightly at the insult to her friend. "Thank you, No-No. And now . . . I'd like to introduce you all to the lovely young ladies who will be in our Queen's Court. They will all be competing for the title, but only one of them . . . just one . . . will be chosen to be our Summer Solstice Queen."

The audience applauded as each of the young ladies got up from their seats at the Queen's Court table, displaying the smiles they'd practiced to look attractive on camera, and waving at the audience.

Hannah began looking around at the other tables next to her as Stephanie walked down the stairs and over to the Queen's Court table to greet all of the candidates before announcing them. Hannah noticed that the table directly behind them held a middle-aged gentleman who was leaning forward in his chair and staring daggers directly at No-No, with a scowl so black on his face that Hannah felt a bit frightened. "Boy, if looks could kill, No-No would be pushing up daisies right about now," Hannah said. "I wonder what he did to earn that murderous look from that man?"

"You didn't hear about No-No's first scandal in the majors, Hannah?" Lonnie questioned.

"No, I haven't heard anything about it. What was No-No's first big-league scandal, and while we are at it, who is that man with the laser-beam eyes? You know, the one who is sitting at the table behind us and staring a hole right through No-No? You know, the guy who is looking at him like No-No should be six feet under, rather than here in Lake Eden?"

"That's a sad tale, Hannah," Lonnie replied, looking Hannah in the eyes. "There once was a journeyman baseball player named Zack Edwards who was never that great as a fielder, but man, could he ever hit that ball a ton! I mean, on the right day, and with the right pitcher to hit against, he could drive that ball like nobody's business. And he was an even better hitter in pressure situations. He was on the back side of his career as a ball player, though, and usually he spent most of his time down in AAA ball, dreaming of a big finish, the one year in which he might win a World Series ring. Don't get me wrong. He was not really a big league mainstay, due to his concrete glove, but Zack would get called up, regular as clockwork, every fall when the parent club needed some punch in the lineup for the playoff run. That is, up until that tragic year his career ended for good."

"Okay, Lonnie, you've got my attention now. This is pretty good stuff, but what does this have to do with No-No and the scowling man?"

Lonnie chortled. "Wow, that sounds like a title for a detective novel, doesn't it? *The Case of No-No and the Scowling Man*! Now hush, Hannah, and let me finish. This is too good a story to rush . . . Now, where was I? Ah, right . . . all throughout that fateful last year, Zack was hitting the cra . . . I mean, hitting the heck out of the ball! He had been leading the minors in hitting throughout the whole first half of the season. His batting average was hovering around .350, he'd already racked up twenty-seven home runs, and he was putting up record RBI numbers for the Royals' AAA league affiliate. He even got to play in the AAA All-Star Game, something he'd never accomplished before! That led to him getting called up to the bigs a lot earlier than he'd ever been called up before."

"Come on, Lonnie! This is fine, but what about No-No?" Hannah ground her teeth, thinking Lonnie was dragging the story out.

"Calm down, Hannah," Lonnie said soothingly. "It's almost over now. Hmm . . . Okay, well, Zack Edwards is called up to the Kansas City Royals in early August that last season, and he continues the batting tear he had been on in the minors for that year, but hitting even better and with a lot more power. I mean, Zack was smacking the best pitchers in the majors around like they owed him rent or something! He was having a game-changer of a season, hitting the ball to every field with power, clearing the bases, and he even managed to improve his fielding a bit."

Hannah leaned closer to Lonnie and asked, "But how did it all go bad, Lonnie?"

"On August 17 during that epic season the Kansas City Royals were playing the Twins, who'd just called up their latest prospect, a guy called Bernie *No-No* Fulton. He was a fire-baller, said to have triggered the radar gun at one hundred miles per hour plus, and what No-No wanted, more than anything else in life, was to be a starting pitcher in the big leagues for the Twins. It was his very first pitching appearance for the big team that evening, and our big-headed friend got shelled! The main culprit in this absolute shellacking was a somewhat older player, a player who for most of his adult life was a minor leaguer. A player with one last chance to prove that he was worthy of the big leagues, and who just happened to be having the best season of his life. Yup, you guessed it! Good old Zack Edwards went three-for-five, with six RBIs off of No-No that night, including a three-run jack, which not only knocked No-No out of the ball game, but also knocked him out of the majors. He was sent back down to an Iowa farm team, and boy, was he angry about it."

Hannah sighed, reluctant to show Lonnie that she was enjoying his storytelling skills but wanting him to keep on going until the end. "I suppose I have to ask once again, Lonnie, what this has to do with the man behind us and why he's scowling at No-No."

"Almost there, Hannah." Lonnie grinned. "We're heading down the homestretch. Now, because of what has happened with your mother and No-No, I know that *you* understand this. But not many people knew back then that No-No was, and still is, a petty, vindictive man who has a mad-on for anyone who challenges him head-to-head, and even more so for anyone who reveals him as the insignificant little gnat that he is. So picture this . . . here is No-No, sent down to the minors, stewing in his anger and resentment toward Zack Edwards, and plotting his revenge . . . said revenge only waiting for No-No's triumphant return to pitching in the majors. Well, it took a while, but No-No actually applied himself toward controlling his temper, as well as his tendency to groove the fastball. Sure enough, No-No returned to the Twins late that season, just in the nick of time for the final push to the playoffs. And guess which two teams were running neck and neck for the pennant?"

"Just tell me, Lonnie!"

"It was the Royals and the Twins with one game to go and the pennant riding on it."

"And . . . ?"

"Dickie Kominski of the Royals and No-No Fulton of the Twins were the starting pitchers. No-No pitched really well, striking out ten hitters in the first eight innings. The only one who really crushed the ball for the Royals was Zack Edwards, who hit two-for-three off No-No, including a stand-up double, and a rocket of a triple, which just missed leaving the yard by a foot. However, the rest of the Royals team couldn't solve No-No's fastball, and the Royals stranded Zack on base after both hits, as No-No struck the batters who followed Zack out. The game was tied and the Twins finally scored with one out in the top of the eighth. A walk, a stolen base, a passed ball, and a perfect sacrifice squeeze play got the Twins in front, one to nothing, until the Royals batted in the bottom of the eighth. Zack Edwards came up to bat with runners on second and third, but two outs. Zack hit No-No's best fastball so hard, and so far, that the ball should have had its own area code . . . but it hooked just foul. Zack stepped out of the batter's box, knocked off the dirt on his cleats with his bat, and gave No-No a little smirk . . . and that's when it happened. According to fans who were there, No-No went into his wind-up and threw a screaming fastball, right at Zack! Zack froze for one second, and that was his undoing. That single pitch by No-No shattered Zack's left elbow joint into powder, and by doing so, it completely ended not only the best year of Zack's life, but completely ended Zack's baseball career forever." Lonnie took a sip of his iced tea and, looking at Hannah, said, "Do you understand who that man glaring at No-No is now, Hannah? And why he is looking like he would like nothing better than to bury No-No in a shallow grave, hopefully while he is still breathing?"

Hannah looked over at Lonnie in amazement. "You don't mean that's . . . Zack Edwards, do you, Lonnie?"

"I knew that you'd figure it out, Hannah. That's Zack, all right. His son, Phil, plays for the Grey Eagle Warriors as their shortstop, and Zack is here in Lake Eden to support him during the All-Star tournament."

Hannah looked up as Stephanie began to speak once again. "May I have your attention, please . . . While Jordan High Home Economics students deliver coffee to our tables and cut slices of the beautiful Pink Lemonade Cakes, I'd like to introduce each of the lovely young women who will be competing for the title of Lake Eden's Summer Solstice Queen. Ladies, I will call you, one by one, by name, and I will ask you to join me here on stage, forming a single line on my right, as your name is called." Stephanie paused to look down at the sheet of paper she'd placed on the podium. "But before that, I'd just like to remind you that our Summer Solstice Parade will begin at ten o'clock tomorrow morning. Every high school participating in the Winnetka County All-Star Baseball Tournament has provided a float for their Summer Solstice Queen candidate, and this float will be accompanied by its corresponding high school marching band. The first float will be from Jordan High School, right here in Lake Eden. Which leads us to our first contestant. A warm Lake Eden welcome, please, for one of our own, Jordan High's candidate for Queen of the Summer Solstice, Miss Dorothy Peters. She loves classical music and this is her third year playing violin in the Jordan High Orchestra as first chair. Come on up here, and stand just behind me to my right, Dorothy."

Everyone applauded as Dorothy walked up to the podium and stood a bit behind Stephanie.

"Our second Summer Solstice Queen candidate is Donna Jensen from Browerville High School.

She is the head cheerleader for the Browerville Tigers, who are competing in our All-Star tournament. Come up here, Donna, and stand next to Dorothy." Stephanie motioned, and Donna made her way to the stage, standing to the right of the first candidate.

"Our third candidate is Princeton High School's Carrie Matthews. She has led the Princeton Monarchs' high school debate team to two consecutive Minnesota State championships." A stunning red-haired girl strode confidently to the stage and shook Stephanie's hand, getting in line next to the others.

"The next contender for the throne of Summer Solstice Queen hails from Little Falls, Minnesota, and her favorite team is the Little Falls Bisons. Her name is Paige O'Connor, and she is the head baton twirler for the Bisons' award-winning marching band." A petite young lady with a short, pixie-style haircut made her way up the stairs to where the other girls waited, and stood there, smiling and waving.

"We are more than halfway through now," Stephanie informed the crowd. "Lucky candidate number five is someone known throughout Minnesota for her portrait paintings in acrylics . . . In fact, she has already had her first gallery show in her hometown of Long Prairie, Minnesota, and she is a huge fan of the Long Prairie Lions baseball team . . . Please welcome Miss Faith DeMarco."

Faith joined the other girls on stage to scattered applause, looking around as she awaited the final three contestants for Summer Solstice Queen.

"On to our number six contestant," Stephanie said, smiling widely. "She comes to us from Elk

River, Minnesota, and she is representing the Elk River Stags, not only as their reigning Homecoming Queen, but also as their candidate for Winnetka County Summer Solstice Queen. Her name is Miss Amelia Tremaine. Amelia is known for her outstanding GPA in Biology and Chemistry at Elk River High School, and she was just offered a full scholarship to the University of Chicago for next year."

Amelia gracefully walked to the stage and up the stairs, joining the rest of the young ladies standing there. Stephanie leaned forward into the microphone and, lowering her voice in tone and in volume, she smiled, knowing full well that she was nearing the end of the candidates, and it was time to ramp up the drama.

"Our second-to-last contestant comes from Upsala, Minnesota, and she plays piano in competitions all throughout the Midwest, recently winning a Jack Kent Cooke Music and Arts Scholarship to attend the University of Minnesota. She is also a huge fan of the Upsala Beavers baseball team. Ladies and gentlemen, please give a warm welcome to Grace Sweeney, who is here tonight to support the Upsala Beavers baseball team.

"Our final talented contestant is of Native American heritage. In fact, she is a member of the Mille Lacs band of the Ojibwa tribe. She loves her Grey Eagle Warriors baseball team, and has since childhood. She is widely known, not only for her beautiful singing voice, but also for her charity work. She can often be found reading to the elderly at local nursing homes. Miss Dawn Sweetwater, please come to the stage and take your place as the final candidate for Summer Solstice Queen!"

Hannah leaned over to Andrea and spoke softly. "It's time for me to leave. I've got a lot of cookies to make. How about you?"

"Oh yes, Hannah, I've been ready to leave for a while now. Can I help you with the cookies tomorrow?"

Hannah gave a little smile. "That would be great! Hey, should we ask Mother and Michelle if they are staying, or if they want to go, too?"

Andrea looked at Hannah with a grin on her face. "I think we'd better, Hannah. Mother would just notice us trying to sneak out anyway. Remember the last time we tried to sneak out . . . at Denny's birthday party?"

"Oh, Andrea, we were very young at the time," Hannah said. "I'm sure that our ninja skills have gotten much better since then!"

Andrea leaned over to talk to Michelle. "Hey, Michelle. Hannah and I are getting ready to duck out of here. Are you in?"

Michelle leaned in. "Thanks, but Lonnie and I are going to stick around for the dancing."

"How about you, Mother?" Andrea asked.

"I'm in. Ready when you are!" Delores said eagerly.

Andrea slid back toward Hannah and said, "Mother's ready. Because Doc's hung up at the hospital, Bill and I will drive her home."

Hannah looked over at Norman and Bill. "Will you boys pull up in front in the getaway vehicles?"

Bill looked at Norman and they exchanged determined nods. "We got this, Hannah," Bill said.

"We'll meet you out front!" Norman chimed in, rising from his chair.

A minute after Bill and Norman had left, the

ladies rose to leave. Hannah went first, followed up the stairs by Andrea and their mother. After they'd reached the lobby, Delores gave a sigh of relief and spoke to Hannah. "Thank goodness we're leaving. I just want to go home, have a glass of champagne, and wait for Doc to get back from the hospital."

"I understand how you feel, Mother. Let's go!"

Chapter
Eighteen

H annah stretched as she took the final baking sheets, filled with Chocolate Lace Cookies, out of her industrial-sized oven and placed them into her large rolling bakers rack to cool. She would wait just a few minutes before transferring the cookies—still on the parchment paper which lined the baking sheet—off the baking sheet and onto the surface of her stainless steel work station to their final cooling before serving.

She gave a satisfied nod of accomplishment to Andrea, very pleased with the way they turned out. True, the cookies needed a bit more attention than most, due to their delicate nature, but they looked fantastic!

"Andrea, are you willing to try one of these yet?" Hannah asked her sister in a teasing tone of voice.

"It's a sacrifice, but I suppose I could *take one for the team*." Andrea teased Hannah right back, in the same tone of voice Hannah had used. "That, along with one more cup of coffee, would almost make me feel human again."

They had both come to The Cookie Jar early in the morning, as Hannah did every day, but it had felt even earlier than usual this morning, after spending so much time at the Summer Solstice banquet the night before.

Andrea was finishing off the last bite of her very first Chocolate Lace Cookie, and exclaiming how crisp and chocolaty it was to Hannah, when the door between the coffee shop and the kitchen burst open, and Lisa came flying in. "Let's go! The parade's starting," she said in a rush. "Come outside, guys. I've got a table reserved for you on the sidewalk."

Hannah and Andrea followed Lisa through The Cookie Jar, then out the front door to an area that was roped off on the sidewalk for a couple of small tables.

"Here you go," Lisa said, lifting the rope and ushering them over to one of the tables. "Herb just called me and he said the parade is going to start any minute now."

"How many bands will there be again?" Andrea asked her.

"Eight. One band is stationed behind every float. And there are eight floats, with one of the Summer Solstice Queen candidates from each high school on top!"

"How about the Jordan High band?" Hannah asked. "Are they wearing their summer uniforms?"

"Yes. Jordan High has white long-sleeved shirts and navy blue pants. Herb told me he feels sorry for a couple of the other bands. They've got heavy wool uniforms, and it's supposed to be hot today."

"I feel sorry for Upsala in those itchy, scratchy uniforms," Hannah said, once the first band had passed their table. "They must be really sweltering in those heavy things."

"Does the Jordan High Marching Band have a winter uniform?" Andrea asked.

"Yes, they do. I know because I helped pay for them! They look just like the letter sweaters made for Jordan High's sports team members, but the band's letter sweaters all have a treble clef embroidered on the back," Hannah replied.

"That's a clever idea."

"Actually, it makes a lot of sense," Hannah answered. "Some of the football games can be chilly, especially at the tail end of the season."

Once Andrea and Hannah were seated, Aunt Nancy and Lisa came out to join them. "If anyone wants to buy anything, we'll run back inside the coffee shop to get it, but I doubt there'll be much action before the parade is over."

"I wonder if Stella's cable guy got out to her lakeside cottage yet," Hannah said. "Mike said he wanted to watch the parade."

"Do you want me to call Stella to ask?" Andrea offered.

"Yes, call them on your cell phone. I'm curious to know if their cable is hooked up by now. You got this, Andrea, right? I have to get ready to go work at the Snack Shack."

"Go ahead. We've got it handled."

Chapter Nineteen

"Hello, Hannah!" Delores called out, raising her voice above the noise of the baseball crowd.

"Mother?" Hannah turned around from her position at the popcorn machine to greet her. "Did you come to watch the game?"

"Yes, for a little while. Then I have to go over to the park and join Andrea and the girls. Can you take a few minutes off?"

"Go ahead, Hannah," Shirley LeBlanc told her. "We've got this."

Hannah escorted her mother to the bleachers that had been set up behind home plate. As they climbed the stairs, Hannah asked, "What brings you out here, Mother?"

"I just came to compliment you on your Pink Lemonade Whippersnapper Cookies, dear. I stopped by one of the other venues to taste them and they're excellent!"

"Thank you, Mother." Hannah led Delores up

the steps at the side of the bleachers and they took a seat near the top. "Is Michelle here somewhere?"

"Yes, she's with Lonnie." Delores sat down on the bench and gave a little smile. "I'm sorry to say that No-No won his game this morning, but at least it wasn't against Jordan High."

"I don't think he pitches again until the Browerville Tigers play Upsala, and that game doesn't start until three-thirty."

Delores unfolded her baseball schedule and checked. "You're right."

"What time is it now?"

Delores pulled her phone out of her purse and looked at the time. "It's only . . . Oh, dear! I just dropped my phone! I have to go after it, Hannah. I promised Doc I'd keep my phone with me in case he called."

"Do you want me to go with you and help you locate it?"

Delores shook her head. "No, dear. I'll just duck under the bleachers and look for it. I saw it fall between the boards right here. It probably landed directly below where we're sitting. I just hope it didn't break into a million pieces when it hit the ground!"

"It shouldn't have broken. You've got a top-of-the-line, impact-resistant case on it. I heard Doc say that when he put the case onto your phone for you. But if you can't find it when you get down there under the bleachers, give a holler and I'll call your number for you."

While she was waiting for her mother to return, Hannah got out her own cell phone. She made a quick call to Stella out at the lake and learned that both Stella and Mike were watching the baseball tournament. She told Stella where she was sitting, just in case KCOW-TV panned the crowd in the bleachers, and then she hung up and waited for her mother to come back.

It seemed to take forever and Hannah was beginning to get a little worried. After a few minutes had gone by, she decided to go beneath the bleachers herself and look for Delores.

"Mother?" she called out, ducking under the bleachers. "Where are you?"

There was a long moment of silence and then Delores answered, "I'm . . . I'm . . . here!"

Because the sides of the bleachers were lined with tarp, it was very dark at first and it took Hannah's eyes a moment or two to adjust to the dimness. When they did, she glimpsed her mother standing a few feet away from her.

"What's wrong?" Hannah asked, moving forward.

"It's . . . it's him!"

Hannah drew her breath in sharply as she saw her mother was standing, with something in her hands, over a bulky figure lying there.

Suddenly there was a loud noise, and Hannah reached down for the phone whose screen was aglow and vibrating on the ground close to her feet.

"Hello?" she answered.

"Hannah! It's Doc. Where is your mother?"

"Right here with me. Mother dropped her phone and came under the bleachers to find it. I need you to come right away, Doc. And bring Bill with you."

"What's wrong, Hannah?"

"Murder," Hannah said. "Call Bill at the sheriff's station and have him bring Lonnie and Rick out with him. KCOW is out here televising the baseball tournament, and I have to get Mother out of here before they see us. Doc, the tournament directors set up the stands with big canvas sheets on both sides of the bleachers from top to bottom, with more canvas sheets that go all the way from the very top seats of the stands down to the ground on the back side of the bleachers. It was probably set up that way to keep people from getting under the stands and fooling around. But listen to me . . . There's an overlap between two of the canvas panels in the back where you can slip in to get to the body. I can show you what I mean when you get here. For now, just pull your car up in back of the bleachers. You'll see us standing there. I'm going to take Mother outside to wait for you and the crime scene boys."

"Good idea," Doc said quickly. "Give me a minute to call Bill and I'll be there."

"It was Doc?" Delores asked, looking at Hannah with a shocked expression as Hannah hung up the call. "He doesn't think that I . . . that I had anything to do with this . . . does he?"

"I'm sure he doesn't. It will be okay, Mother," Hannah reassured her. "Just put down the baseball bat, right there at your feet, and step away with me."

"But . . ."

"Just do it, Mother. We'll go outside to wait for Doc and Bill. That way we can keep anyone else from coming in here."

"But . . . I think he's dead, Hannah."

"You're probably right." Hannah gave her mother

a nod to show Delores that she understood. "But don't think about that now, Mother. All you need to do is gently place the bat down on the ground, right there at your feet, then take three steps away. I'll be right there to take your arm and lead us both outside to wait for Doc."

"They're going to think that I . . ." Delores stopped, then swallowed hard before continuing. "That I . . . I killed him, won't they?"

"Nobody in their right mind would think that, Mother," Hannah reassured her. "It's going to be all right. I'm going to take you outside and when Doc and Bill and the boys come, we'll head down to The Cookie Jar so that you can wait for Doc to meet you there when he finishes."

"Hannah?"

"Yes, Mother." Hannah took her mother's arm and led her toward the back of the area.

"Hannah?" Delores said again, in a small, trembling voice.

"Yes, Mother."

"Will Doc think that I . . . that I . . ."

"That you killed him?" Hannah asked, realizing that her mother was in shock.

"Yes! I . . . I felt for a pulse and . . . and . . . there wasn't any. I watched Doc do that once, so I knew how."

"That's all right, Mother. No one is going to think that you killed him."

"But . . . but I had the bat in my hands. And Hannah, I *was* mad enough to kill him! Everybody knows that!"

"But you didn't and that's what counts." Hannah pulled her mother toward the back of the stands, then in between the massive canvas sheets that led to the outside. Once the two of them had gotten out from under the stands and into the clean, fresh air and sunshine, Hannah spoke once again. "Let's just stand here and wait for Doc, Mother. He should be here any second now."

Hannah propped Delores up against one of the support posts that held up the bleachers and kept an eye out for Doc's car. "Just stay here and breathe deeply, Mother," she said, still hanging onto her mother's arm. "He'll be here any minute now. And when he sees us, he'll know where to come."

"Yes." Delores's voice was still shaky, but she seemed a bit calmer now. "Will I be the prime suspect?"

"Of course not!" Hannah said staunchly, thinking that her mother must be watching too many police procedurals on TV again. "Really, Mother, who would think of you as the *prime suspect* for a murder?!"

"But I vowed to get even with him for dunking me at the fair!" Delores reminded her. "I said I'd get even, Hannah. At the banquet last night, everyone heard me say I would get revenge on him for ruining my favorite summer dress in that dunk tank! What if people think that I killed him because I vowed to get even? Then I'd be a *prime suspect* in his murder for certain! Hannah, you've got to help me! You have to find out who really killed No-No so that you can clear my good name!"

"Not to worry, Mother. I'll do just that. Just stand here and breathe deeply. And the minute that Doc gets here, I'll take you to The Cookie Jar and give you some chocolate to calm you down."

"But . . . I thought you didn't believe that chocolate would help."

"Well, then, we'll just have to try it to see if it works, or not."

"I . . . I can do that," Delores agreed, and Hannah noticed that a little color was coming back into her mother's face.

"Good. And I think I see Doc pulling up right now." Hannah gave a wave as Doc got out of his car and hurried over to them. Before he could say a word, Hannah spoke quickly. "If it's okay with you, Doc, I'll take Mother to my truck now. I'll drive her back to The Cookie Jar and give her some chocolate."

"Good idea. No coffee for her, Hannah, but a small glass of wine wouldn't hurt her at all. I'll come there, just as soon as I finish up here."

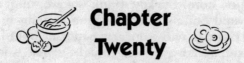

Chapter Twenty

"Why are we stopping here, Hannah?" Delores asked as Hannah pulled up in front of the Lake Eden Liquor Store.

"Doctor's orders," Hannah told her. "Just wait here. I'll be right back."

"Whatever." Delores sat back in the seat and closed her eyes. "I'm really tired, Hannah."

"I know. You've been through a lot today. Just a few more minutes and we'll be back at The Cookie Jar. I've got something new that I want you to try."

"A new cookie?" Delores asked, perking up slightly.

"Yes. They're called Chocolate Lace Cookies, and I need your honest opinion of them, Mother."

"I'd love to taste the new cookies," Delores responded. "And . . . believe it or not . . . I am getting a little hungry. I think it's because I didn't bother to have breakfast this morning."

The moment Delores closed her eyes, Hannah got out of her Suburban and walked rapidly into the liquor store. Luckily, Hank was working, and had several bottles of champagne chilling in his cooler. Hannah chose one, rushed back out to the Suburban, and drove them straight to The Cookie Jar.

"We're here, Mother," she said as she pulled into her parking spot. "Let's go inside. I picked out a nice bottle of champagne for you."

"How lovely!" Delores said, unhooking her seat belt and reaching for the door. "Is Doc coming soon?"

"Yes." Hannah waited for her mother to get out of the car, then led her through the back kitchen door and into the kitchen. "Just have a seat, Mother. I'll get you a little something to drink first, then some cookies."

"But . . . are you *sure* I should have champagne?" Delores asked, sitting down on her favorite stool at the stainless steel work station.

Hannah nodded emphatically, pouring Delores a glass immediately. "I'm quite sure, Mother. In fact, it was recommended by your favorite physician that you have some, strictly for medicinal purposes, just as soon as you got settled here. You might say that it was doctor's orders!"

Delores chuckled faintly, looking quite content. "Well . . . Doc knows best, I'm sure. What kind of wine is this again, dear? It's champagne of course, but what brand is it?"

"It's Korbel Brut. I know that you prefer Veuve Clicquot, but this was the only decent champagne that Hank had chilled."

"It's fine, dear." Delores took a ladylike sip. "Actually . . . it's rather good. I don't always have to drink expensive champagne, you know?" Delores took another sip and smiled. "Actually, I feel a little better now."

"I'm sure you do. Just relax and wait for Doc to get here."

"Yes, and I'll be sure to eat some of the new cookies you just offered me, too. What kind of cookies are they again?"

"Chocolate Lace Cookies. They're made with oatmeal and chocolate, so they'll be perfect for your breakfast."

Delores laughed. "I used to try to get you to eat oatmeal in the morning when you were little," she reminisced. "You didn't like it then."

"Well, I do now." Hannah plated a half-dozen cookies and set them directly in front of her mother.

Delores reached for a cookie, took a bite, and started to smile. "Is this your way of getting me to eat chocolate, so that I'll calm down?"

"Yes," Hannah answered honestly. "Do you think it'll work?"

"Yes, I think it will. And oatmeal is so nutritional . . . isn't it?"

"I'm not sure. You'll have to ask Doc when he comes."

"These are wonderful!" Delores said, finishing a cookie and reaching quickly for another. "If I had these every morning for breakfast, I'd gain a ton of weight." She took another bite, set the last cookie down on her plate, and sighed. "I suppose I'll have to tell the police exactly what happened under the bleachers, won't I."

It was more of a statement than a question, and Hannah nodded. "Yes, I'm sure they'll want a statement."

"I hope I remember everything that happened," Delores said, looking slightly worried. "I wouldn't want anybody to think that I killed No-No!"

"It's okay, Mother. Don't worry about that now."

"You're right. Instead of worrying, I think I'll have another of these delicious new cookies."

Hannah waited until her mother had finished the rest of her second cookie, and started to reach for a third, before pouring her mother another small glass of champagne.

"You really ought to get champagne glasses for down here," Delores told her. "Champagne is much better if it's served in a proper champagne flute. It enhances the flavor."

Hannah just smiled. "I'm sure you're right," she agreed, pouring a bit more into the small juice glass she'd given to her mother.

"The next time I'm at CostMart, I'll pick up some nice glasses for you," Delores promised, taking another sip of her champagne. "This is very good."

"I'm glad you like it."

Doc had been right when he said that a little wine would help Delores feel better. Hannah glanced over and was glad to see that some natural color had returned to her mother's cheeks.

"Hi, I'm here," Doc greeted them, striding in the back door without knocking. "And Lonnie, Rick, and Bill are right behind me." Then he crossed to the work station, gave Delores a hug, and sat down beside her. "You look better, honey."

"Thank you. They're going to want me to give a statement about finding No-No, aren't they?"

"Yes, but I'll be right here with you."

"What if I can't remember everything?"

"It will be fine, Lori," Doc assured her. "You just do the best you can."

"I've don't think I've ever been a prime suspect in a murder before, that's all," Delores said, looking a bit frightened.

"We're here!" Lonnie and Rick arrived just in time to save Doc from answering.

"Are you going to interview me?" Delores asked them.

"Yes, if you're up to it," Lonnie answered.

Before she could say a proper hello to Doc and the two deputies, Hannah's cell phone rang. She hurried to answer it, briefly turning her back on the others, and moving a bit deeper into the kitchen. "The Cookie Jar. This is Hannah."

"Thank God I caught you, Hannah! This is Stella, and I'm calling you from my bathroom. I've got Mike's cell phone in here with me."

"That's different . . ." Hannah said for lack of something better to say. "Why do you have Mike's cell phone in the bathroom with you?"

"Because I didn't want him to call you before I was able to talk to you first. I've got his car keys, too, so he can't get to Lake Eden unless I give them back to him."

For one moment, Hannah was thoroughly confused, but then she understood. "Your cable man came and hooked you up to KCOW, didn't he?"

"Yes, and Mike saw them carrying out the body. He's going to call you just as soon as I give him back his cell phone, Hannah. Do you remember when I said that it might be time for a little reverse psychology?"

"I remember."

"Good. I want you to tell Mike that you don't

need him for this case at all! Tell him that between you, Bill, Rick, and Lonnie, you have everything handled, without his help."

"Do you think Mike will actually believe me?" Hannah asked doubtfully.

"Yes, if you're convincing enough. Just say that everything's fine at your end and Mike should just relax and enjoy his vacation at the lake."

"Whatever you say. You're the expert."

"Thanks. I just hope I'm right. I know that Mike is going to start chafing at the bit, but I'm determined to keep him here for now."

Hannah hung up her phone and walked back over to the work station where Delores was sitting. She had just finished properly greeting Lonnie, Doc, and Rick with a few fresh cookies and some coffee, when Bill came striding in through the back door.

"Hi, Bill. Did you come to take my statement, too?" Delores asked.

"That's right," Bill answered for all of them. "It's just a formality, Delores. No one here thinks that you killed No-No."

"Really?" Delores asked, and it was clear that she was surprised. "You mean that I'm not the prime suspect?"

"No." Bill shook his head, looking a little perplexed. "You sound almost disappointed, Delores. Did you *want* to be the prime suspect?"

"Well . . . perhaps. I did say that I'd get even with him for dunking me in that tank, didn't I? And all of you know full well that I'm good at wielding a baseball bat. I'm the prime suspect, Bill, whether you want to believe it or not. No, I didn't kill him, but I would have if I'd had the chance!"

"Oh . . . well . . . whatever you say, Delores. If you want to be the prime suspect, we'll consider you our prime suspect." He turned to Rick and Lonnie. "How about you two?"

"Sure," Lonnie agreed quickly.

"Yes, that's okay with me, too." Rick seconded Lonnie's opinion.

"Then get out your notebooks and interview me," Delores instructed.

Rick and Lonnie exchanged glances and then both of them got out their notebooks. "What time did you enter the area under the bleachers, Delores?" Lonnie asked her.

"I have no idea. All I know is that I dropped my phone and I went under there to try to retrieve it." She stopped speaking and glanced at Hannah. "Do you know what time that was, dear?"

"Yes . . . approximately. Hand me your phone, please, Mother."

Hannah took the cell phone from Delores, pressed on the phone icon to reach the recent calls menu, scrolled down through it, and then looked up. "It was between one-fifteen and one-thirty today," Hannah informed them.

"How did you come up with that range of time, Hannah?" Lonnie asked.

"Because, according to Mother's recent call log, under incoming calls, Doc called her phone at one thirty-five today. I answered that call *after* I had found Mother under the stands already, and it had to be at least ten minutes before that time when I actually got worried enough that she hadn't come back yet and started down the stairs to find her. Given that it took a few minutes to get down the bleachers, walk around the back, then find a way for me to get under the bleachers, that gives us a timetable of around one-twenty when Mother went under there. Well, plus or minus five minutes for error . . . that would give us a time span between one-fifteen p.m. and one-thirty p.m. when Mother headed down the stairs."

"Well done! And why did you go under the bleachers, Hannah?" Bill asked.

"I thought that I just told Lonnie, didn't I? I went there to find Mother, because she hadn't come back yet, and I got worried that she couldn't locate her phone under the bleachers and might need my help."

"So, it was at one thirty-five p.m. that Doc called Delores on her phone?" Rick chimed in.

"That's right. I told Doc to call in the murder, then for him to get to us as quickly as he could."

Bill jumped in. "Hannah, Mike doesn't know there's been a murder, does he?"

"I'm afraid he does. Maybe five minutes before you got here, Stella called me. Mother and I had been back here at The Cookie Jar for a while. Lonnie, Rick, and Doc had just come in, and Mother had finally calmed down a bit. Stella told me that they had been watching the tournament coverage on KCOW and had seen a sheet-covered body being wheeled out. She wanted to assure me that she was going to keep Mike with her, and she wouldn't let him come back to Lake Eden to get involved in the investigation."

"How was she going to do that?" Rick interjected. "I mean, how could she stop Mike from coming back to Lake Eden if he wanted to? A two-by-four?"

Hannah laughed. "Not quite. Stella's a genius.

Not only did she hide his cell phone, but she also confiscated his car keys so he couldn't just take off! Stella also reminded me that she wants all of us to practice a little reverse psychology on Mike. She told us to say that we have it all under control and we really don't need him for this investigation. In other words, gently but firmly stonewall him. She doesn't want anyone encouraging Mike to come back to Lake Eden for work until she thinks he has gotten his passion back for the job, or as she puts it, *until he's got his head back in the game.*"

"And you went along with that reasoning?" Bill asked Hannah.

"Yes, of course I did. Stella's the expert in things like this. She's dealt with a lot of cop burnout, and she knows Mike better than anyone. If she feels that Mike isn't ready to come back to Lake Eden yet, I'm more than willing to trust her judgment."

"Okay," Bill said, "I guess I'll trust her, too, at least for right now . . . And now, I'd like to get back to what Delores saw and heard while under the stands." Bill walked over to the work station to give Delores a gentle pat on the shoulder. Then he addressed her directly. "Are you ready to tell us what you remember about finding No-No, Delores?"

"Yes. But you should really try one of these new cookies, Bill. Hannah made them this morning and they're delicious."

"I will in a minute," Bill said, motioning for Lonnie and Rick to come closer to the work station. "All right, boys. I believe Delores is calm enough to give you her full statement now."

"What do you want me to say?" Delores asked him.

"Just tell us what you remember in your own

words. Hannah's already told us her perspective on how this all started, that you dropped your phone and it fell through the gap in the boards of the bleachers."

"That's right," Delores said quickly. "They had the sides of the bleachers draped with tarps, so I had to go all the way to the back, that is, once I'd walked down the steps to reach field level. I found the gap between the canvas tarps to get under the stands and I slid between them to try and retrieve my phone."

"How high up were you sitting in the bleachers, Delores?" Rick asked her.

"We were near the very top. I think there were only five rows that were higher up than where we were seated."

"Okay," Lonnie prompted. "So once you walked down to the ground level, you found the gap in the canvas panels at the back of the stands and ended up beneath the bleachers. Is that right?"

"Yes. I walked inside for a little while, but then I almost tripped over something. Something that rolled out from under my feet as I stepped on it. I picked it up and I realized that it was a baseball bat! It was pretty dark under there, and I couldn't really see where I was going, so I picked up the bat and carried it with me."

"Why did you do that?" Bill asked her.

"Because I kept hearing noises. At first, I thought there might be some sort of animal under there with me, like an opossum or a raccoon. It was bright sunlight outside, but it was a little scary in the darkness under the bleachers. What little light there was underneath the stands was so scattered, that it reminded me of swimming underwater out at the lake and trying to see the bottom in those last few moments before the sun goes down. I was more than a little frightened of getting turned around and lost under there!"

"That's totally understandable." Rick gave her a sharp nod. "You are doing great. Go on, Delores. Tell us exactly what happened next."

"I didn't see much at first, but then my eyes adjusted to the light, just a little. There was something lying on the ground ahead of me, and I moved slowly toward it. I thought it might be just a pile of trash or a bundle of old clothes at first, but as I got closer, then I saw . . ." Delores stopped and swallowed hard. Her hands were shaking and she picked up her glass with both hands to take another sip. "Then I saw that it was more than clothes. It was . . . a person lying there, someone in some sort of a uniform. I moved even closer, and that's when I realized that it was a baseball uniform and . . . that the person was No-No!" Delores took a deep breath and blinked away tears. "I . . . I felt for a pulse on his neck, and then on the inside of his wrist, but . . . I couldn't feel any pulse."

"How did you know to check there for a pulse, Delores?" Lonnie asked.

"I'd seen Doc do that before. And Hannah, too. I'd seen Hannah feel for a pulse on someone's neck. I thought perhaps, if there was a pulse, I'd hurry back out and get help for him. But . . . there was nothing. No pulse . . . and No-No wasn't breathing. No-No didn't move at all when I touched him. I wanted to scream or run away, but . . . I think I just stood there for a while, just standing there over his body . . . wanting to scream, or cry or run or do anything other than stand there, but I couldn't seem to move!" Delores turned toward Bill, and tears began to run down her cheeks. "I'm sorry, but I'm not exactly sure how long I stood there, Bill. It felt like it was all a bad dream, you know, like the ones you get when you have a bad fever? And I kept thinking *If I just wake up now everything will be all right again,* but I . . . I couldn't wake up, you see. All I could seem to do was stand there looking at him, growing colder and colder, shivering . . . and I couldn't stop. I only looked up when I heard Hannah calling my name."

"So you said something back to Hannah?" Rick asked.

"I guess I must have, because the next thing I remember is that Hannah was telling me to set the bat down, and take a couple of steps away. The next thing I remember we were standing outside in the sun, waiting for Doc."

"Thank you, Delores," Bill said quietly. "You've been very helpful. I know that couldn't have been easy for you to remember. You've done very well."

"I have?" Delores seemed to awaken from a daze, looking up in surprise at Bill. "But . . . that still makes me the prime suspect, right, Bill? I mean . . . I found him and I had the bat in my hand. That was the murder weapon, wasn't it?"

"Yes," Bill confirmed.

"Doesn't that make me the prime suspect? Nobody else was there except me. And I had the murder weapon in my hand."

Bill exchanged wry glances with Hannah. Then he reached out to pat Delores's shoulder. "That's correct, Delores. But we are going to need you to help us."

Delores looked startled. "Me? How?"

Bill answered Delores with a serious expression on his face. "Don't tell *anyone* about the baseball bat, OK? We need to keep that a secret."

CHOCOLATE LACE COOKIES

Preheat oven to 350 degrees F., rack in the middle position.

Ingredients:

    ½ cup salted butter *(1 stick, 8 Tablespoons, 4 ounces)*, softened

    ¾ cup brown sugar *(packed down in the measuring cup)*

    2 Tablespoons all-purpose flour

    ½ cup Hershey's Cocoa Powder

    2 Tablespoons whipping cream

    1 Tablespoon water

    ½ teaspoon coconut extract

    1 and ¼ cup old fashioned oats *(I used Quaker)*

    ¼ cup of finely ground pecans

Directions:

Line a cookie sheet or baking sheet with parchment paper.

Spray with Pam or another non-stick cooking spray.

Using an electric mixer, beat the butter and brown sugar on HIGH for 2 minutes.

Add in the flour, cocoa powder, whipping cream, water, and coconut extract.

Beat on HIGH until thoroughly combined.

Remove the bowl from your mixer.

Add the oats and pecans.

Stir them in gently until everything is well mixed.

Flour your impeccably clean hands, and form 1-inch balls, 12 to a cookie sheet. Press your cookies down slightly.

Bake at 350 degrees F. for 11-13 minutes *(mine took 12 minutes).*

Remove the cookie sheet or baking sheet from the oven using oven mitts and place it on a cold stove burner or wire rack.

Let cool for 3 minutes, then remove the parchment paper and cookies from the cookie or baking sheet to another area to finish cooling.

Yield: 36-42 delicious light and chocolatey cookies that your family will love.

Serve with strong, hot coffee or icy-cold glasses of milk for a real treat.

Chapter Twenty-one

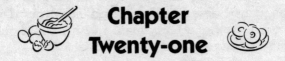

Hannah had just set out a plate of cookies for Doc, Bill, and the detectives when Bill's cell phone rang. "That's probably Mike," she alerted Bill. "KCOW probably had some sort of an alert or a breaking news banner on the screen. Remember, Bill, to tell him that we've got this covered and we don't need his help on this one!"

"Got it!" Bill reached for his phone and answered. "Hi, Mike," he said when the caller had identified himself. "What can I do for you? Really, you saw them take out a body from under the stands?" Bill repeated the conversation on the other end of the line for everyone's benefit. "No, Mike. We don't need you on this one. Just stay there at the lake with Stella so you can relax and recharge your batteries. We're good to go here."

There was a moment of silence and then Bill laughed. "Not now, Mike. We've got all the horses we need to pull this wagon. As I told you . . . we've got this handled. You just go catch a big fish for dinner out on the lake, then go on back to the cabin, maybe have a little nap, and enjoy your day out there. You're a lucky man. I wish I could get out there and relax with you at the lake."

There was a raised voice on the other end of the line making a heck of a racket, and Bill held the phone way out, away from his ear, all the while grinning a mile-wide grin to the rest of them in the kitchen. After the tirade from Mike had quieted down, Bill returned the phone to his ear and then spoke to Mike, this time in his most soothing, syrupy-sweet voice. "Now, now, Mike. Is that any way for a member of my elite team to speak to his superior officer? Even one who is out on administrative leave?"

Another bout of caterwauling broke out from Mike's end of the phone, and Bill once again had to yank the phone away from his ear and wait for Mike to calm himself.

"Well, Mike. I don't believe I care to speak to you any further about this matter, at least not until you can get yourself under some sort of control. You really need to cool down! I guess it's a very good thing that you are relaxing at a lake, so you can literally go soak your head. Goodbye, Mike!" And with that, Bill shut off his cell phone rapidly, with a laugh. "Boy, oh boy, he's blowing off more steam than a Great Northern locomotive! He's so tightly wound up right now, they could rent him out as a yo-yo for kids' parties."

"Perfect!" Hannah told Bill.

"I don't know . . . He seemed a tiny bit disappointed in your responses to his questions, Boss," Lonnie said, trying to keep a straight face.

"You might be right, Lonnie. I think Mike wanted me to say that we needed him back here."

"I'm sure he did," Hannah agreed. "I'm glad I remembered to charge my cell phone this morning. Mike will probably call me next."

"And you'll tell him nothing about the case, except that we've got this and don't need his help, right?" Rick asked her.

"Yes. We . . . all of us . . . we should trust in, and stick to, Stella's plans for Mike. She'll be closest to him out there, and he will vent to her, because she will be the only one giving him a sympathetic ear, so she should be the one to decide when Mike will be truly ready to come back here. Though, I'm more than a bit surprised, given the way that Bill just spun him in circles, that my cell phone isn't blowing up with calls from Mike already!"

As if in answer to her statement, Hannah's cell phone rang. "I bet that's Mike," she said, picking up her phone to answer.

"Mike!" Hannah greeted him on her cell, giving a little nod at everyone gathered around the work station. "What can I do for you?"

Lonnie began to smile. "He's chomping at the bit all right."

"Yes." Hannah responded to something Mike had said. "Mother's here, but she's a little too upset to talk to you right now. I don't know if KCOW mentioned this or not, but Mother is the one who found the victim's body."

Now it was Hannah's turn to hold the phone away from her ear as Mike squawked and sputtered. Hannah let him get it off his chest, then she calmly said, "Now really, Mike. Be reasonable. This investigation is already completely staffed and fully under control! Honestly, Mike, we don't need you on this one. Bill is a great investigator, and you trained Lonnie and Rick yourself. And if they need basic legwork or research done, they can always count on me and Norman! We will catch this killer, Mike. We won't let the fine folks in Winnetka County down! All we want you to do is just relax, have a beer to cool down, maybe take the rowboat out on the lake, catch some walleye for dinner, and stay there with Stella, okay?"

You could hear a pin drop as Hannah softly, but emphatically, hung up the phone on Mike.

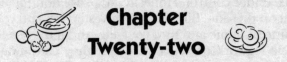

Chapter
Twenty-two

Hannah had just finished making the last batch of cookie dough for her Don't Ask, Don't Tell Cookies when Lisa poked her head through the swinging doors that led from the coffee shop into the kitchen.

"Hi, Hannah. Gee, you are looking a little frazzled. Have you taken a break yet, since Delores and Doc left? You've had a really long day so far, and you look like you need a break."

"You're probably right, Lisa. Maybe I need to take a walk outside for a bit. Can you and Aunt Nancy cover The Cookie Jar for a while?"

"Absolutely! We have got everything under control here. Take as much time as you need. Go listen to the birds chirp, breathe some air that doesn't have any flour in it, and enjoy the late-afternoon sunshine."

"Thanks, Lisa. You're the best partner ever!"

"Aww, you're only saying that 'cause it's true." Lisa chuckled, but nevertheless looked pleased at

Hannah's compliment. "Go on, get while the getting is good!"

"You don't have to tell me twice," Hannah said as she took off her apron, hung it on the rack on the back wall, and walked out the back kitchen door into the great outdoors.

Maybe I'll just go visit my neighbors and see how their Summer Solstice Sales are going, she thought. *That should take my mind off of things.*

Hannah looked up rather absently to find that her feet had taken her over to the back door of the Beau Monde Dress Shop. A look of contentment came over Hannah's face briefly. *Yes*, she thought to herself, *this is just what I needed. It will be good to see Claire and just chat for a minute about nothing at all.*

"Hello, Hannah," Claire greeted her when Hannah knocked on the back door of Claire's dress shop.

"Hi, Claire. I'm just kind of floating around Lake Eden this afternoon, visiting my friends and seeing how they all are doing. Have you had many customers today?"

"Quite a few," Claire reported with a smile. "All the shops are cooperating, referring customers to one another, and keeping the sales chain going. We're all doing good business, as far as I know."

"That's good to hear. I believe I'll go on over to Florence's Red Owl and see how her Summer Solstice Sale is going, too."

Just then the bell over Claire's door rang, signifying that someone had come into her shop. "Just let me check and see who's come in, Hannah. Stay right here, and we'll have something to drink when I come back. I just took some white grape juice out of the refrigerator, and it should be nice and cold. Or . . . better yet . . . come up front with me and greet my customers."

Hannah followed Claire into her shop and waited until the Beau Monde owner had greeted the new arrivals. "This is Hannah." Claire introduced her. "Hannah owns The Cookie Jar next door."

"I love your cookies!" one of the women responded. "Darla and I were at the next table from you during the parade."

"Which parade?" Hannah asked. "The one with the floats? Or the *parade of one?*"

Both ladies started to laugh at Hannah's description. "We were there at the first one," the first lady responded. "It was the one-car parade starring Mr. Big Shot himself. And, unfortunately," she pointed to her friend, "her daughter was up on the back of his convertible."

"That was quite a show, all right," Hannah said quickly. "Is your daughter all right with . . . uh . . . the most recent developments?"

"You mean No-No's murder?" the other woman asked.

"Yes," Hannah said.

"Yes. Darla was actually . . . maybe it's not nice to say so, but she told me that Susan was relieved."

"It's true." Darla sighed. "My husband, James, and I were both worried that my daughter would fall for No-No's fame and fortune and throw her future plans for getting engaged and graduating from college right out of the window. I was actually relieved when I heard he'd . . . well, you know."

"I can't say I blame you," Claire said quickly. "Young girls can be easily fooled by celebrities."

"I know," Darla admitted. "Usually Susan is a very levelheaded young woman, but No-No was handsome, and he had a certain appeal."

"But Susan had everything all worked out in her plans for the future," her friend said.

"I know. Susan and Tony, the boy she'd been dating for over four years, were going to go to college together. They wanted to get married after they graduated, and perhaps they would have, but neither one of them wanted children until they'd gotten their degrees. James and I thought that waiting to have a child until after college graduation was a reasonable decision to make, and our family doctor gave Susan birth control pills so there wouldn't be any unexpected surprises."

"So was your husband worried that all your daughter's plans for the future would go by the wayside if she decided to be with No-No?" Claire asked her.

"Yes, and I've never seen him that angry about something before! I assured him that I'd had *the talk* with Susan, but he was still furious about Susan defying him, and terrified that she might throw her entire future away for some no-good, puffed-up, no-account baseball player. James said that No-No had better hope James didn't catch up with him before No-No left town, or that jumped-up little weasel would regret ever talking to our daughter in the first place! And then . . . all of a sudden, No-No was out of the picture for good, and Susan's future looked bright again."

"Did your husband . . . uh . . ." Hannah hesitated, not wanting to bring up anything too personal.

"Did he think it could happen?" Darla asked, understanding why Hannah was asking immediately. "Of course he did. And even though it's not very nice, I've got to say that he looked relieved when he heard about No-No's death."

"I'll be right back, Claire," Hannah said quickly, deciding to go next door for the steno pad she called her murder book. "I want to get a sample of my new cookies for Darla and her friend."

It didn't take Hannah long to dash next door, bag up some of her Pink Lemonade Whippersnapper Cookies, and come back.

"This is so nice of you, Hannah," Darla said, accepting a bag of cookies. "We're going to have one just as soon as we look at the colors Claire has in these sweaters."

Hannah watched while Claire opened a large box and arranged some sweaters by color.

"Remember what I promised," Claire reminded them. "If this new material doesn't work the way it's supposed to, all you have to do is bring back the sweaters and I'll be glad to refund your money."

"And the material is supposed to be cool during the day and keep in the heat at night?" Darla's friend asked.

"That's right. I'm not sure exactly how it works, but the salesman assured me that it all had to do with the brand of hollow fibers that were featured in the weave."

The two ladies chose several colors, Claire bagged what they had purchased, and they left Beau Monde smiling.

"Offering to refund their money was nice of you." Hannah complimented her friend. "Do you think the sweaters will actually work the way they're supposed to?"

Claire gave a little shrug. "I really don't know. I gave one to Grandma Knudson and she said it was perfect for day or night."

"I'm sure she wouldn't say that unless she thought it was true."

"You're right. She wouldn't," Claire replied with a smile. "You can always count on Grandma Knudson to give an honest opinion. I didn't decide to make the sweaters my featured item until she'd approved them." Claire glanced at the bag of cookies Hannah had just placed on her counter. "Are those for me?"

"Yes."

"Thank you! I noticed that you brought back your steno pad. Are you going to list Darla's husband as a suspect?"

"Absolutely. From what Darla said, he was worried about their daughter being . . . uh . . ." Hannah paused, trying to find the right word.

"About being too enamored by No-No?"

"Exactly. It sounded to me like their daughter had her life all planned out until she met No-No. And that makes her husband a suspect."

"So you are going to help with the murder investigation."

"I have to. Mother was very clear about that. She's worried that since everyone knows how upset she was at No-No, people will think that she killed him. I know that sounds silly, but she did pick up the murder weapon. And her fingerprints are all over it."

"Do you think that Rick and Lonnie will ask for your help when they question suspects?"

Hannah took a moment to think about that. "I don't know, but I hope so. If I'm actually there, I won't have to pry information out of them. And I may discover other people with motives on my own."

"I'm sure you will," Claire assured her. "You're a very good detective, Hannah."

"Amateur detective." Hannah corrected her. "I wouldn't want to be a real detective. Look what happened to Mike. He burned out on the job, and if that could happen to him, it must be the pressure of being a full-time police detective! Stella told me that this job *burnout* has also happened to a couple of other detectives she's trained."

"Well . . . just let me know if there's anything I can do to help. And I'll keep my ears open for any tips that I hear. Are you going to check with some other people here in town?"

"Yes. I thought I'd go bag up some more cookies and then check in with Florence."

"Good idea! Florence always keeps her eyes and ears open. And . . . maybe it's a little uncharitable of me to say so, but Florence likes to pass on what she hears."

"Very true." Hannah headed for the door. "Save one of those sweaters for me, will you, Claire?"

"Of course. Are you going to test it out for me, Hannah?"

"No, but I'm sure Mother will. It'll give her something else to do besides worrying about whether people will think she's guilty of murder!"

Chapter Twenty-three

"Hello, Florence," Hannah greeted their local grocer at the meat counter.

"Hello, Hannah. I was wondering when you'd be in to hear the local gossip." Florence looked down at the distinctive cookie bag that Hannah was carrying. "Are those for me?"

"Yes, they are."

"Great! And it's just in time for my break," Florence said, motioning to Donna Logan, who was making an end cap display of soup cans.

"Watch the meat counter for me, will you, Donna?" Florence asked her.

"Of course I will. Is there anything in particular that you want me to point out to your customers?" Donna asked her.

"Yes, please offer them the Braunschweiger, Donna. The expiration date is only four days from now, so we need to move it, but it's delicious. I prepared a plate with samples earlier and you can give them out to anyone who's interested." Florence turned to Hannah. "Come with me. We'll have a cup of coffee on my break."

Hannah followed Florence to her back room and took a chair next to the kitchen table that Florence had placed there. "Try these," she invited, placing the bag of cookies she'd brought on the table.

"Wild horses couldn't stop me!" Florence declared, pouring Hannah a cup of coffee, sitting down, and reaching for a cookie. "What are these?"

"Raspberry Crisps. They're a variation on my Watermelon Kool-Aid Cookies, but instead of watermelon Kool-Aid, you use raspberry Kool-Aid."

"Well . . . I love those, so I should love these, too," Florence declared, biting into a cookie. "Mmmmm!" She made a sound of enjoyment. "They're wonderful!"

"Thank you. I like the *twang* you get with the raspberries."

"So do I!" Florence finished her cookie and reached for another. "These will be a huge hit at the Snack Shack."

"I hope so."

Florence looked at Hannah quizzically. "What brings you here, Hannah? Are you making the rounds today?"

"You could say that . . . Just wanted to find out what everyone chose for their Summer Solstice Sale item. What about you, Florence?"

Florence smiled. "Did you see the other end cap display that Donna just finished?"

"The one with all the sample boxes of cereal?"

"Yes. That's going to be my special Summer Solstice offering. There are two kinds of cereal. The sugared samples, like Froot Loops, and the regular ones, like Cheerios. All my customers have to do is buy two of the little sample cereals and they get a ballot to vote for Summer Solstice Queen. I compared notes with Rose over at the café. We didn't want to duplicate, so I decided to sell car snacks."

"'Car snacks?'" Hannah repeated. "What are those?"

"They're snacks that aren't too messy, which you can keep in your car for the kids in case they get cranky. My supplier had these darling little one-serving boxes of cereal and they come in different twelve-packs."

"What a good idea!" Hannah complimented her. "And they'll keep for a while in the car, won't they?"

"Yes. My supplier said they wouldn't be stale for at least six months, and I'm sure they'll be long gone before then."

"Have you sold many?"

"Yes, a lot. It's a good thing I ordered a bunch from my supplier. By the way . . . if you see Bill, tell him that everyone thinks it's a great idea that the Winnetka County Sheriff's Station is counting the Summer Solstice Queen ballots."

"How about Hank at Lake Eden Liquor? Do you know what his Sale item is?"

"Beer, of course. But he's going to check IDs and make sure his customers are of age."

"It sounds like everyone's got things figured out."

"I hope so. This is going to be fun. People are really excited about the baseball tournament despite . . . well . . . you know."

"Despite No-No and his untimely demise?"

"Yes. And despite the fact that your mother is the prime suspect. Of course no one I know thinks she did it, but without Mike here . . ." Florence took another sip of her coffee and sighed. "You *are* going to help in the investigation, aren't you, Hannah?"

"Of course. Norman and I will be happy to help if we're needed."

Florence gave a little laugh. "You're needed! There's no doubt about that! Now that Stella has spirited Mike off to the lake, Lonnie and Rick will need your help. After all, they're used to having Mike right there, leading the questioning of suspects." Florence gave Hannah a curious look. "I don't think either Rick or Lonnie feel confident about handling things themselves, do you?"

"You may be right, Florence. How about Rose? What's she selling?"

"I talked to Rose this morning and she said she's selling little blue cheese mini-meatloaves, made in muffin pans."

"That sounds good."

"They are. She gave me a sample."

Both Florence and Hannah sipped their coffee for a moment and then Florence smiled. "Did you know that Andrea dropped in this morning?"

"No."

"She said she was up early because she wanted to see me to thank me for the pointers I gave her on using the frosting tips and the pastry bags. She told me she had a lot of fun figuring out how to use the frosting tips with Tracey and Bethie. Bethie practiced and practiced writing all the first names of the Swensen and the Todd families using instant mashed potatoes."

Hannah laughed. "I bet that was messy!"

"That's exactly what I said, but she said no, that the girls were extra careful. Tracey showed Bethie how to write DAD in instant mashed potato letters first, and Andrea said Bethie just ran with the idea. She created a special *DAD* place mat to set in front of Bill's place at the head of their dining room table, made entirely of instant mashed potatoes!"

"I'll bet Bill thought that was wonderful."

"He did. He got so silly about it that he told Andrea that he wanted to shellac the mashed potato *DAD* that Bethie made for him on the place mat, frame it, and stick it up on the fridge as art! As you can imagine, that idea got squashed in a hurry though, by Andrea!" Florence doubled over in laughter, just thinking about the sad look that must have appeared on Bill's face when he was denied his grand scheme for Bethie's instant mashed potato creation. "Andrea said it was tricky for the girls to use the pastry bag tips at first, but they figured it out eventually."

Hannah finished her coffee and stood up. "Thanks for the coffee, Florence. Sorry, but I've got to run along now. I want to stop at Hal and Rose's Café to see how they are doing."

"Okay. I'll see you later, Hannah. I have to get back to the meat counter anyway. I have some smoked salmon I want to sell today while it's nice and fresh."

"Norman loves smoked salmon," Hannah said, following Florence out of the room. "I'll buy some of that. We can have it on bagels tomorrow for breakfast."

"Good idea! I'll even give you a discount. And I've got some bagels in the bread aisle."

Several minutes later, Hannah left with her smoked salmon and bagels, and hurried down the street to Hal and Rose's Café. She walked in the door, pleased at the crowd she saw lining the booths, and took a seat at the counter.

"Hello, Hannah," Rose greeted her. "Did you want coffee?"

"No, thanks. I just had coffee with Florence, so I think I'll switch to lemonade."

"Good idea. It's hot out there and lemonade is refreshing. Would you like regular lemonade, or strawberry lemonade?"

"What's in the strawberry lemonade?"

"Grenadine. I like the flavor."

"So do I. I'll have the pink lemonade, Rose." She glanced around. "It looks as though you've been busy today."

Rose handed Hannah a glass of pink lemonade, and nodded her head in response to Hannah's question. "I have been. And we're not even selling beer! Hank and I discussed it and I'm leaving that to him at the liquor store. To tell you the truth, I just didn't feel like checking IDs all day."

"I understand." Hannah took a sip of her pink lemonade and smiled. "This is good, Rose. Did you use Kool-Aid?"

"Yes, strawberry. I heard that they were going to be selling 7th Inning Slushes at the Snack Shack so I decided to do something different here."

"That was smart, Rose."

"Thank you!" Rose looked pleased. "If you're hungry, I can make you a Blue Cheese Meatloaf Mountain."

"A Blue Cheese Meatloaf Mountain? Andrea mentioned those . . . How do *you* make them, Rose?"

"It is a little meatloaf, made in a muffin tin, with instant mashed potato piped on as its snowy mountain top, and little sprigs of parsley acting as trees along either side of the mountain. If our customers want us to do it for them, we can drizzle on melted butter or gravy, just like ski runs, making their way down the mountain. Otherwise we just serve the gravy on the side in a little dish and they can create their own mountain trails. I think it is going to be a very popular Summer Solstice Sale special for the whole family, and we are going to run it all week!"

"What a great idea!" Hannah complimented her. "I wish I were hungry—I'd get one right now—but I have to go out later with Norman."

"Norman's taking you out to dinner?"

"Yes, but he didn't tell me where. I guess we're playing it by ear."

BLUE CHEESE MEATLOAF MOUNTAINS

Preheat oven to 375 degrees F., rack in the middle position.

Meatloaf Ingredients

    2 cups crumbled blue cheese (*16 ounces*)
    1 large egg, beaten
    2 and ¼ pounds ground beef
    ⅔ cup crushed potato chips (*crushed finely in a food processor, or crushed up with a rolling pin in a large zip-lock bag*)
    ½ cup yellow onion (*finely chopped*)
    2 Tablespoons chopped fresh parsley
    4 garlic cloves, minced (*about 2 Tablespoons*)
    2 and ½ teaspoons kosher salt
    2 teaspoons Worcestershire sauce
    1 and ½ teaspoons red wine vinegar
    1 teaspoon dried thyme
    ½ teaspoon black pepper

Meatloaf Glaze

    ¾ cup ketchup
    ¼ cup tightly packed Brown Sugar
    1 teaspoon dry mustard (*I used Colman's*)

Directions:

Spray a 12-cup muffin tin with Pam or another non-stick cooking spray.

In a medium-sized bowl, with your impeccably clean hands, combine the crumbled blue cheese, the beaten egg, the ground beef, and the finely crushed potato chips.

Add in the finely chopped yellow onion, the chopped parsley, the minced garlic, salt, Worcestershire sauce, red wine vinegar, thyme, and black pepper.

Combine thoroughly.

Roll the mixture into balls with your hands and place them in the cups of the muffin tin.

Mix the ketchup, brown sugar, and dry mustard in a small bowl.

Paint the top of each Blue Cheese Meatloaf Mountain with the ketchup/brown sugar/dry mustard mixture you just made.

Bake at 375 degrees for 25 to 30 minutes (mine took 27 minutes).

Remove the muffin tin, with oven mitts, from the oven and set the muffin tin on a cold stove-top burner or wire rack to cool.

Make two 8-ounce packages of Instant Mashed Potatoes in your Microwave or on the stovetop, according to the Instructions on the back of the packages. *(I used Idahoan Buttery Homestyle Mashed Potatoes.)*

Place the finished mashed potatoes aside to cool slightly for 3 or 4 minutes before either piping or scooping the mashed potatoes on top of the Blue Cheese Meatloaf Mountains.

To Serve:

After 5 minutes, remove the Blue Cheese Meatloaf Mountains from the muffin tins with a fork or tongs to a serving platter, and bring the platter to the table.

When your mashed potatoes are ready and slightly cooled, carry them to the table, along with a disher or small ice cream scoop.

Everyone can scoop their own amount of mashed potatoes onto the top of their individ-

ual Blue Cheese Meatloaf Mountains for a snow-topped treat.

Don't forget to bring some melted butter or some gravy to the table so everyone can decorate their own Meatloaf Mountains with ski trails that run down the snow-capped tops.

Now, all you need are some small sprigs of parsley, just in case anyone wants to decorate their mountains with little parsley trees!

This recipe makes 12 mini Blue Cheese Meatloaf Mountains per muffin tin.

CHERRY CRISPS

Preheat oven to 325 degrees F., rack in the middle position.

Ingredients:

1 packet *(0.13 ounce, 3.6 grams)* Cherry Kool-Aid powder *(don't get the kind with sugar or sugar substitute added)*

1 and ⅔ cup white *(granulated)* sugar

1 and ½ cups softened butter *(3 sticks, 8 ounces)*

2 large eggs, beaten *(just whip them up in a glass with a fork)*

½ teaspoon salt

1 teaspoon baking soda

3 cups all-purpose flour *(pack it down in the cup when you measure it)*

½ cup white *(granulated)* sugar in a bowl

Directions:

Mix the Cherry Kool-Aid powder *(the kind without sugar)* with the granulated sugar.

Add the softened butter and mix until it's nice and fluffy.

Add the eggs and mix them in.

Mix in the salt and the baking soda. Mix to make sure they're well incorporated.

Add the flour in half-cup increments, mixing after each addition.

Spray cookie sheets with Pam or another nonstick cooking spray. You can also use parchment paper if you prefer.

Roll dough balls 1 inch in diameter with your hands. *(We use a 2-teaspoon cookie scooper at The Cookie Jar.)*

Roll the cookie balls in the bowl of white sugar and place them on the cookie sheet, 12 to a standard-size sheet.

Bake the Cherry Crisps at 325 degrees F. for 10-12 minutes *(mine took 11 minutes)* or until they're just beginning to turn golden around the edges. Don't overbake.

Let the cookies cool on the cookie sheets for no more than a minute, and then remove them to a wire rack to cool completely.

Yield: Approximately 6 dozen pretty and unusual cookies that kids will adore, especially if you tell them that they're made with Kool-Aid.

7TH INNING SLUSH

Ingredients:

    2 cups of club soda
    1 packet Kool-Aid Pink Lemonade Drink
       Mix Unsweetened
    ½ cup of white (*granulated*) sugar
    3 cups of ice cubes
    2 scoops vanilla ice cream

Directions:

Place the 2 cups of club soda, the packet of Kool-Aid Pink Lemonade Drink Mix Unsweetened, and the white granulated sugar into a blender.

Add 2 scoops of vanilla ice cream and blend well.

Add 3 cups of ice cubes or crushed ice, and blend again until smooth.

Yield: 4 to 6 Glasses of ice-cold summer relief!

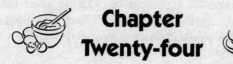

Chapter
Twenty-four

"Hannah?" Hank called out to her as she walked past the liquor store. "Could you come in for a minute, please?"

"Sure." Hannah went around the side of the building and went into the door that led to the on-sale bar. "What's up, Hank?"

"I've got some . . . well . . . I'm not sure if it's important or not, but Roman Ganz came in here today, and I think I should talk to you about him. Have a seat, and I'll pour you a glass of wine."

"Thanks, but no thanks. I'll have something non-alcoholic. What do you have?"

"Diet Coke, regular Coke, root beer, Sprite, and"—Hank glanced down at the label on the tap—"Diet Sprite."

"I'll have a Diet Sprite," Hannah decided. "Norman's taking me out to dinner tonight and I don't want to drink anything with alcohol this early."

"Here you go," Hank said, placing a glass in

front of Hannah. "I might be wasting your time here, but . . . as I said, Roman Ganz was just in today, and he said a couple of things that I thought you should know."

Hannah took a sip of her drink. "What did he say?"

"He looked odd, and he wanted a drink immediately. His hands were shaking, and he looked really upset about something."

"Did he tell you why he was so upset?"

"Yes. It took a little prying, but he wanted to talk, so I convinced him that I wanted to listen."

Hannah smiled. "I think maybe you should be working for the sheriff's department, Hank. That's one of the best techniques that a good detective can use, convincing someone that you really want to hear what they have to say."

Hank looked pleased. "Thanks, but I'm a bartender, Hannah. Bartenders do this sort of thing all the time. People come in and they need to talk. And all we have to do is listen."

"What did Roman have to say?" Hannah asked the important question.

"He'd been upset and angry with his granddaughter's behavior lately. You may recall that Roman and his wife had been taking care of her, ever since her parents were killed in that auto accident."

"I do remember hearing something about that."

"Well . . . Roman told me he was still very upset because his granddaughter sneaked out of the house a couple of days earlier without saying anything about where she was going, or who she'd be with. I guess she'd walked down to the end of their driveway, out to the main road, and got herself picked up by that baseball player. The same one who came into town for the All-Star Tournament, showing off to the girls in his flashy convertible. You know who I'm talking about. That fool baseball player who hung around Lake Eden a while back, and dunked Delores at the fair?"

"Are you talking about No-No?"

"Yes, that's him! Mr. Big Shot, himself. Now, Roman didn't realize that his granddaughter had snuck off the farm until his neighbor called him to warn Roman that he saw Emily riding down the road to town, just as bold as brass, sitting up on the back of that convertible in what appeared to be a little short skirt and a bikini top. Well, ma'am, Roman got in his old pickup in a hurry and he drove lickety-split toward town to try and stop Emily from shaming herself in front of the whole town and God himself!"

"You know, his granddaughter wasn't the only one riding with No-No, Hank. There were three girls sitting up on the back ledge of that convertible," Hannah pointed out.

"I know that, Hannah," Hank said a little heatedly, "but I'm not talking about those other girls right now! Anyway, Roman made it to the junction right outside of town before the convertible did. No-No took the time to stop and pick up two more young girls, just to show what a big deal he was. What an idiot! Imagine him driving that new, flashy convertible slowly into town, with those young girls up on the back, just waving away at everybody like he was a big man." Hank chuckled for a minute and went on. "What's funny is that all the while No-No was trying to make us think he was a Big Man, the hero come home to a small town, we were

all thinking what a fool No-No was for showing off!
Now, let's see . . . Oh, yes . . . Roman could have
caught them all easily before No-No started parad-
ing those girls through the center of town, but at
that point in time, Roman wasn't thinking too
clearly. He took a guess on which route No-No
would take to get into town . . . and boy, was he
ever upset that he picked the wrong way in!"

"I'll just bet Roman was so mad he was spitting
tacks when he figured out they had come a different way into town, right, Hank?" Hannah asked,
caught up in the story. This was starting to sound a
little like a daytime drama she'd watched years before.

"Sure enough," Hank said, winding up Roman's
story. "Of course by the time Roman realized that
No-No had come into town the other way 'round,
No-No's little mini parade was already done. Roman
finally managed to spy No-No's car by sheer luck!
Seems they drove out the back side of town and
right past the junction where Roman was waiting.
I'm here to tell you, right then and there, Roman
pulled out and skidded his pickup truck sideways
across the road. Heck, Roman managed to block
the whole junction off. Then Roman got out of
that old truck and gave No-No a real good taste of
what Roman thought about city slickers with fancy
new cars, trying to corrupt naive young farm
girls."

"Oh boy!" Hannah said, smiling at the mental
image of No-No getting dressed down by the old
farmer, right there in the middle of the road.
"That really must have been something to see, and
to hear, too."

Hank chuckled again, and said, "I'm surprised

they didn't hear Roman takin' No-No to task way up there in Brainerd! *Good riddance to bad rubbish.* That's what I told everybody today, after I heard No-No got himself killed. Just the thought of Emily perched up there on top of the back seat in that car, wearing that skimpy little outfit, while all three girls waved and rode around so prideful in that convertible, makes my blood boil. They drove right through downtown Lake Eden, did you know that? I reckon Roman was madder than a wet hen mostly because Emily had snuck out while dressed like that. I mean, after all they'd tried to teach her about staying modest and humble. That made Roman think that maybe he and his wife were . . . falling down on the job in trying to raise Emily in the proper manner for a respectable, church-going young lady. It's a darn shame!"

"Roman's very religious?" Hannah asked.

"Yes. Sometimes . . . well . . . it's not up to me to judge, but I think he's a little over-religious, if you know what I mean."

"I understand."

"Anyway . . . when I saw him earlier today," Hank went on, "Roman seemed so upset, and he was shaking real bad, when he sat down in here and asked me for a whiskey to calm down. He drank it like it was water, and then he got a second one! Hannah, Roman only drank beer before, so far as I know . . . Then, after he drank his second whiskey down, Roman told me that he had to get going because one of his Jersey cows was about to calve, and Roman was worried that she was pretty small for birthing."

"So Roman said the reason he was shaking was because he was worried about the calf?"

"Yes, well . . . that's what he said. It seemed a little strange to me, so I asked him if he'd called Dr. Haggaman. I mean, if he was that nervous about the birth and all, you'd think that he'd call the vet over, in case there was trouble, right? But . . . he said no, he hadn't, because he was raised on a farm, and he was used to things like that. He told me that he'd be fine without any hand-holding from *some city vet* like Doc Hagaman. But he surely was shaking a lot for someone who didn't want the vet there and was used to delivering breeched calves himself!"

"So he was going to take care of the calving alone?"

"That's what he said, and he left straightaway after."

"Was this before or after No-No was killed, Hank?"

"That's just it. It was before, I think, but if it was before, it sure couldn't have been that much before. I had the TV over the bar on, and KCOW showed the body on the stretcher no more than thirty minutes after Roman left here. And that made me wonder if . . . I hate to say it, but . . ."

"You wondered if Roman could have killed No-No?"

"Yeah. The timing fits. He was really upset, Hannah, and I don't think it all had to do with that calf. I'm pretty sure he was still fuming about his granddaughter, and you know, people who are upset sometimes do crazy things. I've been in this business long enough to know that. It's always the quiet ones you have to watch out for, Hannah."

Chapter
Twenty-five

"Hi, Norman," Hannah greeted him when he came in the back door of The Cookie Jar. "I just finished baking and I'm ready to go if you are."

"Great. Sally called me and asked us to come out there for dinner tonight. She said it was on the house."

Hannah began to smile. "That sounds wonderful to me. Should we go back to your house to feed the cats first?"

"No need. Your mother called me earlier and asked me to bring them over to her place, so they could play in the garden. She said Doc gets a real kick out of watching Moishe and Cuddles try to catch the ladybugs there."

"I just hope neither one of them ever catches one."

"I don't think they will. Although it is funny thinking about the shocked expression that would be on their faces . . . if they ever did catch one. But Doc says they just like to nudge the ladybugs with their paws and watch them fly."

"Does Mother have enough food for them?"

"Yes, the same kind that we feed them. And she's got the water bowls that we took over there last time they played in the dome."

"So we're all set, and we can go straight out to Sally and Dick's?"

"That's right. Sally told me she has a couple of specials on the menu tonight that we're bound to like."

"I always love Sally's specials," Hannah responded, going over to the rack by the door and grabbing the sweater she'd bought from Claire earlier. "I'm ready if you are."

It didn't take long to get to the Lake Eden Inn. Norman pulled up in the space for deliveries, instead of into a regular parking place out front, and Hannah looked at him curiously. "Are you sure it's okay to park here?"

"Yes. Sally said they've gotten all their deliveries for today." Norman walked around the car and opened Hannah's door. "Come on, Hannah. I'm getting hungry just thinking about Sally's specials."

"Hello, Hannah . . . Norman," Dot greeted them as they walked into the restaurant. "Sally told me that you two were coming out here tonight." Dot picked up two menus and led the way to one of the private booths that were situated on a level above the rest of the restaurant. "Here you are. Would you like one of Dick's special drinks to start?"

"Ginger ale for me," Norman said quickly, and Dot nodded.

"I knew you'd say that, Norman." She turned to Hannah. "How about you?"

"I'll have a glass of white wine."

"Any wine in particular?"

"No, just tell Dick to choose whatever he thinks I'd like. He's the expert when it comes to wine, not me."

It only took a few moments for Dot to bring their drinks. Hannah took a sip of her wine and leaned back with a sigh. "I love to come out here. It's so relaxing."

"Yes, it is. And it's not that far to drive home. Do you want to pick up the cats tonight, or leave them over there? Your mother said that they're welcome to stay overnight."

Hannah thought about that for a moment. "Let's leave them there overnight then. I know they love to play in the garden, and Mother and Doc always take good care of them."

"Perfect. Then we can have a night by ourselves. I've got a new movie I recorded that we can watch."

"That sounds good. What is it?"

"Something called *Squared Love.*"

"I've heard of that. It's a romance, isn't it?"

"Yes, and a comedy at the same time. We can make microwave popcorn and stay up late."

Hannah laughed. "You know that I'll probably fall asleep, don't you, Norman?"

"Yes, but you fall asleep with your head on my shoulder, and I like that."

"So do I," Hannah said, smiling at him again.

"Let's check out the specials Sally has on the menu."

They both picked up their menus and Hannah gave a big smile. "Sally's got goose! I wonder if that's wild goose or domestic goose."

"We'll have to ask. It doesn't say. What difference does it make?"

"Domestic goose is fat, and you have to roast it on a rack. Wild goose doesn't have enough fat since it's been traveling for a while, so you have to lard it."

"What does that mean?"

"I'm not sure what it means now, but it used to mean that you had to keep basting it with lard."

"And it doesn't mean that anymore?"

"I'm not sure you can even buy lard in stores anymore."

"What do you do if it's wild goose and you don't have any lard?" Norman asked.

"I'm not sure what Sally does, but I'd probably use bacon and lay it all over the top of the goose. And then I'd keep an eye on it and replace the cooked bacon with more fresh bacon when it was needed."

"Interesting. You know a lot about cooking, Hannah."

"Thank you, but there's a lot I don't know." Hannah sighed, shaking her head.

"Hello, you two!" Sally said, pulling back the privacy curtain and giving them a smile. "Did you notice that I have goose on the menu tonight?"

"It was the first thing I noticed," Hannah told her. "I'm going to have the goose. I absolutely hate geese!"

Sally looked puzzled. "Wait a second. You're going to have the goose, but you hate geese?"

"That's right. And I'll be very happy to eat them instead of being chased by them."

"I sense a story in the making here. Do you have time to sit down and listen to Hannah's tale, Sally?"

"I do. Dot's got everything covered for me and . . ." The curtain pulled back and Dot reached in with a glass of wine for Sally. "See what I mean? Now tell me about those geese that chased you, Hannah."

"It was when I was three years old. I went out to Grandma and Grandpa Swensen's farm for the first time. I was all dressed up for the occasion. I think it was my Uncle Jim's birthday, or something like that. I had on a beautiful pink dress with lace around the collar and cuffs, and white patent leather shoes."

"Your grandparents lived on a farm?" Norman prompted.

"Yes, and I'd never been there before. The farm was on a hill and there was a path leading up to the house. I started up the path and three big geese chased me with their wings flapping. They were hissing and I was so scared, I slipped and fell down. What I fell in was a puddle of . . . well, you can guess."

"You . . . oh no! You poor thing!" Sally sympathized.

"My dad picked me up and held me out in front of him so he wouldn't get you-know-what on him. Then he took me in the back way, through something he called the *mudroom.* It was a room with a sink and a spigot of water that acted like a shower."

"So they washed you off in the mudroom?"

"Yes. And then they washed my clothes, too. And since I couldn't wear wet clothes in the house, Grandma Swensen wrapped me in a blanket."

"That must have been embarrassing," Norman commented.

"It was, especially since the blanket kept slipping and everyone else there had nice clothes on."

"And that's why you hate domestic geese?"

"Yes. I'll never forget the way they flapped their big wings and hissed. And that they nipped really hard at my legs and ankles. I know it's probably silly of me, but I've hated geese ever since."

Sally smiled. "And you want to eat them to get even?"

"Exactly! I'll definitely have the goose, Sally."

"And so will I," Norman concurred.

"You're doing it to support me?" Hannah asked him.

"Yes, partially. And since I've never had goose before, I want to try it to see if I like it."

Sally giggled, then took a larger sip of her wine. "Hannah," she said, "Dick said that he has something he'd like you to try out for him. It's an appetizer that we are thinking of putting on the bar menu, and he'd like to get your opinion on it. He also said something about bringing it over himself. Is that okay with you two?"

Hannah shot Norman a quick glance, and then answered for them both. "Sally, you know how much we love being Dick's favorite guinea pigs when he's working on his new bar appetizers! Tell him to come by the table whenever he is ready. We will be right here with either forks or fingers waiting on his latest creation."

Sally nodded, then left Norman and Hannah alone in the booth, heading toward the bar to tell her husband of their decision. Hannah and Norman sat for a moment or two in companionable silence, then Norman spoke. "Hannah, I want to thank you."

"For what?"

"I know that it might seem silly, but I'm very pleased that you answered for both of us just now, when Sally asked about the appetizers."

Hannah arched one eyebrow, in her best Mr. Spock impression. "Why would you be pleased that I answered for both of us?"

Norman looked amused at Hannah's single raised eyebrow, which kept jumping up and down, sometimes being joined by its twin, despite her best efforts to keep it as a solo act. "It's just . . . moments like that when we can share just a look, and you know exactly what I'm thinking, make me realize all over again that you *are* the one for me, Hannah. And you always will be."

Hannah blushed, and she looked at Norman out of the corner of her eye. Her heart seemed very full when Norman spoke in so direct a manner about his feelings for her, but it also made her feel a bit . . .

"Isn't it awfully warm in here to you, Norman? Maybe we should ask Sally if she'll turn the AC up a little bit."

There was booming laughter from just beyond the booth curtains. A large hand held an even

larger platter with a great many small compart-
ments, filled with many different items. This was
followed rapidly by the rest of Sally's husband,
Dick, the other co-owner of the Lake Eden Inn.

"Passions rise, where flames of love burn ever
bright," Dick stated in a theatrical tone, with an
impish grin plastered widely on his oh-so-slightly
smug face. "But I will ask Sally to turn up the air-
conditioning regardless."

"Dick!" Hannah glared at her favorite bartender
with a look of exasperation on her rapidly redden-
ing cheeks. "Sometimes I think you enjoy teasing
me more than you should. It merely seems a bit
warm here, that's all."

"Aha!" Dick said, giving Norman a conspirator-
ial wink. "Methinks the lady protests too much."

"The real quote is *the lady doth protest too much,
methinks.*" Norman laughed at Dick's wink. "It's
Queen Gertrude speaking about the *play within a
play* in *Hamlet* by Shakespeare. The line quoted is
in act three, scene two."

"You are not helping, Norman!" Hannah somewhat sheepishly joined in their laughter. "So, anyway . . . what appetizer do you have for us to try,
Dick?"

"I have just the thing you want, Hannah," Dick
said as he placed the platter, two tiny forks, and
two small appetizer plates on the table in front of
them. "We call this a *plentitude of pickles,* and it has
six different pickled vegetables, each in their own
little compartment on the platter. There are pickled beets, cornichons, pickled baby corn, pickled
cauliflower florets, pickled wax beans, and for
dessert, sweet, pickled watermelon rind! We find

that pickles are light and easy on the digestion, they cool down your body temperature (*unless they are pickled jalapenos, of course*), and best of all for the restaurant, they make you thirsty!"

"What do you mean, best of all, they make you thirsty?" Norman asked slyly, knowing the answer already.

"Think about it, Norman," Dick chortled happily. "If customers at a bar are eating something that makes them thirsty, they naturally will want to . . . ?"

Hannah swept into the conversation, smiling at Dick. "They will buy more drinks, of course." Hannah turned to him, her embarrassment all but forgotten, smiling at him in her acknowledgment of a fine marketing tactic.

"Well, I will let you try the *plentitude of pickles* and then eat your supper in peace," Dick said. "Although, I would like you to come see me before you leave tonight, to speak to you about No-No and give you some information you may need for the investigation. Will that be all right with you both?"

"That's fine with me, Dick!" Norman said, loading the two small plates, one for each of them, full of different little pickled things, and handing one of the plates to Hannah.

"That sounds great, Dick," Hannah agreed. "See you later, then."

Norman began to nibble on one of the pickles, unable to resist their siren call, even before Dick had left the booth. After a second, Hannah started eating, too, and the next five minutes were spent exclaiming in happiness to one another over the varied flavors and tastes that seemed to envelop their mouths. Then they went even further, analyzing and breaking down in detail what they thought were the different types of spices Dick had used on each little vegetable variety that he pickled. Soon they were smiling and laughing with each other and having a wonderful time together just eating, talking, and squabbling good-naturedly over which pickle they liked the best.

Hannah looked up as Dot cleared her throat from outside the booth's curtain at precisely the same instant they had finished the appetizers. When she heard them call out permission to enter, Dot rolled in a cart featuring a main course consisting of lovely moist goose with beautiful crispy-brown skin which was piled high on two plates of Sally's best china. The goose was accompanied by a tart blackberry sauce in one of the two sterling-silver gravy boats on Dot's cart, with a second gravy boat of thick dark brown gravy sitting right next to it. The cart also held some very tasty-looking baby brussels sprouts which had been slow-roasted earlier in the day over low heat in Sally's ovens with a reduction of balsamic vinegar and bacon pieces. The brussels sprouts glistened and gleamed in the low light of the booth, looking almost as though they had been candied with a sugar glaze, from the balsamic vinegar. One final thing caught their attention almost immediately: a large bowlful of some sort of mashed golden-hued vegetables, seeming to glow with deliciousness, and which looked whipped into perfection with what surely must have been an entire cow's daily production of cream and butter.

After they had finished their dinner, and they

had ruefully declined dessert, at least for the moment, Hannah turned to Norman and spoke. "Norman, Dick said that he had some information for us which might help out the investigation into No-No's murder. Let's stop to see what he meant?"

"That's fine by me, Hannah."

Chapter
Twenty-six

Dick was standing behind the bar polishing bottles while he awaited the slow trickle of drink orders from Dot, when Hannah and Norman walked into his mostly empty bar. Dick motioned to two comfortable captain's chairs located directly in front of him, indicating they should sit there.

"Bit of a slow crowd this evening, Dick?" Norman asked him, looking around at the mostly vacant tables and booths in the bar.

"Not really. You guys just managed to *hit the seam* between our happy-hour rush and the newest piano bar player coming in."

Hannah quizzed Dick. "Earlier you said that you might have some information about the investigation into No-No's death. What have you heard, or what do you know that might help us in the investigation?"

Dick leaned toward them, so only they could hear him, first motioning for the other bartender to cover for him. "What this is . . . it could be considered deep background about why No-No left major league baseball a little over a year ago, plus other certain curious things I've seen and heard lately while working here. Odd things, ones which led to me asking around about a couple of No-No's *former associates* who happen to be here in town for the tournament. In fact, they are staying right here in the Lake Eden Inn!"

Hannah leaned in closer to Dick. "What do you mean *why No-No left baseball?* Everyone knows he left the majors because he blew out his arm pitching in spring training the year following the Twins winning the World Series! That's right, isn't it, Norman?"

Norman looked a little reluctant to say anything at first, but finally he spoke up. "There were some slightly unsavory rumors of No-No associating with quite a few shady characters in the Twin Cities, characters who might have been involved with racketeering and high-end sportsbook operations."

Hannah looked over at Dick, who nodded along solemnly, and leaned in toward the bar. "Go ahead, Dick. We're listening. Tell us what really happened when No-No *retired* from the big leagues."

"Background first," Dick said, lifting one index finger in the air as though he were giving a lecture. "Do either of you know of any surefire ways to get booted out of organized baseball forever? I'll give you a hint. The clue is contained in Major League Rule Twenty-One, the one regarding player misconduct."

Hannah shook her head, but Norman, after looking thoughtful for a moment, lifted a hand slowly into the air. "Dick, I think trying to bribe an umpire to influence a game in order to make the opposing team lose is an automatic lifetime ban, isn't it?"

"Good job, Norman. Yes, under Major League Rule Twenty-One, Section C, giving or trying to give an official either a bribe or a gift for services rendered in defeating a competing team, or in attempting to defeat a competing team, shall be declared permanently ineligible to play in major-league or minor-league baseball. But that's not the reason No-No got booted. Hannah, are you sure you haven't heard any reasons to get kicked out of organized baseball permanently?" Dick leaned back and smiled at Hannah encouragingly.

Hannah thought hard and recalled something her father had said once. "I think I remember that Dad said something to me about getting kicked out of baseball, when I was a little girl. He said that no one was allowed to shove an umpire for a bad call, or violently confront any official in the majors, or else they were booted out!"

Dick looked up at the ceiling for a second, as though reading a list which was stuck up there, then he answered Hannah. "It's not a surefire way to get banned for life, but yes, a physical attack by players on umpires, or umpires on players for that matter, can be met with fines, suspensions, or worse. So, yes, if the Commissioner of Baseball finds the violent act egregious enough, that player or umpire could be made ineligible for life in the major and the minor leagues . . . But that's not it either."

Norman snapped his fingers. "Pete Rose!" he yelled out, confidently.

"You are absolutely correct, Norman," Dick stated. "Pete Rose was drummed out of baseball, and most feel he never got inducted into the Hall of Fame because of gambling, and his alleged betting on baseball games while he was a player on the Reds, Phillies, and Expos and even later on as a manager of the Reds. It got so bad, that he was accused of signaling his bookie from the dugout! However, he always bet *on* his teams, he never bet against them!"

Hannah burst in, a little incensed at what she felt was wrong. "That's not fair! He bet *on* his team to win, right? That means he was trying his hardest for his team to win. He wasn't betting for them to lose! Why would that be an issue?"

"I guess they felt that if he only bet on his team to win certain games, maybe he wasn't giving his all for games which he didn't bet on? Which is a lot of horse-hockey, if you ask me. Everyone knows *Charlie Hustle* gave all he had when he was out there. Every game!" Dick stated, with all the fervor of someone who was a true baseball fan and had been for his whole life.

"And before you ask, Hannah, *Charlie Hustle* was a nickname for Pete Rose because of the all-out effort he threw into every game he played," Norman informed her.

"Actually, I knew who that was already, Norman. Dad only truly watched two teams, the Reds and the Twins," Hannah said with a slight smirk. "He and I used to listen to the games on our old porch radio, and sip lemonade that Mom used to bring out to us. He actually made me a promise that if I could look up, and then memorize, the key players on the Big Red Machine from the World Series winning year of 1976, he would buy me a new bike!"

"Did you get the bike?" Dick asked her, looking at her very curiously.

"Let's see . . . Davey Lopes, Johnny Bench, George Foster, Pete Rose, Joe Morgan, Dave Concepcion, Tony Perez, Ken Griffey, Cesar Geronimo, with Sparky Anderson behind the bench. I think that's about right!" Hannah answered, furrowing her forehead in concentration. "I might have forgotten the pitchers on the team, though."

Norman smiled widely at Hannah. "That's amazing!"

Dick nodded and continued. "Now, back to the man at hand . . . In No-No's case, rumors began to intensify in the days shortly following the game in which he ruined Zack Edwards's baseball career by shattering his elbow. Rumors of No-No betting big on the Twins to win for every game he started. This rumor ran around the league dugouts and locker rooms for most of the season. A rumor, mind you, if proven true, would have been enough all by itself to spell the kiss of death for No-No's baseball career. However, there was something No-No did which was far worse than just betting on his team to win, at least in the eyes of the Commissioner of Major League Baseball. And I suppose, in the eyes of the federal government, too."

"What are you talking about, Dick?" Hannah interjected. "The Feds got involved when No-No placed bets on the Twins to win when he pitched? That seems a little far-fetched. I mean, it wasn't like he was involved in organized crime, right?" She puzzled aloud. "Wait a minute . . . or was he?!"

"Yes, I am afraid that No-No did get involved in bookmaking himself, especially when he was sent down to the farm leagues. Remember that there was a real fight for bets coming in from online sports gambling groups. The Feds got involved, but they needed to find a way to get information from inside the crews to shut it all down. Enter No-No, a man who they already had leverage on, mostly because the Commissioner of Major League Baseball himself was strongly leaning toward the idea of throwing No-No very publicly, and very directly, to the mainstream media wolves for violating Major League Baseball's Rule Twenty-One. The Feds pressured Major League Baseball to let them have No-No, using the old *we are all working toward the same goal* approach. They convinced the commissioner that getting No-No to work from inside the illegal sportsbook operations and then pass on info to the Feds would slow down the betting which was occurring all over the league."

Norman looked skeptical, and questioned Dick further. "Well, okay, but what about No-No? He still had to give up something, obviously. He didn't get off scot-free. We know that."

Hannah nodded her head, seeing the big picture now. "No, Norman. He still had to give up playing or working in Major League Baseball forever, and I bet my bottom dollar that helping the Feds take down those bosses, from the inside of their own gambling operations, was no picnic for him, either!"

"Right!" Dick agreed with Hannah. "Believe it or not, after MLB put out a press release about No-No *retiring due to an injury he suffered in spring training,* he went on to gather some serious trust from the big bosses of one of the online operations, who brought him even further into the business. I imagine that they figured, if he was slick enough to pull the wool over the eyes of Major League Baseball's best investigative team, that he must have some heavy leverage on MLB and could get the sportsbook bosses some new money. In the eyes of the top brass of the biggest sportsbook operators, he was more than a superstar attraction. They all were convinced, as a draw for new gamblers, No-No could give them a ton of new business! He worked closely with the Feds to get the goods on the top tier of illegal sports bookies and really made a dent in illegal online sports betting. All with no one the wiser, or so he thought."

"What do you mean, *or so he thought,* Dick?" Hannah sat bolt upright in her captain's chair, staring at Dick worriedly. "Do you think the people working for the illegal sportsbook operations found out and tracked him down to Lake Eden?"

"Well, if you think about it," Norman stated, "he wasn't exactly keeping a low profile while he was here in Lake Eden. I mean, first he drove a new convertible down Main Street in the middle of the day honking his horn and acting like a big shot with three young ladies who were wearing next to nothing and waving to everyone in sight. Then, the next evening, No-No attended the banquet and got called up on stage by the mayor of Lake Eden. Finally, and perhaps the worst if you wanted to remain unseen, *No-No pitched on the main field in the opening game of Lake Eden's Tri-County All-Star Tournament.*"

"You're right, Norman. Dick, is that what you meant when you said *or so he thought*?"

"No, although Norman is right about No-No being very visible in Lake Eden. Using the *invisible bartender trick*, a homemade twist on your *invisible waitress trick*, I managed to overhear the conversation between two *very* well-dressed gentlemen, with the shoes to match. And they got louder the more they drank. When I say very well-dressed, I'm talking about Italian leather shoes worth at least five hundred dollars a pair, and bespoke suits that probably cost a couple of thousand dollars each! Not the sort of guests that we usually get in such a small town. Here's the kicker . . . They spoke about No-No a lot!"

"What did they say? Did they sound angry about No-No's helping the Feds? Were they looking for payback?" Hannah asked in a curious voice.

"That's the strange part," Dick answered quickly. "They didn't sound angry at all! They were speaking about the Feds busting the big bosses, all right, but in a joking sort of way. It was as if No-No had helped them get lucrative new positions, or *a new contract.*"

Dick looked at them both and looked a little upset. "Here, I've been talking your ears off and I haven't even made you a drink yet. Hannah, I have a new spin on an old classic that I'd like you to try. I call it the *How Now, Brown Cow.* I also make a virgin version of it, with no alcohol, that Norman might enjoy! Want to try it?"

Hannah answered without even glancing Norman's way. "That sounds great, Dick. It sounds like a great dessert drink or an after-dinner drink . . . Is that what kind of drink it's supposed to be?"

Dick beamed. "That's it exactly. The version with alcohol in it is my take on a classic called a Brandy Alexander, but my version uses chocolate ice cream. Norman's drink, the *How Now, Brown Bessie*, is the one I make for anyone who doesn't want alcohol. That's basically just a super-rich chocolate malted milkshake. I'll be right back . . ."

While Dick made his way out to the back freezer area, Hannah sat quietly for a bit and thought about what Dick had said earlier. Dick's comments about the sharp-dressed strangers who spoke too loudly about No-No bothered her, but she wasn't sure at first why it did. She looked at Norman, who was lost in his own thoughts, then Hannah chewed her bottom lip waiting for Dick to return.

Dick proudly strode back into the bar with two large glasses filled to the brim with something that appeared to be thick, dark brown, creamy, and delicious. Norman started to say something, but then Dick put the drinks down in front of them and stood behind the bar, grinning and looking like a fox loose in a henhouse.

Hannah took her first sip of the velvety-smooth concoction and moaned. It was incredible! Her taste buds swooned in delight, crying *more, more,* so she sipped faster, almost gulping it down, hurrying to get as much of the liquid to her taste buds as she could. The spike headache hit her hard on about her fourth sip. "Ouch," Hannah said, as the cold seemed to spread as fast as wildfire through her entire head. "I know I shouldn't drink really cold things that fast, but this is so good!"

Norman smiled over at Hannah, but he drank his own non-alcoholic *How Now, Brown Bessie* much less quickly than she, learning from Hannah's painful experience. Norman hummed appreciatively after he sipped, glanced over at Dick, and asked him in a speculative tone of voice, "Dick, about those two snappily dressed gentlemen you overheard, the ones with the volume control issues . . . You don't think that they were in town to . . . ?"

Hannah spoke at almost the same time as Norman finished, her voice overlapping his slightly. "Dick, you can't honestly think they were here . . ."

"To rub No-No out? To fulfill a contract on his life, one given by the big bosses, before they went down for their crimes? It's possible, certainly, but I'm just not sure," Dick answered quickly.

"But to speak so loudly about a contract, and in a public bar?" Hannah asked, with doubt twisting her lips sideways. "It seems a little far-fetched."

"I only told you what I overheard them say. I inferred the rest! What I heard them speculating about was how easy No-No would be to hit. And that they could easily hit him here, in a small town like Lake Eden."

"They said they could *hit No-No easily here*? Are you certain about that?" Norman questioned.

"Absolutely, but that's not all! In fact, I overheard one of them mutter something to the other, before they went up to their rooms. The bigger one told the other, he knew *how they could hit No-No so hard, that no one would ever forget it.* And then he said, *After all, we are both great hitters.*"

"Wow! That sure sounds suspicious. I know that it's asking a lot, Dick, but if you could keep an eye on them and tell Sally to call us if they suddenly check out, that would help a lot! We will let Bill know about those two right now."

NUTELLA TRIFLE

(You will need 6 Large Margarita or Dessert Glasses)

(This is a no-bake recipe)

Ingredients for the first layer:

24 Ladyfingers, or premade Sponge Cake
cut into strips 2 inches wide by 4 inches
long

8 ounces of Buttershots *(a butterscotch
liqueur/schnapps)*, or 8 ounces of
Chambord *(a Raspberry liqueur)*

Directions for the first layer:

In a large-sized metal bowl, place 24 ladyfinger-
like cake pieces (these could be pieces of pound
cake cut into finger-sized strips, or even sponge
cake strips you tear yourself) side by side in the
bowl.

Sprinkle 4 double shots (8 ounces) of either
Buttershots (a Butterscotch Schnapps) or four
double shots (8 ounces) of Chambord (a great
Raspberry liqueur), but not both types of
liqueur, as evenly as you can over the top of the
ladyfinger/cake pieces in the metal bowl. (All
right, I cannot deny it . . . I used a water pistol

which belonged to my neighbor's little boy. I cleaned and re-loaded with eight ounces of Buttershots. After I loaded it, I squirted the Buttershots all over the ladyfingers. In my defense, I did rinse it out before I gave it back to him!)

Cover the bowl with Saran Wrap, then place the bowl in the refrigerator for 30 minutes to chill and come together.

You will be lining the bottom and sides of your Large Dessert glasses (or Margarita glasses) with these tasty treats before adding the rest of the ingredients to follow.

Directions for the second layer:

NUTELLA MOOSE (MOUSSE) LAYER

Ingredients:
    3 cups heavy whipping cream
    ⅔ cup powdered sugar
    1 cup Nutella

Directions:

Pour the three cups of heavy whipping cream and the ⅔ cup of powdered sugar into the bowl of a stand mixer, or into a medium-sized metal mixing bowl. Use a hand mixer, or the whisk attachment on a stand mixer, to whip up the cold whipping cream until stiff peaks form.

After your stiff peaks have formed, scoop the one cup of Nutella into your stand mixing bowl, or your medium-sized metal bowl. Mix it all together with the now really whipped whipping cream by using a rubber spatula and folding it over and over, gently, until all the whipped cream and Nutella are combined into a uniform brown/tan color and the mixture loses any streaks.

Refrigerate for at least fifteen minutes, or until you're ready to serve.

Third and Final Layer:

RASPBERRY WHIPPED CREAM

Ingredients:

    1 medium-sized glass bowl

    2 cups heavy whipping cream

    ½ cup powdered sugar

    2 small packages of fresh raspberries (eight- or twelve- ounce prior to mashing up). You can mash these raspberries with a potato masher or a fork in a glass bowl, along with the one-quarter cup of granulated sugar—see below—then stick them in the refrigerator.

    ¼ cup of granulated white sugar *(for mashing up the berries)*

Hannah's 1st Note: Chill a metal bowl and the two whipping beaters from your hand mixer or the whipping attachment from your stand mixer for at least 30 minutes before you start this whipped topping.

Directions for the third layer:

Beat whipped cream and sugar on medium-high until mid-firm peaks form, being careful not to over whip this (mine took 4 and a half minutes).

Fold in two cups of mashed raspberries.

Set aside in the refrigerator until you are ready to assemble this dessert.

To serve:

Remove the bowl with Ladyfingers or Sponge Cake pieces from the refrigerator, place it by your Margarita glasses or large dessert glasses.

Using a large serving spoon, divide the contents evenly between the 6 margarita/dessert glasses, lining the bottom and the inside of the glasses with the marinated pieces. If someone should happen to get a bit more of this deliciousness than the others do in their glass, that just means they win!

Remove your second bowl (the one with the Nutella Mousse) from the refrigerator and,

using the same serving spoon you used for the Ladyfingers/Sponge Cake pieces, divide the Nutella Mousse evenly over the top of the Ladyfinger pieces for each of the 6 glasses.

Finally, take the bowl with the mashed raspberry whipped cream and place dollops of the mixture on top of the Nutella Mousse in the glasses.

Hannah's 2nd Note: You can make this dessert super-fancy by the addition of a few sprigs of mint placed on top of the whipped topping, or some shaved chocolate curls, or a bit of melted seedless raspberry jam. The sky is the limit here. Heck, you could even top it with crushed Butterfinger pieces.

HOW NOW, BROWN COW

(This is usually served in a margarita glass or any other glass which not only looks nice, but holds a lot.)

Hannah's 1st Note: There is a non-alcoholic version of this cocktail called *How Now, Brown Bessie*. That recipe will follow this one.

Ingredients:

    4 ounces of Brandy
    4 ounces of Crème de Cacao
    2 ounces Kahlua
    4 Tablespoons Chocolate Malted Milk
       Powder *(I used Carnation)*
    2 Tablespoons Hershey's Chocolate Syrup
    2 scoops Chocolate Ice Cream
    2 cups of Heavy Whipping Cream
    Reddi-Wip topping in a can

Directions:

Place the Brandy, Crème de Cacao, Kahlúa, Malted Milk powder, and Hershey's Syrup in a blender.

Put the lid on the blender, and turn it on LOW until combined.

Shut off your blender, remove the lid, and add the 2 scoops of Chocolate Ice Cream and the Heavy Whipping cream in (*NOT the Reddi-Wip*, the Heavy Whipping Cream). Blend it all on whatever the medium setting on the blender is until combined.

Hannah's 2nd Note: If the resulting drink is not thick enough for you, the blender may be filled up all the way to the ¾ full mark on the blender's glass body (either with crushed ice, or with more chocolate ice cream) and then re-blend the beverage until it matches your icy-headache tolerance level.

Hannah's 3rd Note: I like it so frosty and thick that a plastic straw will stand up on its own if left unattended in the glass . . . but then again, I AM a Minnesota girl!

Serve in large glasses, like margarita or dessert glasses, replenishing ingredients as needed to keep yourself and your guests happy. Top with a spritz of Reddi-Wip, and perhaps a maraschino cherry or two.

However, just a heads-up . . . Although this drink tastes like the world's best malted milk-shake, the alcohol in it may sneak up on you! Please do NOT drink and drive, okay? If you do not want to drink alcohol at all, or desire a non-alcoholic version of this drink, here it is—see below!

HOW NOW, BROWN BESSIE

(This is usually served in a Margarita glass or any other glass, which not only looks nice, but holds a lot!)

Hannah's 1st Note: This is the <u>non-alcoholic version</u> of HOW NOW, BROWN COW!

Ingredients:

4 cups of Heavy Whipping Cream
4 Tablespoons Malted Milk Powder
6 Tablespoons Hershey's Chocolate Syrup
8 ounces of crushed ice (for icy goodness)
3 scoops Chocolate Ice Cream
Reddi-Wip topping in a can *(for top of the milkshake)*
Maraschino cherries (to garnish)

Directions:

Place the 4 cups of Heavy Whipping Cream, the Malted Milk powder, the Hershey's Chocolate Syrup and 8 ounces of crushed ice in a blender.

Put the lid on the blender and turn it on LOW or CRUSH mode until combined.

Shut off your blender, remove the lid, and add the 3 scoops of Chocolate Ice Cream.

Blend it all on whatever the medium setting on the blender is until combined and smooth. Pour into large dessert glasses or margarita glasses. Top with Reddi-Wip and a maraschino cherry!

Hannah's 2nd Note: If the resulting drink is not thick enough for you, the blender may be filled up all the way to the ¾ full mark on the blender's glass body (either with crushed ice, or with more chocolate ice cream), and then you can re-blend the beverage until it matches your icy-headache tolerance level.

Hannah's 3rd Note: I, myself, like it so frosty and thick that a plastic straw will stand up on its own if left unattended in the glass . . . but then again, I AM a Minnesota girl!

Serve in large glasses, like margarita or dessert glasses, replenishing ingredients as needed to keep yourself and your guests happy. Make this special with a topping with a spritz of Reddi-Wip and perhaps a maraschino cherry or two.

Chapter
Twenty-seven

Hannah took her latest creation, Berry Excellent Strawberry Pie, out of the industrial oven at The Cookie Jar. She'd just set it onto a cookie sheet and was placing it into her bakers rack to cool, when there was a certain rhythmic knock on the back kitchen door.

"Hold on for just a second," Hannah called out. "I'm coming, Andrea." Hannah rushed over to the back kitchen door and flung it open with a smile.

"Hannah! You never even looked through the peephole," Andrea said, giving her sister a small frown. "How do you know that I wasn't some axe murderer at your door?"

"That's just silly," Hannah replied with a slight grin. "Murderers don't know your special knock!"

That stopped Andrea for a moment, then she shook her head rapidly. "Nice try. But someone could watch me and duplicate my knock to fool you."

Hannah looked past Andrea and noticed that

Bill, Lonnie, and Rick had all followed her to the door. "Or maybe some shady characters, like the ones right behind you, might slip on in while you stand there reminding me to check the peephole!"

Andrea almost broke her neck, whipping around to see who Hannah was talking about. She managed to look a bit sheepish as she realized that it was only Bill and his two-person team of detectives. "Ha, ha! Very funny, Hannah. Shady characters indeed!" Andrea said, striding in the door and rather-too-firmly hanging up her Lake Eden Realty jacket on one of the coat hooks positioned there.

Hannah glanced at Bill, Lonnie, and Rick as they followed closely behind Andrea into The Cookie Jar. All of them seemed to be either hiding a smile or trying not to chuckle at Andrea's overreaction to Hannah's comment. "Why, Andrea . . . I was agreeing with you! One can never be too careful with desperate characters like these three about. Coffee, anyone?" Hannah asked with an impish look on her face.

"Yes, please!" Bill answered her. "All kidding aside, Hannah, we came here to ask for your help."

"You've got it," Hannah said, answering Bill without any hesitation. "What's the problem?"

"Interviews," Lonnie responded, breaking into their conversation. "We want you and Norman to sit in when we interview persons of interest."

"That's right, Hannah," Rick spoke up, silent until now, but wanting to be involved. "We are not used to doing these interviews by ourselves, and we might miss something that we'd catch if Mike were here."

"What do you say, Hannah?" Bill followed up, jumping back in the conversation before his deputies ran away with it. "Will you sit in on the interviews with us? We would really like to hear your thoughts on what the interviewees say, and what they *don't* say."

"Of course I'll help," Hannah promised quickly, "and I'm positive that Norman will say yes, too!"

"That's great!" Lonnie told her. "The first interview is later this afternoon. Do you have time to sit in then?"

"Is it before, or after, the second game in the All-Star tournament's quarterfinals today?" Hannah asked. "I'm supposed to premiere a couple of new popcorn recipes while I'm working at the Snack Shack, sometime around noon today."

"Popcorn recipes?" Andrea asked her sister, a little perplexed. "What's the big deal? All you do is pop and serve, right? What popcorn recipes could possibly need a *premiere* at the Snack Shack?"

"Aha!" Hannah answered, in a slightly mysterious voice. "But if I told you all now, it would spoil the debut!"

"If it's okay with you, we thought we might have the initial interviews here, in the kitchen of The Cookie Jar. That might put the people being interviewed more at ease about being interviewed. The first one, James Connor, isn't until three this afternoon. That should give you plenty of time to *premiere* the new popcorn recipes at the Snack Shack, and still get back to The Cookie Jar. How's that?" Bill asked.

"Sounds smart," Hannah replied. "We can soften them up with coffee and a cookie or two, while they're asked the warm-up questions, then hit them with the stuff we really want to know after they're relaxed!"

"Brilliant, Hannah!" Andrea interjected. "That should work perfectly."

Bill nodded and moved toward the door. "Right! We'll be leaving now. Come on, boys, let's go. Hannah's got work to do, and so do we. Hannah, we'll meet you here later, right?"

"See you this afternoon, Bill. I will call Norman and make sure he is here, too. Bye, Rick, bye-bye, Lonnie!" Hannah waved at the boys as they walked out the kitchen door, and then she turned to her sister. "Could you hang around for a few minutes, Andrea? I might need a little of your help with a new cookie recipe before I go to the Snack Shack."

"New recipe? Sure. What are you calling the new cookies?"

"Curveball Cookies. They're a variation on the usual sugar cookies we serve here, but the cookies look like a baseball. Well, really, they look like a baseball which has been run over and flattened by a road roller. But what I need you to do is frost the sugar cookies to make them white on top, like a baseball. Then, when they're dry, you can help pipe on the red cookie icing for the baseball's seams."

Andrea beamed at Hannah, rolled up her sleeves, and strode determinedly over to the sink. Andrea began to wash her hands, then she turned back to her sister and stated with certainty, "I was born to decorate things. After the Pink Lemonade Cakes I decorated, and after these Curveball Cookies, I'll change my job description to *Lake Eden's Queen of Frosting!*"

CURVEBALL COOKIES

Preheat oven to 375 degrees F., rack in the middle position.

Hannah's 1ˢᵗ Note: This first part of this recipe (the sugar cookies themselves) is a really good "pitcher's mound" for the Curveball Cookie recipe. But what makes these cookies stand out is the shape of the cookie, the white "baseball" frosting on top of them, and the red icing "seams", which really make these Curveball Cookies pop!

Ingredients:
> 1 cup Softened butter (**2 Sticks, 16 Tablespoons, ½ Pound**) I used Land O' Lakes salted butter
>
> 1 cup Vegetable Oil *(I used Wesson)*
>
> 1 cup Confectioners *(Powdered)* Sugar
>
> 1 cup White *(Granulated)* Sugar
>
> 2 Large room-temperature Eggs *(beaten in a glass or small bowl)*
>
> 1 teaspoon Vanilla Extract
>
> 4 and ½ cups All-Purpose Flour *(I used Gold Medal AP Flour)*
>
> 2 teaspoons Baking Powder
>
> 1 teaspoon Baking Soda
>
> 1 teaspoon ground Cinnamon *(optional)*

Directions:

Take out 2 cookie sheets and spray them with Pam or another non-stick cooking spray, or you may cover your cookie sheets with sheets of parchment paper instead of spraying with non-stick spray.

In your Stand Mixer or a large mixing bowl, add in the salted, softened butter, vegetable oil, powdered sugar, and granulated sugar and mix until combined.

Add in the 2 beaten eggs, vanilla extract, and the cinnamon (if you decide to put in the cinnamon—which is optional) and combine together with the sugar mixture you just made.

Place the 4 and ½ cups of all-purpose flour in a medium-sized bowl.

Add the baking powder and the baking soda.

Combine using a fork or small whisk.

Add this into your mixer bowl. Make sure that you add the flour one cupful at a time, mixing after each addition, until everything is combined.

Remove the cookie dough from your mixer and cover with plastic wrap.

Place the bowl in the refrigerator for at least 30 minutes to chill.

Then pop the bowl into the freezer for an additional 15 minutes.

In the meantime, get out a bread board and flour it lightly.

Find your trusty rolling pin and flour that, too.

Then get your cookie dough from the freezer and turn the dough out of the bowl and onto your bread board for rolling.

Hannah's 2nd Note: You may also use a clean, dry kitchen counter as a surface to roll out your cookie dough, but make sure to flour the counter and your rolling pin lightly first.

Roll your dough out to a uniform thickness of about one inch thick, then take a regular-sized water glass from your cabinet and dip the rim of the glass in either white, granulated sugar

or in flour. Be sure to dip it enough to coat the rim of the glass, because this will become your cookie cutter!

Taking the rim of the glass, cut out cookie dough circles and, using a spatula, place them on your baking/cookie sheet.

Hannah's 3rd Note: Make sure that you leave at least two inches between cookies on the sheet. And don't place any more than 12 cookies to a sheet.

Put the Curveball Cookies in the oven—which has been preheated to 375 degrees F. already—and bake them for between 8-10 minutes.

Remove the Curveball Cookies from the oven and place them on a cold stovetop burner or wire rack for two minutes.

Then take them from the cookie sheet, parchment paper and all, and place them on another wire rack to finish cooling completely (at least 20 minutes).

Let them set for at least 4 hours (or overnight, if you'd like) before doing the next step, which is making the cookies look more like baseballs by using a powdered sugar frosting **(recipe follows).**

POWDERED SUGAR FROSTING:

Ingredients:

2 cups powdered *(Confectioners')* sugar
3 Tablespoons of heavy whipping cream
1 teaspoon vanilla extract

Directions:

Place the powdered sugar, the heavy whipping Cream, and the vanilla extract into a medium-sized bowl.

Stir with a wooden spoon or a wire whisk until they are well combined. This is your frosting!

Cover the cookies with the frosting you've just made using a pastry brush, or by carefully dipping them (with the top of the cookie down) into the frosting and swirling to coat.

Put your newly frosted Curveball Cookies aside for an hour or two on some parchment paper or a wire rack (frosting side up) to set. Then you can do the final step in decorating your Curveball Cookies.

The Final Step:

When the Powdered Sugar Frosting has hardened completely, your Curveball Cookies should look quite a bit like a baseball . . . but wait! Where are the red seams on the baseball? You can't throw a curveball without having any seams on the ball!

It's true . . . I used a shortcut here. I went out and found a product that is perfect to make the seams on the Curveball Cookies. It's called Betty Crocker Red Decorating Cookie Icing and it comes in a 7-ounce pouch. Now, I am certain that if you wanted to make this yourself (or a substitute at least), you could make another batch of Powdered Sugar Frosting, and instead of adding vanilla extract, you could probably add in the same amount of grenadine (a non-alcoholic pomegranate syrup) as you do the extract and it would make a slightly red frosting for the seams. However, if you use the Betty Crocker Red Decorating Cookie Icing, all you do is unscrew the top of the tube and follow the directions to get the icing out.

Making the Seams:

One third of the way into the left-hand side of the cookies, you will make a mark using the red icing that looks like half of a circle. It will look like a closing parenthesis symbol, a bit like this one:).

On the opposite side of the same cookie (the right side), again one third of the way in from the side of the cookie, make the other half using the red icing. This one will look just like the last symbol but reversed. It will look a bit like a reversed closing parenthesis or a capital "C", a little like this one here: C.

Together, they will look like the two symbols at the end of this sentence.

) (

Got it? Good! Finish the rest of the cookies using the same method.

Let them set for an hour before you do the very last step.

After 1 hour has passed, take the Red Decorating Cookie Icing and make small 45-degree

lines upward about every inch or so across each seam (on a diagonal up on one side of the seam, and down on the other side of the seam) on both sides of your Curveball Cookies. They will look like a slightly flattened pyramid, or an upside-down capital "V". These are the baseball stitches on the seams and they are the final part of the Curveball Cookies.

Yield: This recipe makes 3 to 4 dozen Curveball Cookies (depending on the size of your water glass).

Serve these with tall glasses of icy-cold milk, big cups of hot chocolate, or steaming hot coffee.

BERRY EXCELLENT STRAWBERRY PIE

Preheat oven to 400 degrees F., rack in the middle position.

Ingredients:

> 1 Frozen Pie Crust (*I used a Pillsbury Deep Dish Frozen Pie Crust*)

FILLING:

> 5 Cups of Strawberries, hulled and cut in half lengthwise
>
> ¾ Cup of White *(Granulated)* Sugar
>
> 1 Tablespoon fresh Lemon or Lime Juice
>
> 1 and ½ tsp. grated Orange Zest
>
> ¼ Cup *Minute* Tapioca (*I used a single quarter-cup taken out of an 8-ounce box of Kraft Minute Tapioca*)
>
> For the topping:
>
> ½ Cup White (*Granulated*) Sugar
>
> ½ Cup ground Pecans
>
> ¾ Cup All-Purpose Flour
>
> ½ Cup Sweetened, Flaked Coconut (*I used Baker's Angel Flake Coconut, Sweetened*)
>
> ¾ Stick of Salted Butter (*6 Tablespoons, ⅓ Cup, 3 Ounces*) cut up into ¼ -inch pieces,.

Hannah's 1st Note:
I have tried a few different kinds of Frozen Pie Crust for this pie. I guess I really wanted to like the Marie Callender's Deep Dish Pastry Pie Shells (probably because I really like their pot pies), except their frozen Deep Dish Pastry Pie Shell came out a bit too doughy for my taste. I'd also heard raves about the Wholly Wholesome Pie Shell, but I found it super-bland, and it cracked a little too easily. I used the Pillsbury, and it turned out great!

Directions:

Set aside a large metal or stoneware bowl along with a big mixing-type spoon.

Hull all the strawberries, split them in half lengthwise, and place them in the large bowl.

Add the ¾ cup of sugar to the strawberries in the bowl and use the mixing spoon to stir together until totally combined. Let sit for 5 minutes on your counter, then give it another stir.

Add in the grated orange zest, the lemon or lime juice, and Minute tapioca to the bowl with

the strawberries and sugar. Combine all the ingredients well using the mixing spoon.

Set the bowl aside for about 20 minutes to let all ingredients marinate together while you work on the topping for the pie.

Hannah's 2nd Note:
Do NOT cook the Minute tapioca before placing it in this pie! It will cook in the oven along with the rest of the filling.

Get out your food processor, or blender.

Place the white, granulated sugar, and the ground pecans in the food processor/blender.

Combine them together thoroughly.

Add the all-purpose flour and the flaked, sweetened coconut to the food processor and pulse it a couple of times to mix, but just a couple of times!

Place the cold, sliced pieces of salted butter from the refrigerator into the food processor a couple at a time, pulsing just a time or two after each addition until all the butter is in and the

mixture has little pieces of topping the size of fish tank gravel.

Remove the mixture to a bowl and, using your impeccably clean hands, rub the topping between your hands until all the topping pieces look the same size.

Cover and refrigerate this topping until it's time to bake the *Berry Excellent Strawberry Pie*.

After 20 minutes have passed, place the still-frozen Deep Dish Pie Crust on a cookie sheet or on a jelly roll pan.

Remove your strawberry filling mixture from the refrigerator and after stirring once more with your spoon, pour it into your pie shell.

Smooth the filling evenly across the pie with a rubber spatula or the back of the mixing spoon.

Place the pie in the oven and bake for 30 minutes (<u>without the topping, for now</u>).

After 30 minutes have passed, remove the pie from the oven and place on a cold stovetop burner. DO NOT turn off the oven!

Take your topping out of the refrigerator, and VERY carefully spread it over the top of the pie as evenly as you can.

Return the pie to the oven for an additional 30-35 minutes to bake, or until the topping is golden brown, and any juices that peek through the topping bubble thickly.

Remove the *Berry Excellent Strawberry Pie* and transfer to a cold stovetop burner and let it sit for at least 25 minutes or more to cool before serving.

Hannah's 3rd Note:
I like to serve this Pie with Vanilla Bean Ice Cream, Whipped Cream or sometimes, if I am feeling a little daring, a slice or two of sharp cheddar cheese (Hey, don't knock it, until you've tried it. Cheddar cheese is not JUST for apple pie, don'tcha know?). Make sure to give your guests or family either tall glasses of ice-cold milk or strong, hot coffee with this pie.

Chapter
Twenty-eight

After the frosting on the last batch of Curveball Cookies had set, and Andrea had finished piping on the red stitching, Andrea and Hannah sat at the work station to relax. They had just lifted their coffee cups in a toast, when a knock rattled the back kitchen door. Hannah got up to answer, but something made her look over at Andrea first. Sure enough, Andrea was staring at her hard and clearly waiting for Hannah to do something. *Aha*, Hannah thought, *I know what she's waiting for me to do now.* As Hannah reached the door, instead of casually flinging it open, as she usually did, she very deliberately and very slowly put her eye to the peephole to see who was there. She glanced over her shoulder and saw her sister looking back at her with a smile as bright as morning sunshine and nodding her head in approval.

"It's for you, Andrea," she said with a laugh, just as a second, more impatient knock came at the back door.

Andrea's smile disappeared and, practically running across the kitchen to the door, she opened it only to find Bill, Lonnie, and Rick standing there for the second time that morning.

"Hey, Andrea," Bill said with a chuckle, "I'll bet a week's worth of dish duty that you didn't look through the door peephole first before answering, did you?"

Andrea stammered, because Bill was correct. Sure enough, after chiding Hannah about not looking through the peephole earlier, she had made the same mistake herself. "I . . . I . . . well, gosh! Bill, you're right, but how did you know I didn't look first?"

"That's easy, Andrea. After all, I am a highly trained professional. When I knocked for the first time, I noticed that the peephole was briefly obscured for a second. That meant someone had placed their eye there to check out who was at the door. However, enough time had lapsed between my first and second knock to know that someone else had likely come to the door to answer, and that person had not blocked the peephole with their eye first! I assumed, since you were the one who finally opened the door, you must have been the second person to arrive at the door. And since the second person to the door did not obscure the peephole, that means you didn't look out to see who it was first before you opened up!"

As Andrea pondered this logic, Hannah decided to take over. "Hello again, boys. What's going on? Did you decide you were hungry and you needed something to munch on before canvassing the neighborhood and tracking down the bad guys? How about some Lemon Muffins?"

"I would love a little something, Hannah," Lonnie replied quickly.

"Count me in, too!" Rick said, hot on Lonnie's heels.

"Bill? How about you?" Hannah inquired of her brother-in-law.

"I could eat," Bill admitted. "It's been a while since breakfast. But that's not really why we came back to see you."

While Andrea got them all coffee, Hannah walked through the kitchen doors into the coffee shop and grabbed five Lemon Muffins out of the display case.

"We'll need to put another batch of those in the oven sometime today," Lisa called out as Hannah started to walk back into the kitchen. "But don't worry about that now. Come to think of it, don't worry about a thing, Hannah! What are you bringing with you to the Snack Shack today?"

"I've got a bunch of cookies all ready to take out there for the game."

"Wonderful! What do you have ready?"

"I've got two big batches of Lazy-Daze Summertime Cookies and two big batches of Root Beer Cookies, all ready to go. There are a few more already mixed up in the walk-in cooler in case they run out."

"You're the best, Hannah. You're always so creative! I'm glad you're my partner."

Hannah gave Lisa a thumbs-up, thinking for the umpteenth time what a smart thing it had been for her to make Lisa a partner in The Cookie Jar. She was very happy that Lisa excelled at, and appeared to thrive on, handling the day-to-day operations of The Cookie Jar, leaving almost all the creative aspects of the business to Hannah. It really was a perfect match!

ROOT BEER COOKIES

Preheat oven to 350 degrees F., rack in the middle position.

Ingredients:

2 and ½ cups of all-purpose flour *(I used Gold Medal, but you may use Pillsbury or any all-purpose flour)*

½ teaspoon regular salt

½ teaspoon baking soda

1 stick salted butter, softened *(½ cup, 8 Tablespoons, 4 ounces)*

1 cup white *(granulated)* sugar

⅓ cup brown sugar

1 egg

1 teaspoon vanilla extract

6 Tablespoons root beer

1 cup white chocolate or vanilla chips

Directions:

Place parchment paper on the cookie sheet.

Spray the parchment paper with Pam or another non-stick cooking spray.

In a medium-sized bowl, mix the flour, salt, and baking soda. Set aside for now.

In another bowl, mix the softened butter, the white sugar, and the brown sugar. Mix together until light and fluffy.

Add the egg and the vanilla extract to the butter mixture and mix it in until well combined.

Add root beer and mix until everything is combined.

Take the flour mixture you combined first *(the one in the bowl you've set aside),* stir it into the bowl with the root beer mixture *(the one you've just done),* and mix until well combined.

To finish, stir in the white chocolate or vanilla chips.

Hannah's 1st Note: The resulting mixture should be smelling really good by now. Resist the urge to eat the raw cookie dough. These cookies will be even better if you bake them first.

Drop the resulting dough by the spoonful, no more than 12 to a cookie sheet and leaving at least an inch between cookies.

Bake at 350 degrees F. for 8-10 minutes, or until golden brown.

Remove the cookie sheets from the oven to a cold stovetop burner or wire rack.

Let cool on the cookie sheets for at least two minutes, then move the cookies to another wire rack. *(This is easy if you have lined your cookie sheets with parchment paper first. Then all you have to do is grab the parchment paper by the corners and move the cookies and the parchment paper to the wire rack.)*

Yield: 36-48 cookies, depending on cookie size.

Serve with strong, hot coffee or cold glasses of milk. Everyone will think you're a genius.

Hannah's 2nd Note: We served these at the baseball tournament, in the Snack Shack. They were a huge hit.

LAZY-DAZE SUMMERTIME COOKIES

Do NOT preheat oven first. You will be chilling this dough.

Ingredients:

- 1 cup salted butter, softened to room temperature *(2 sticks, 16 Tablespoons, 8 ounces, ½ pound)*
- ¾ cup white *(granulated)* sugar
- ¾ cup brown sugar
- 2 eggs
- 1 teaspoon vanilla extract
- ¼ cup of good orange juice *(I used Tropicana—No Pulp orange juice)*
- 1 teaspoon of table salt
- 1 teaspoon baking soda
- 3 cups all-purpose flour
- 1 Tablespoon of orange zest, grated *(just the orange part of the peel, not the inner white part)*
- 2 cups vanilla baking chips *(I used Nestle)*

Hannah's Note: This recipe is much easier if you use an electric mixer.

Directions:

In a large bowl, mix your salted butter, white sugar, and brown sugar.

Add the eggs and vanilla extract, and mix thoroughly.

Drizzle in the ¼ cup of orange juice and blend that in.

Sprinkle in the salt and baking soda and mix well.

Add in the flour, one cup at a time, mixing thoroughly after each addition.

Sprinkle in the orange zest and vanilla chips and mix them in by hand.

Cover the bowl with plastic wrap, and place in the refrigerator to chill for at least an hour.

After an hour, remove your bowl from the refrigerator

Turn your oven to 375 degrees F.

Prepare your cookie sheets, using parchment paper to line them and spraying them with Pam or another non-stick cooking spray.

After the oven reaches 375 degrees F., drop your cookie dough by Tablespoonsful, or use a 1 Tablespoon disher on your cookie sheets (leaving at least one inch between each cookie).

Place no more than 12 cookies to a sheet.

Flatten your Lazy-Daze Summertime Cookies with the bottom of a water glass dipped in granulated sugar, or the back of a metal offset spatula.

Bake for about 9-11 minutes or until the cookies are golden brown on top.

Remove the cookie sheets from the oven to a cold stovetop burner or wire rack.

Let cool on the cookie sheets for two minutes, then remove the cookies to another wire rack. *(This is easier if you have lined your cookie sheets with parchment paper first. Then all you have to do is grab the parchment paper by the corners and move the cookies and the parchment paper to the wire rack for cooling.)*

Yield: 3 to 4 dozen delicious cookies, which everyone will enjoy.

Serve with strong, hot coffee or cold glasses of milk. Everyone will think you're a genius.

CINNAMON TOAST POPCORN BALLS

Ingredients:

6 Tablespoons of salted butter, softened *(¾ stick, 3 ounces)*

16 ounces of mini marshmallows *(I used Jet-Puffed brand mini-marshmallows. I used the entire 1-pound bag.)*

12 cups of popcorn, popped *(This popcorn is <u>measured after it's been popped</u>, not prior to popping!)*

For the Cinnamon Toast Spice:

1 Tablespoon cinnamon

¼ cup of white *(granulated)* sugar

Directions:

Hannah's 1st Note: When you are done popping all the popcorn for this recipe, make sure you only use the kernels which have popped. Throw away any popcorn which hasn't popped the first time, because if it didn't pop then, it's not ever going to pop!

Hannah's 2nd Note: This recipe can be made in two batches if you don't have a bowl that's big enough to fit all 12 cups of popped popcorn.

Hannah's 3rd Note:

Cut out several 10 inch by 10 inch squares of wax paper and spray them with non-stick cooking spray. Next, wrap one of the squares around each Cinnamon Toast Popcorn Ball, and pop them, one to a bag, into small individual plastic or paper bags/baggies. They won't stick to the wax paper this way, and they will be easier to transport to the ball game!

Mix the cinnamon and white sugar together in a small bowl with a fork, until totally combined. Set aside until seasoning portion of the recipe.

Melt butter in a large pot on LOW heat.

Add the mini marshmallows and stir the mixture continuously until almost all the mini marshmallows have melted completely *(when you pour in the hot, popped popcorn, it should melt any remaining stragglers)*.

Remove the mixture to a cold stovetop burner.

Add the 12 cups of hot, popped popcorn into the pot with the butter and marshmallow mixture.

Sprinkle in your cinnamon toast spice mixture quickly, then stir the hot mixture all the way through the popcorn.

Let sit until it's quite cool to the touch.

Using a stick of cold butter, coat your palms with butter. Then, using those buttered hands, form popcorn balls about the size of a small of baseball.

Place each of your Cinnamon Toast Popcorn "baseballs" on one of your ten inch by ten inch, non-stick sprayed wax paper squares to prevent baseballs from sticking together. Twist the wax paper around each popcorn ball to close it shut. Then pop the popcorn "baseballs" in bags or baggies for easy transport, and you're good to go!

Yield: This recipe makes 12-14 popcorn "baseballs" depending on how big you form the popcorn balls.

COTTON CANDY POPCORN

This is from one of Doc's nurses, Tami.

Ingredients:
- 2 and ½ quarts of popped popcorn
- ½ cup white *(granulated)* sugar
- ½ cup pink cotton candy sugar
- ½ cup butter
- ¼ cup light Karo syrup
- ½ teaspoon salt
- ½ teaspoon baking soda

Directions:

Cook butter, Karo syrup, white sugar, pink cotton candy sugar, and salt in a large saucepan on HIGH.

Heat the mixture, stirring occasionally, until bubbles form on the edges.

Turn heat down to MEDIUM and cook for another five minutes.

Remove saucepan from heat.

Quickly stir in the baking soda, stirring the entire time.

The mixture will foam up, so hopefully you made sure to use a large saucepan.

Spray a large disposable roasting pan with Pam or another nonstick cooking spray.

Place your popped popcorn into the roasting pan.

Quickly pour the hot sugar mixture over the popcorn and stir to coat until evenly distributed.

Place in the oven and bake at 200 degrees F. for 1 hour, stirring the popcorn every 15 minutes or so.

Yield: 2 and ½ quarts of yummy, sweet popcorn that's sure to tickle everyone's sweet tooth!

Hannah's Note: I gave some of this Cotton Candy Popcorn to Norman, who said, "Please eat lots of this popcorn! My dental clinic needs the business."

EGG AND BACON PASTA SALAD

(This is a recipe from Michelle's college friend, Shelley B.)

Ingredients:

1 2-pound package of corkscrew pasta
(cooked according to the directions on the box and chilled after cooking)

8 hard-boiled eggs, peeled and chopped

3 stalks of celery, halved and diced

⅔ cup of diced sweet onion

1 and ⅓ cups of cooked, crumbled bacon
(only use 1 cup now and save ⅓ cup to sprinkle on the top of the salad)

1 small can of sliced black olives, drained

12 ounces of frozen petite green peas *(I used about ¾ of a 16 ounce bag of Birds Eye Early Harvest Petite Peas)*, thawed and drained

1 cup of sweet pickle relish *(I used Del Monte Sweet Pickle Relish in a jar)*

1 and ½ cups of mayonnaise

⅓ cup of white *(granulated)* sugar

2 Tablespoons of red wine vinegar

3 Tablespoons of heavy cream

1 Tablespoon country-style Dijon mustard

2 teaspoons of salt

1 teaspoon cracked black pepper

Directions:

In the largest bowl you have, mix the first eight ingredients all together.

In a smaller bowl, toss the last 7 ingredients together to make the dressing for your salad.

Combine the bowls together into one, and mix until they are well incorporated.

Cover and refrigerate until you are ready to serve.

Just before serving, sprinkle the ⅓ cup of crumbled bacon you reserved over the top of the pasta salad.

Yield: 1 potluck-sized bowl of yummy pasta salad which will serve your whole family.

"Hannah, I don't think I've ever had your Lemon Muffins before," Lonnie said.

"That's probably because I've never made them for you before," Hannah replied, placing them on a platter in the center of her work station in front of the boys. She grabbed a bowl of softened butter, some small plates, and a couple of butter knives.

"I'm really looking forward to trying out the muffins," Andrea said.

"So am I," Hannah admitted, delivering the butter, plates, and knives to the top of the work station and setting them down next to the muffins.

There was a quiet time in the kitchen as everyone grabbed a Lemon Muffin, divided up the plates and knives and, buttering their muffins, took a large bite of them.

"Yum!" Bill said, with a huge smile as he devoured half of the muffin in one enormous bite. "I really like these."

"Gosh, Bill," Hannah said, smiling back at him

with a laugh in her voice. "You'd never know it from the dainty little bite you just took!"

Everyone laughed at Hannah's comment, then Lonnie chimed in.

"I like them, too. They've got a nice little twang to them."

"Right!" Rick agreed with his brother. "They really do. How did you do that, Hannah?"

"Lemon zest. I might have gone with orange zest instead, but I ran out of oranges yesterday."

"Well, when you do try out the orange zest muffins, I volunteer to taste test them for you!" Rick said quickly.

"You'd be surprised how often folks volunteer to be taste testers when we test out new recipes," Hannah mused out loud.

"No, I don't think I would be surprised at all, Hannah," Lonnie said. "Everything you've ever made for us has been delicious!"

"Could you use oranges *and* zest in these muffins, as well?" Bill asked. "Oranges are my favorite."

"Yours and Bethie's both," Andrea spoke up with a little laugh. "They are her favorite as well. I swear, Bethie is so crazy for them, she would even use orange-flavored toothpaste if I could find it for her."

Hannah laughed, thinking about her niece brushing her teeth with orange toothpaste, and then took a moment to think about Bill's question. "I think I could do it. I'd have to adjust the recipe accordingly, but . . . Yes, I know I could make them."

Once again a knock came at the back kitchen door, and Andrea got up first this time to answer it. Giving a pointed look at her sister and her husband first, Andrea, slowly and with greatly exaggerated care, bent down and looked through the peephole. Hannah and Bill glanced at each other while rolling their eyes, and with hard-fought efforts somehow managed to restrain their mirth at Andrea's antics.

Once Andrea had finally decided it was safe enough, she opened the door wide, and Norman strolled in.

"Hi, guys, what's happening?" he inquired.

"Nothing really," Hannah quickly replied for the group. "Come in and have a muffin, Norman. I was going to call you later, but I'm glad you're here now."

Hannah came over to join Norman, bringing him a muffin, silently thanking him for not taking her favorite stool.

Bill cleared his throat and spoke directly to Hannah. "We heard that you were going around town yesterday asking questions. Did you learn anything that we should know?"

"I learned a couple of things," she said. "I was checking to see how the Summer Solstice Sale was coming along. Claire had two customers who were very impressed with her miracle fiber sweater."

"Did Claire's customers say anything interesting?" Rick asked her, taking out his notebook.

"Yes," Hannah admitted with a sigh, knowing that she would share the clues she'd gathered. "One lady said that her husband was very upset about the fact that No-No had picked up his daughter and she was riding on the back ledge of his convertible."

"She wasn't the only one riding up there," Norman pointed out.

"I know," Hannah said quickly.

"You're right. There were other girls sitting up there," Lonnie agreed.

Bill jumped into the conversation. "We really should find out how the parents of those girls feel."

"Do you really think that's a motive for murder, though?" Rick asked.

"It could be," Bill responded. "In any event, it's something we should check out." He turned back to Hannah. "Anything else we should know?"

"There were a couple of people at the banquet upset over the way No-No was acting around Mother."

"Who?" Lonnie asked.

"Irma York for one, and I'm sure Stephanie Bascomb was upset, too. After all, Mother *is* one of her closest friends!" Hannah answered. Hannah looked up toward the ceiling, thought for a second, frowned a bit, then continued speaking. "There is someone else, too. They had a different reason for being upset about No-No, though . . . There was also that ex-pro baseball player who was sitting at the table close to us . . . you know, Zack, the one whose son is playing in the Winnetka County All-Star Tournament as a freshman short-stop. Zack Edwards was staring daggers right through No-No when he got called up on stage. It was during the part of the program where Stephanie was honoring the Winnetka County All-Star Alumni who were playing in the tournament. Boy, if looks could kill, we would have been calling Digger Gibson right about then to come and pick up the body! You told me that No-No's fastball shattered his elbow, destroyed the best year of

Zack's career, and knocked him out of baseball forever. Remember, Lonnie? You told me all about it at the banquet!"

"That's right," Lonnie exclaimed excitedly. "I completely forgot about Zack! I suppose we had better add another name to our suspect list."

LEMON MUFFINS

Preheat oven to 350 degrees F., rack in the middle position.

Ingredients:

⅔ cup of white *(granulated)* sugar

½ cup vegetable oil *(<u>I used Wesson</u>)*

2 large eggs *(just zoop them up in a glass with a fork)*

½ teaspoon lemon zest *(that's the yellow part, none of the white part)*

1 and ⅓ cups all-purpose flour

¼ teaspoon of baking soda

¼ teaspoon salt

½ cup buttermilk

2 Tablespoons fresh lemon juice

1 teaspoon vanilla extract

Directions:

Spray the 12 cups of a muffin tin with Pam or another non-stick cooking spray.

Next, line the muffin tin with cupcake papers.

Hannah's 1st Note: This will make it very easy to remove the muffins after baking.

Place the white sugar and the vegetable oil in the bowl of an electric mixer and process on MEDIUM until thoroughly combined.

Add in the eggs, vanilla extract, and lemon zest and mix well.

Add in half of the flour and all of the baking soda, and process until they're combined.

Add the rest of the flour and mix thoroughly.

Add the buttermilk and mix.

Remove the bowl from the mixer and stir in the lemon juice by hand.

Take the batter and fill each muffin cup ⅔ of the way full (the muffins will rise while baking).

Bake at 350 degrees F. for 25-30 minutes or until the tops of the muffins are golden brown.

When the Lemon Muffins are done, remove them from the oven and place them on a cold stovetop burner to cool and await the Lemon Glaze.

LEMON MUFFIN GLAZE

Hannah's Note: *If your powdered sugar has hard lumps or appears to be chunky, rather than smooth, replace it before you make this glaze.*

Ingredients:

⅔ cup powdered *(confectioners)* sugar

2 Tablespoons of fresh lemon juice

Directions:

Place the powdered sugar into a small bowl.

Stir in the lemon juice and whisk well until it forms a glaze.

When muffins are cooled, remove from the muffin tin and transfer to a pretty platter.

Drizzle the glaze over the top of each muffin.

Yield: 1 dozen scrumptious, lemony muffins.

Serve with strong, hot coffee or ice-cold glasses of milk.

ORANGE MARMALADE MUFFINS

Preheat oven to 375 degrees F., rack in the middle position.

Ingredients:

1 cup buttermilk

¾ cup white (*granulated*) sugar

½ cup of good marmalade (*I used Smucker's Sweet Orange Marmalade*)

2 large eggs

¾ stick of salted butter, melted, then left to room temperature (*6 Tablespoons, 3 ounces*)

3 Tablespoons Triple Sec or 2 Tablespoons frozen concentrated orange juice

1 teaspoon orange zest (*just the orange part, not the white*)

2 and ½ cups all-purpose flour (*I used Gold Medal*)

2 teaspoons baking soda

½ teaspoon salt

Directions:

Spray 2 12-cup muffin tins with Pam or another nonstick cooking spray.

Line the muffin cups with cupcake papers.

In the bowl of the electric mixer, place the buttermilk, sugar, and orange marmalade.

Turn the electric mixer on LOW and mix until smooth.

Turn mixer off.

Add the eggs, butter, Triple Sec, and orange zest.

Mix together on LOW until well combined.

Turn off mixer.

Add the flour ½ cup at a time into the bowl of the electric mixer, mixing after each addition on LOW until all of the flour is in.

Add the baking soda. Combine.

Add the salt and combine.

Fill the muffin cups ¾ full.

Bake at 375 degrees F., for 18-25 minutes, or until the tops are golden brown.

Remove from oven using oven mitts and place them on a cold stovetop burner or wire rack.

Cool for at least 10 minutes before serving.

Yield: 18-24 incredible orange muffins.

Serve with strong, hot coffee or ice-cold orange juice for a lovely start to your morning!

ORANGE HONEY BUTTER

Ingredients:

> 1 stick salted butter, softened to room temperature (*¼ pound, 4 ounces, 8 Tablespoons*)
>
> 3 Tablespoons of Orange Blossom Honey (*I used Sue Bee Orange Blossom Honey*)

Directions:

Mix the butter with the honey.

Stir thoroughly.

Yield: A little over 1 stick of sweet, sticky, orangey goodness.

Serve with Orange Marmalade Muffins.

Or on English muffins.

Or on toast.

Or for something a bit strange, but fun . . . Over popcorn for a late-night treat!

Hannah's Note: This is Bethie's favorite . . . and Bill's, too!

Chapter
Thirty

"Hi, guys," Hannah greeted Bill, Rick, and Lonnie when they came in the door later that afternoon. Then she smiled as she turned to speak to the rather tall, academic-looking man wearing stylish rimless glasses who had just followed them in. "And you must be James Connor. Welcome to The Cookie Jar, James. If anyone's hungry, I just made some Chocolate Cherry Oatmeal Squares and there's fresh coffee ready, if you're interested."

"I thought that this was going to be a police interview," James told her.

"We're not really that far along in the process yet," Hannah answered for all of them. "Think of this as us just having a chat with you and gathering some information." Hannah stopped to ask, "How does everyone take their coffee? Or would you rather have some Pink Lemonade Iced Tea instead? We just made up a batch this morning."

"Coffee, please. With a little cream and sugar for me," Rick answered her.

"Coffee, yes! But just plain and black for me," Lonnie responded.

Bill spoke up next, nodding his head. "Yes, please. I'll take a cup, Hannah."

"How about you, James?" Hannah asked, heading for the kitchen coffeepot.

"I'll give the Pink Lemonade Iced Tea a try, thank you. Is there a lot of sugar in it?" James asked.

"Well, there is a little sugar added in during the making of the Pink Lemonade part of our Pink Lemonade Iced Tea, but other than that . . ."

"That'll do nicely then, and thanks," James stated, finally smiling for the first time since entering The Cookie Jar kitchen.

Once Hannah had poured the coffee, poured James his Pink Lemonade Iced Tea, and delivered a plate of her newest Chocolate Cherry Oatmeal Squares to the work station where they were all waiting, she took her favorite chair, which was directly across from where James was seated. "I talked to your wife yesterday morning, James, and she seems like a lovely person. Would you say Darla was upset when she heard that your daughter was riding on the back of No-No's convertible as it slowly cruised its way down Main Street through the entire town of Lake Eden?"

James sighed. "You betcha, she was furious! See, our daughter, Susan, had her whole life after high school all planned out. She discussed it all with us, and we approved of her plan. Susan and Tony were going to go to college together, but they'd live in separate dorms while they were on campus. Both of them were good students, and they both got academic scholarships to attend college, so it sounded like a great idea to Darla and me. But then Susan went a little crazy for that idiot ball-player and ended up accepting a ride through town on the back of his convertible with the other girls, dressed in next to nothing. Hannah, I am positive that if you asked anyone in Lake Eden, they would say that Susan getting into No-No's car at all, much less hopping up on top of the back seat with those other girls, was probably the dumbest decision Susan ever made! We were really worried that Tony would see her as a . . . well . . . that Tony would decide that he didn't want to have anything to do with her anymore."

"Is that what Tony decided?" Bill asked.

"Not at that point, but you have to understand this . . . I really didn't know how he was going to react to the whole No-No thing. I was far more concerned that she might be throwing her whole future down the drain."

"I sure can't blame you for that," Hannah sympathized. "Were you . . . uh . . . this may be a little difficult for you to answer, but were you relieved when you found out that No-No was dead?"

"Of course I was!" James took a bite of his Chocolate Cherry Oatmeal Square. "But, I was more concerned that maybe Susan's boyfriend, Tony, might have had something to do with No-No's demise."

"Are you sure he didn't?" Bill asked.

"I . . . I don't think so. Tony is a levelheaded kid. He might have been jealous, but I really don't

think he would have been outraged enough to actually . . . uh . . ."

"Kill No-No?" Lonnie suggested.

"Exactly!"

"When did you find out that No-No had been
murdered?" Rick asked him.

"Not until that evening, when it was on the
news. I heard that there'd been a murder, but
KCOW-TV didn't say who the victim was until
then."

"Do you know how Susan felt about No-No's
murder?" Hannah asked him.

"Yes. She cried at first, but then I read her the
riot act! I asked her how she thought it would look
to the good folks of Lake Eden, her bawling her
eyes out over that sleazeball. I mean, her reputation was already spiraling down because she wore
that skimpy outfit in front of the whole town,
right? By sitting up there on the ledge of the convertible, just waving and grinning at everyone, it
had made Susan seem like some kind of bobble-
head doll to just about everyone! I said, *Congratulations, Susan, you've become the latest in a long line of
pretty little playthings that No-No had collected for his
summer fun-time, then abandoned.* I know that the only
reason that oily creep of a ballplayer had her around
in the first place was so No-No could show off to
the whole town what a big man he was. I told her
that, too! She cried a little more then, because I
was plenty harsh in my words to her, but she apologized to us right away. Susan promised to her mother
and me that she would *never, ever*, appear in public
like *that* again.

"Darla and I brought Susan back home and we

banished her to her room. Darla came in to see her, after a little while, and gave Susan a stern talking-to. Darla told her how worried we'd been about her, and how Susan might have blown up all of her future plans by being duped by No-No! Good riddance to bad rubbish. After we'd heard he'd been killed, I couldn't help thinking, Susan is a good girl, Hannah, and she really didn't deserve to be made a fool of by a little weasel like No-No. He made her look cheap, and low-class, in front of everyone in Lake Eden, and for that alone, I'm glad he's dead!"

"When you heard the local news say he was killed, that's the point that you knew that No-No wasn't a threat to Susan's future any longer?"

"Yes. He could no longer hurt our family, because he was dead! Later that night, after we'd both talked to Susan separately, we came into her room together, advised her to call Tony, and to tell him immediately that she was sorry that she'd acted so foolishly. In fact, we told her that she should beg for his forgiveness. It's like my father used to tell me . . . *When you screw it up, you've got to clean it up.* And part of Susan's *clean-up* had to be to try and make things right between her and Tony."

"And did she call him and make things right between them?"

"Well . . . She called him all right, and she said that she asked him to come over right away."

"So did he come over?" Hannah asked.

"Yes. They went into the other room to talk, but maybe five or ten minutes later, Tony came out with his head hanging down and his shoulders slumped. He walked right past us, straight out the front door, without even saying goodbye! That's when I started thinking their relationship might be a goner."

"How about Susan? Was she heartbroken?" Hannah asked sympathetically.

"Yes. At least, I think she was. All I know is that after Tony left, she just locked the door to her room, and we didn't see her at all until the next morning. I might have heard crying coming from behind the door, but I just don't know for certain."

"Is she all right now?" Lonnie asked.

"She's a little better, but . . . I think she knows that she made a mess of things, and that the way Tony feels now is *her* fault. She's still going away to college at U. of M.–Duluth, and so is Tony, but I don't know if they'll be together there."

Hannah cleared her throat. It was time for some hard questions. "I can only imagine how upset you must have been about this whole thing. Your wife said she'd never seen you so angry before."

"Darla's right. It was just the thought that my usually smart daughter had jeopardized her whole future for . . . some moron in a flashy convertible that got me so angry. The thought of her horrible mistake in judgment made me question everything I thought I knew about her. I know Susan's bright, Hannah. She wouldn't have gotten an academic scholarship unless she was a smart girl. Maybe I shouldn't say this, but when I saw her on the back of that convertible, all I wanted to do was yank that no-account baseball player out of the car and throttle him with my bare hands!"

"I can't say that I blame you," Bill said, seeming sympathetic. "But you didn't . . . did you?"

"Of course not. I would never do something like that!"

Hannah glanced over at Rick, who had folded his notebook and placed it back in the inside pocket of his green deputy jacket, and then at Lonnie, who was looking to her for the next step in the interview. "Well, okay, then, James, is there anything else you can think of . . . any fact which you might have inadvertently left out of your story? Something which might give us a clue to help us track down No-No's killer?"

"I don't think so. But just let me state this. I want it known, for the record, that I certainly didn't kill No-No. Neither my wife nor our daughter killed that *idiot* of a ballplayer. No, not idiot. That's far too nice a word for that . . . that S.O.B. who made my sweet little girl look like a common floozy in front of the whole town. I may not have killed him, but make no mistake, if anyone deserved to meet his maker, it was No-No," James stated, while looking Hannah squarely in the eyes.

"Well, unless anyone has anything else to ask about . . . hold on for a second, James," Hannah said, as James had begun to rise out of his chair. "I know that I said this wasn't exactly a formal interview, but we may as well lay the groundwork now. However, since you made a statement *for the record*, let's have you put your answer to this question on the record, too. Please tell us, exactly, where were you and your family when No-No was murdered?"

James thought about it and then smiled widely. "Where were we? We were at the University of Minnesota–Duluth all day. Darla, Susan, and I drove up to Duluth by car, along with another scholarship student who will be attending there. Her name is Mary-Lou Farrell, and her mother, Dianna Farrell, rode up there with us, too. It's easy enough to check our alibi. Just call up Dianna and Mary-Lou Farrell. They are in the phone book. They were with us in the car all the way up, and all the way back. Once we arrived, they were with us the whole time, touring the campus from about noon on the day No-No was killed, until we all re-turned together to our house, just in time to see the evening news at 6:00 p.m. There's your alibi, Hannah, and with that, I believe we are all through here, yes? In that case, good day to you!"

James threw his head back with a snort, then rose to his feet and stalked angrily out the back kitchen door.

"Well, what does everyone think? Is he telling the truth? Should we clear his name from our sus-pect list? I realize he comes across as a bit of a pompous windbag, but him as No-No's killer? I really doubt it." Hannah surveyed the room. "And, if we do decide he's cleared, who's next on our in-terview list?"

"I say let's clear him, and move on to the next suspect," Lonnie said, anxious to find the next clue and nab the killer.

"Hold on just one second there, brother," Rick answered, in his slow, deliberate way. "Like Pres-ident Reagan said a long time ago, 'Trust, but ver-ify.' I agree with Hannah completely. I don't think that James Connor is No-No's killer, either, but we have to follow procedure on this! We will check the Connor family's alibi with Dianna Farrell first, and make sure that they all drove up to U. of M. – Duluth in the morning of the day No-No was killed, and that they were all together up there, on campus, until well into the late afternoon. Then we'll verify with the U. of M. – Duluth admissions office that the Connors and Farrells all signed up to tour the campus that day. Only then can we think about totally clearing Mr. Connor!"

"Right!" Hannah said. "Makes sense, Rick. Who's the next interview?"

"Well . . . in about ten minutes," Rick said, after a quick glance at his wristwatch to look at the current time, "Tony Sloan, Susan Connor's boyfriend, will be here. He said he'd meet us here at four p.m. It's almost four now."

CHOCOLATE CHERRY OATMEAL SQUARES

Preheat oven to 350 degrees F., rack in the middle position.

Ingredients:

    1 21-ounce can of cherry pie filling *(I used Comstock Original Country Cherry)*
    ¼ cup fresh squeezed lemon juice
    2 Tablespoons instant tapioca *(I used Kraft Minute Tapioca)*
    ½ cup softened butter
    ½ cup brown sugar
    1 cup quick oats
    1 cup all-purpose flour
    ¼ teaspoon baking soda
    ¼ teaspoon salt
    1 cup of semi-sweet chocolate chips

Directions:

In a small bowl, mix cherry pie filling, lemon juice, and instant tapioca.

Let stand 15 minutes.

In the bowl of an electric mixer, cream the brown sugar and the softened butter.

Add the oats and mix well.

Mix in the flour ¼ cup at a time, until it's all in.

Add the baking soda and the salt.

Mix them in.

Butter, or spray an 8x8-inch glass pan with Pam or another non-stick cooking spray.

Take ½ the oatmeal mixture and press it down into the bottom of the glass pan (either using a spatula, or your impeccably clean hands, which you have dusted with flour).

Spread your cherry pie filling mixture over the top of the oatmeal mixture in your pan.

Sprinkle the cup of chocolate chips over your cherry mixture.

Take the other ½ of your oatmeal mixture and sprinkle it evenly over the top of the chocolate chips. Smooth it down evenly.

Bake at 350 degrees F. for 50-60 minutes, or until the cherries are bubbling through and the topping is golden brown.

Remove the pan from the oven (using oven mitts) to a cold stovetop burner or a wire rack to cool for at least 20 minutes.

Yield: 1 8x8-inch pan of delicious chocolate cherry delight!

Serve with cups of strong, hot coffee or glasses of ice-cold milk.

Or, if you want to get a little fancy, serve your Chocolate Cherry Oatmeal Squares with sweetened whipped cream or French vanilla ice cream. YUM!

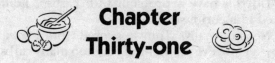

Chapter
Thirty-one

No more than ten minutes had passed, when there was a knock on the back door and a tall young man poked his head inside The Cookie Jar kitchen. "Hello, is this the right place for the interview?" the young man asked, moving the rest of his lanky six-foot, four-inch frame to stand in the doorway.

"That's right, come on in," Hannah assured him with a smile. "You must be Tony. It's a pleasure to meet you. I'm Hannah Swensen, and I have some Pink Lemonade Whippersnapper Cookies here for you, if you'd like to try them."

"I would! I didn't eat breakfast or lunch today. I was still too . . . upset about Susan."

"I can understand that," Hannah said, carrying a plate of cookies over to the work station. "Coffee?"

"Yes, but only if you have sugar-free sweetener to go with it. Except for these cookies, I'm watching my carb count."

"Do you have a problem with carbs?" Lonnie asked him curiously.

"No, not really," Tony answered, "but I have to keep a close eye on them. If I eat too many carbs, it starts having an effect on my game because I put on weight."

"So, you're an athlete?" Hannah inquired, even though she already knew the answer.

"That's right. I'm starting college next year with an academic scholarship *and* a basketball scholarship already lined up!" Tony looked down at the plate of Pink Lemonade Whippersnappers which Hannah had placed in front of him, and gave her a happy grin. "These look really good. I tried to make round cookies once that looked like basketballs, but I couldn't find anything with the right consistency to make the stitching on the cookies."

"Did you try food color gel . . . the kind that comes in the little tubes from the grocery store?"

"Yes, but it never dried. In fact, it smeared all over the cookies, and besides, I just hate to use artificial coloring agents in food," Tony said to her rather firmly.

"Hannah, I have to tell you, those cookies right there are looking awfully good to a hardworking deputy like me," Rick said, angling for some of his own Pink Lemonade Whippersnappers.

"Well, we can't have it said that The Cookie Jar ever turned away a hungry member of our police, can we? I don't suppose anyone else might like a couple?" Hannah asked, with a wry look crossing her face.

"Yes, please!" Lonnie jumped in, always ready for a snack.

Bill stood there with a thoughtful look on his

face, eyes turned upward as if he were considering his position on the offer, then he nodded. "Why, yes, Hannah. I do believe I would like one or two."

"Tony, I am going to let you in on a little secret about why we are meeting you here for your interview at The Cookie Jar, instead of at the Winnetka County Sheriff's Department. We thought that this might be a more relaxing place for you to be interviewed, plus there are cookies here!"

"That's very nice of you," Tony said. "Now, what would you like to ask me?" he continued, while straightening up on his stool.

"We'd like to find out how you felt when you saw your girlfriend riding on the back ledge of that convertible," Rick told him, bluntly.

"At first, I was . . . shocked. I never imagined that Susan would do anything like that, especially dressed the way she was. As far as I know, she'd never worn anything like that before, at least, not in front of me. Susan looked . . ." Tony stopped, and couldn't find the words to go on, his face looking a little lost and vulnerable like a child unable to find his way back home.

"Did you feel the same way about the other girls who were riding up there on the back ledge with Susan?" Rick questioned.

"Not really, because . . ." Tony stopped for a second and then sighed. "I wasn't in love with them, you see . . . !"

"How about No-No? Did you feel an urge to beat him up? Maybe even feel like killing him for what he did to your Susan?" Norman said, getting right to the heart of the matter.

"You bet I did!" Tony snapped. "I suppose I never should have admitted to that, but it was only an urge. At no time did I allow the urge to re-arrange No-No's face take control of me, or of what I did."

"Okay, Tony, but you do understand that this is a little different situation than just wanting to take a swing at him over a girl, right?" Rick pointed out to him. "A man is dead here, and to just about any-one who didn't know you or Susan, it looks like your girlfriend stepped out on you to hook up with No-No!"

"Do we really need to talk about this? It's al-ready hard enough just thinking about Susan and I . . . not being together now. It's even worse when I have to relive that day through your questions." A sigh came from deep inside Tony's chest, and a glimpse of true sadness rose up in his eyes. "I don't want to talk anymore. May I go now?" he asked, his voice very quiet and his eyes seeking the floor.

"No, not yet, son." Bill spoke up sternly. "We need your cooperation for a while longer. In case you missed it, we're trying to solve a murder here. Let's get right down to brass tacks . . . Where were you on the afternoon No-No was murdered?"

"I went out to the lake."

"Did you go with anyone? Can anyone else verify your story?"

"No, I went there by myself, Sheriff. Sometimes I just want to be alone."

"That's not much of an alibi, son. You know that."

"That's all I've got, Sheriff. I want to go home now, okay? I am tired and I'm sad, and I'm disap-pointed in everyone and everything right now. I'm just so tired of it all. I want to go home!"

"I've got one more question for you, Tony," Hannah told him, glancing over at Bill for approval.

Bill nodded at her.

"What did you mean earlier, Tony, when you said that you and Susan aren't together now?" Hannah asked gently.

Tony sat, head hanging, saying nothing, until Bill jumped in. "Answer her, Tony. I'll like to hear the answer to that, too."

"Fine," Tony almost whispered, "but I don't know why you won't just leave me alone. I went to the Connors' house that night, after she rode into town in No-No's car, to tell Susan that I thought it would be a good idea to cool it for a while. That we could reassess where our relationship was after it didn't hurt me so much to see her and to hear her voice." He fell silent then.

"Is that it, Tony? You decided to take a little break? Then why the hurt face?" Rick asked a bit sarcastically.

"You don't get it, do you? I went there that night expecting to hear Susan beg me to stay with her. At the very least, apologize to me for being with No-No and hurting me. I thought she might cry or argue with me when I said we should cool it. You know what she did? Nothing! Do you know what she said to me? *Okay, Tony.* No crying, no begging, just *Okay, Tony.* I wonder if she ever loved me."

Chapter
Thirty-two

Hannah was just taking the last sheet of Chocolate Chip Crunch Cookies out of the industrial oven, when Lisa came through the swinging doors from the coffee shop.

"Your mother is on the phone for you," she said.

"Got it," Hannah responded, reaching for the phone.

"Hello, Mother."

"Hannah, dear, I wanted to see if you could come over for cocktails at our place, after you finish work this evening," Delores said. "Bring Norman of course, and we'd love to see the grandkitties, too!"

"Okay, Mother. We'll bring the cats."

"Oh, good! Doc loves to watch Moishe and Cuddles play in the garden. He promised to stop by the nursery to pick up more ladybugs to chase."

"What happened to the last ladybugs that were there?" Hannah asked.

"The window washer came, and when he opened the access panel, they all flew off."

Hannah breathed a sigh of relief. "For a moment there, I was afraid that Moishe and Cuddles had caught them."

Delores laughed. "No, dear . . . The ladybugs are much too fast for them. And Doc just loves to watch the puzzled expression on Moishe's face when they fly away."

"What about dinner? Do you want me to bring something in the crockpot?"

Delores took a moment to think about that. "That would be lovely. But aren't you too busy to make something?"

"I'm almost through with the baking for the day, and dinners in the crockpot are easy to make. Besides, I've got a new recipe I'd like to try."

"That's very nice, dear. I've invited Andrea and Bill for dinner, and . . . since Stephanie is coming for cocktails, I'd like to invite her to stay for dinner, too."

Hannah quickly added up the guests in her head. "How about inviting Michelle and Lonnie?"

"They're going out to the mall to see the newest Spielberg movie. It's supposed to be *over the top* . . . whatever that means. At least that's what Michelle told me yesterday. And since Lonnie loves the hot dogs at the theater, they're going to eat there."

"So . . . that's seven of us for dinner, then?"

"That should be just fine. What's the new crockpot recipe, dear?"

"Sweet and Sour Chicken, served over rice."

"That sounds perfect. You know Doc loves any sort of Asian dish . . . as long as it's not too spicy."

"What time is cocktail hour?"

"How about seven-thirty tonight? I'll ask Andrea to come a bit early and set the table."

"Fine with me. We'll be there for cocktail hour."

"Wonderful! This will be fun! I just love giving dinner parties!"

When Hannah hung up the phone, she was still chuckling. A *dinner party* to Delores meant one of the roasted chickens from Florence's Red Owl with a choice of ice cream and toppings for dessert. When her mother felt particularly daring, she made something called E-Z Lasagna, which wasn't bad if you felt like eating Italian cuisine from the freezer, or . . . dinner out at an Italian restaurant, if the E-Z part failed.

"Everything okay?" Lisa asked, coming back into the kitchen to fill another cookie jar.

"Everything's fine. Do you have time to check the pantry for me and see if we have any instant rice?"

Lisa stepped inside the pantry to take a look. "I found five packages of Uncle Ben's, the kind you can make in the microwave. Will that do?"

"Perfectly. Thanks, Lisa."

When Lisa left, Hannah checked her recipe folder and took out the recipe for the Sweet and Sour Chicken.

She was just reading through the recipe and looking for ingredients when Aunt Nancy came into the kitchen. "Another phone call, Hannah."

"Thanks." Hannah walked over to the kitchen phone and picked it up. "The Cookie Jar. This is Hannah."

"Hannah . . . it's Hank from the Lake Eden Liquor Store. Rick Murphy called me. He wants to interview me tomorrow at your place."

"I figured they'd get around to you," Hannah

admitted. "Sorry, Hank, but I had to tell them what you said about Roman Ganz."

There was silence for a moment or two and then Hank spoke again. "Okay . . . I understand. It's just that when people tell me things in confidence, I shouldn't really reveal them to anyone else."

"True . . . but what if Roman was so upset, he went to the baseball stadium and killed No-No? Wouldn't you want him arrested?"

"Well . . . of course I would! But . . . do you really think he'd do something like that?"

"I don't know, but you were honest enough about it, to tell me how he acted. I think you should tell the authorities everything you know and let them decide if they want to question Roman."

"You're probably right," Hank admitted. "But you'll be there, too, won't you?"

"Of course I will. Just come to the back kitchen door a little early tomorrow, and I'll get you settled down with a cup of coffee and a muffin. What time did they tell you to be here?"

"Nine o'clock. I'll look forward to that muffin, Hannah."

SWEET AND SOUR CHICKEN

(A Crockpot Recipe)

(A 5-quart or larger crock pot is needed for this recipe.)

Ingredients:
- ⅓ cup soy sauce
- ⅓ cup honey *(I used Sue Bee Orange Blossom Honey)*
- ⅓ cup ketchup *(I used Heinz)*
- 1 Tablespoon balsamic vinegar
- 1 teaspoon garlic powder
- ½ teaspoon ground ginger
- 1½ pounds boneless, skinless chicken breasts, cut into 1-inch pieces
- 1 14-ounce package frozen Bell Pepper Strips, cut into 1-inch pieces *(I used Birds Eye)*
- 1 20-ounce can pineapple chunks in 100% juice *(I used Dole Pineapple Chunks—undrained)*
- 1 package of chicken gravy *(to be added in when you turn the crock pot to HIGH later)*
- 5 packages of microwavable rice *(I used Uncle Ben's Ready Rice Butter and Garlic—prepare this just prior to serving.)*

Directions:

Spray the inside of the crock pot with Pam or another nonstick cooking spray.

Place the 1-inch chunks of chicken, 1-inch chunks of bell pepper, all the canned pineapple chunks (including the liquid), the soy sauce, the honey, the ketchup, the balsamic vinegar, the garlic powder, and the ground ginger into your crock pot.

Give it all a stir, put on the lid, and plug in your crock pot.

Turn the crock pot on LOW.

Cook on LOW for 5-6 hours.

Then sprinkle in your 1 package of chicken gravy, give it all a stir, put the lid back on the crock pot, and turn your crock pot up to HIGH 30 minutes prior to serving.

Right before serving, make your white or mixed rice in the microwave, according to the package instructions *(I used Uncle Ben's Ready Rice Butter and Garlic—5 full packages—made in the microwave according to the directions on the back).*

Hannah's Note: I serve this Sweet and Sour Chicken over rice, with a green salad and garlic bread when I take it to Mother's for dinner.

Chapter
Thirty-three

"Hello, Mother," Hannah called out, entering her mother and Doc's penthouse with Moishe and Cuddles both on kitty harnesses. "Would you like the cats in the garden?"

"Yes, dear." Delores came out from the garden, grabbing the leashes of both of her grandkitties from Hannah's hands. "Stephanie and I were just having our first glass of champagne . . . Where's Norman?"

"Down at the car. He's loading up our big carrying box, so he can bring everything up at once."

"Once I get the grandkitties situated outside, can I come back to the kitchen to take a sneak peek at dinner?" Delores wheedled.

"Of course you can," Hannah answered immediately.

"Good! I'll pour you a glass of champagne, dear. When Norman comes up, have him set it all on the kitchen counter," Delores told her, directing the kitchen operations as only she could. "Andrea will be here in about fifteen minutes to set the table for our dinner party."

"Hello. Anyone home?" Norman asked jokingly as he walked in the door, staggering a bit under the weight of the enormous box in his arms.

"Put it over here," Hannah told him. "I'll help you unload it."

Once the box had been placed on the counter, Hannah reached in and pulled out both crock pots, plugged them into the outlet on the counter, and turned them both on low to heat. "And that's that!" she said firmly. "Norman, come join me when you finish unloading the rest of the items you brought for cocktails."

"I'll do just that!" Norman said as he pulled mysterious juices and ingredients from the box.

Hannah headed out to the garden to check on the cats. She found both Moishe and Cuddles searching the garden for ladybugs.

"They don't . . . eat them, do they?" Stephanie asked.

"Heavens, no!" Delores replied.

"That's a relief," Stephanie declared. "I've seen a cat with a mouse and . . . well . . . it's not exactly fun for the mouse."

"It's not like that at all," Delores reassured her. "The cats just look amazed when the ladybugs fly off. As far as I know, they've never caught one."

"Hello, ladies," Norman greeted them as he came into the garden. "I see the cats are having fun."

"So what did you make for dinner, Hannah?" Stephanie asked.

"Sweet and Sour Chicken, made in a crockpot. I hope you like Chinese food, Stephanie."

"I love it."

"Does that mean you're staying for dinner?" Hannah asked. "I know Mother was hoping you would."

"I wouldn't miss it for the world," Stephanie declared.

"What's all this?" Delores asked, watching as Norman unloaded the box he'd brought with him on top of the bar in the garden.

"I thought I'd make you ladies some special champagne cocktails."

"With domestic champagne?" Stephanie asked, as Norman opened a bottle.

"Yes. It would be almost a crime to use Delores's expensive champagne for cocktails. This is a perfectly good domestic champagne and just right for the cocktail I have in mind."

"I'm game," Stephanie declared. "What's in these cocktails of yours?"

"If these had white peaches in them, I could call them Bellinis."

"But they don't?" Stephanie asked.

"No. These have different fruit juices. I call this first one a Satin Swirl Champagne Cocktail."

"That sounds lovely. What's in it, Norman?"

"My secret! Try it, and see if you recognize the ingredients."

Stephanie took the small glass that Norman handed her and took a sip. "Lovely!" she declared. "It's very refreshing. Is this . . . I know it's not pear . . . but is it . . . apricot?"

Delores walked over just in time to hear Stephanie's question.

"Is what apricot?" she asked.

"The new champagne cocktail that Norman just made," Hannah answered her.

"Here," Norman said, handing Delores a glass. "It's your turn to be the guinea pig."

Delores laughed. "I'm always willing to help a dentist embarking on a new career."

Norman and Hannah cracked up, laughing, and Delores looked gratified. She took a sip of her drink, smiled, and took a second sip. "I like this!"

"It's called a Satin Swirl Champagne Cocktail."

"Delicious! It's a little like . . . a Bellini. That was one of Hemingway's favorite drinks, wasn't it?"

"So they say. I decided to use a few different kinds of fruit juice, and so far, this has turned out to be one of the best."

"Hello, everyone!" Doc greeted them. "Are you ready for the main event?"

"Are you talking about the ladybugs?" Stephanie asked.

"I am," Doc answered.

"I know Moishe and Cuddles are ready," Delores told him. "They've been hunting for the ladybugs ever since they got here."

"Well . . . here they are!" Doc said, walking over to the bushes next to the pool and opening a small container. He shook the contents out on the bushes and everyone watched as the cats ran over to see what was there.

Moishe reached out with one paw, touched a leaf, and then quickly reared back as several of the ladybugs flew past his nose.

"He does look intrigued," Stephanie commented.

"And puzzled. I think he's trying to figure out why they can fly and he can't."

"Hannah, may I speak with you alone for a second?" Doc asked.

"Sure, what's going on?"

Doc led Hannah by the elbow, away from the rest of the party, speaking to her in low tones. "I spoke to that friend of mine, the one who did the reconstructive surgery on Zack Edwards's elbow? You can cross Zack off your list of suspects for No-No's murder. There is no way he could have done it!"

"Why not?"

"Dr. Hirsch informed me that, even after multiple rounds of surgery, and placing in an entirely new elbow joint, there is simply no way Zack could ever generate enough power to smash in No-No's skull. Yes, it's true that the new joint gives Zack a certain amount of control over using his hands. As an example, he can tie his own shoelaces. But the flexibility, the range of motion, and his full arm strength will never be the same. He couldn't have killed No-No with any sort of blunt object that he would have to swing with power."

"Thanks for the update. That's one down anyway!" Hannah replied. She wrapped Doc's arm in hers and while Doc looked down upon her fondly, Hannah walked him back to the party and their friends.

"Hi!" Andrea greeted them, as she strolled from the kitchen into the garden. "Did I miss the launch of the ladybugs?"

"Yes, at least this round. There are scheduled flights all evening," Doc quipped. "We anticipate a tiny bit of low-hanging cloud cover, but we still have clear visibility for ladybug sightings throughout the entire evening."

Andrea laughed as she came in and took her seat between Bill and Stephanie.

"Do you want to try one of my new creations?" Norman asked Andrea, handing her a glassful.

"Sure, why not?" Andrea sipped the contents in the glass and gave Norman a pleased nod. "I like it! It tastes like . . . a wine cooler?"

"Close," Norman replied.

"Would you mind setting the table, dear?" Delores asked Andrea.

"Of course, Mother," Andrea said, getting up and motioning to Bill. "Come on, honey. You can help me."

"I guess I'd better go, Norman. You know how it is . . ."

"Not yet, but I hope to someday," Norman said, looking at Hannah.

Hannah flushed slightly, looking down for a moment. *Norman is a bit like Cracker Jacks,* she thought to herself. *He's a little nutty, more than a little corny, but very comforting to have around.*

Hannah glanced back up and caught her mother looking sideways at her, then over at Norman, then back again, with a small smile twitching in the corners of her mouth, and a speculative look in her eye the entire time. *Oh-oh . . . this looks like trouble. Mother's planning something again!* she thought, as alarm klaxons began to sound, and fire engines began to race around in her mind's eye. She squinted her eyes a little at Delores, but her voice sounded just as sweet as the cotton candy spun at the Minnesota State Fair. "What is it, Mother?" she asked Delores. "Is there something on your mind?"

"It's nothing really, dear," Delores answered her. "I was just thinking how well suited the two of you are. That's all."

SATIN SWIRL CHAMPAGNE COCKTAIL

Ingredients:

> 4 shots (just about 6 ounces) Apricot
> Brandy
> 8 ounces apricot juice *(I used Kern's Apricot
> Nectar, 1 8-ounce can)*
> 1 750 ml bottle of some decent
> champagne *(I used Korbel Brut
> Champagne)*

Norman's 1st Note: I have found that if you add something like a fruit juice into champagne to make a champagne cocktail, it will really stretch out the servings-per-champagne-bottle. For instance, in this recipe, by using an ice-shaken mixture of the Apricot Brandy and the apricot juice, then pouring that mixture ⅓ of the way up each champagne flute before adding champagne, I was able to serve 8 people cocktails while using just one 750 ml bottle of Korbel Brut!

Directions:

Grab 1 regular or fancy 64-ounce pitcher and fill it about ½ of the way up with ice.

Take the Apricot Brandy and Apricot Juice and pour it into the pitcher on top of the ice.

Use a large spoon or cocktail stirrer to combine the apricot mixture thoroughly.

Norman's 2nd Note: I like to use a glass pitcher, shaved ice, and a cocktail rod for this part (a cocktail rod is just a fancy bartender term for a straight glass stirrer). I find it adds to the theatrics when you do it this way.

Strain out the ice and pour about 2 or 3 ounces of the resulting apricot mixture into each champagne flute.

Fill the champagne flutes the rest of the way to the brim with champagne, and voilà!

Norman's 3rd Note: I know it's a lot of notes, but I just keep thinking of ways to make this better! The last time I made these over at Delores and Doc's, I served the Satin Swirl Champagne Cocktails with just a tiny bit of maraschino cherry juice floated on top of each cocktail. Then I placed a maraschino cherry into each flute as a garnish. Everyone seemed to love it!

Norman's 4th Note: This is the last note for this recipe, I promise! I was thinking of changing this version of the Satin Swirl Champagne Cocktail's name (the version with the maraschino cherry juice on top, and the cherry garnish) from Satin Swirl Champagne Cocktail to "Sunrise over the Vineyard." What do you think?

Yield: This will serve between 6-8 people a single flute of this cocktail per 750 ml bottle of champagne, but can easily be doubled or tripled for larger groups. Just use your good old grade school math and multiply each ingredient by 2 or 3!

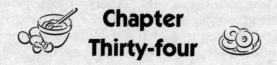

Chapter Thirty-four

"This is delicious, Hannah!" Doc said as he scooped some more Sweet and Sour Chicken onto his plate.

"Thank you, Doc. But I can't take all of the credit. Andrea helped with it, too. She did the shopping for the ingredients, and helped me put it together."

"You did?" Bill looked over at Andrea in surprise.

"Don't look so shocked, Bill," Andrea told her husband with a hint of steel entering her voice. "I've been helping Hannah a lot lately. She's teaching me how to make a lot more recipes than just Whippersnapper Cookies and PB&J's, you know."

"Now, now, Andrea," Bill spoke in a hurry. "Don't get your feathers ruffled. I was just a bit surprised at first, but I'm also happy and proud to hear that my wife helped make something this delicious."

"Aww, thank you, Bill," Andrea cooed to her husband, as her mood swung 180 degrees. She smiled, pleased as punch with Bill's compliment, then she leaned toward him and gave him a peck on the cheek.

Andrea turned away to talk with her mother, and Doc sidled over to speak quietly to Bill. "Nice save, boy. I thought that you were a goner at first, especially when you looked stunned at the idea of Andrea helping Hannah cook. But I'll tell you, I'm most impressed with your recovery time! You managed to turn that whole thing around in the blink of an eye. And I don't think I've *ever* seen anyone maneuver better to get out of a potentially explosive situation. Well, unless you count the time I was literally cornered at the Community Center Dance by Nurse Crockett. I only managed to get away by diving out the window behind me. This was long before I married Delores, of course!"

"Why, of course it was," Bill answered Doc with a twinkle in his eye. "We both know that Delores would have taken Nurse Crockett out of the picture quick as a wink, all by herself."

"So, Bill," Hannah spoke across the table to her brother-in-law, "you know what this means, right?"

Bill looked slightly apprehensive and a bit guilty at Hannah's question, almost as though he were about to be caught doing something shady. "What's that?"

"Since Andrea worked with me on this recipe, she might be able to . . ." Hannah prodded him.

"You mean . . . she might be able to make it at home, too?" Bill asked Hannah, a brilliant smile breaking out on his face, lighting up like sunlight on fresh-fallen snow.

"Don't ask me, ask her!" Hannah grinned back at Bill, who was wriggling about like a puppy on a new blanket, so excited by the thought that he was barely able to keep in his chair.

"Honey? Honey!?" he blurted out, unable to wait any longer. "Oops, excuse me, Delores. I just need to ask Andrea something real quick," he anxiously told his mother-in-law.

"Bill, honey, are you all right? What has gotten into you?" Andrea asked, wide-eyed at Bill's excited burst of words.

"Andrea,Ineedtoaskyousomething,rightnow!" Bill spoke so rapidly that it seemed like his tongue might catch fire.

"Do speak up, Bill!" Delores mock-scolded him, with an impish sort of smile on her face, as if looking amused at the oft-foolish nature of menfolk. Then she went on. "Don't just stand there with your tongue all tangled up, spit it out!"

"Mother, quit teasing him. Can't you see how excited he is? What did you need, honey?" Andrea asked her husband, with her face echoing her mother's amusement.

"Do you think . . . I mean could you . . . could you make it again, *but at home*?" Bill stammered slightly.

"Yes, Bill!" Andrea answered proudly. "I wrote down the entire recipe with all of my notes, and Hannah's too. And the best part is that Tracey and Bethie can help make it, too."

Doc ignored Bill and Andrea and leaned forward. "Hannah, I have an important question for you. One only you can answer!"

"What's that, Doc?"

Doc gave a chuckle and asked, "What's for dessert?"

"I made Chess Bars, Doc. They're a lot like a cheesecake, but you can cut them into squares."

"Cheesecake? Cheesecake? I love cheesecake!"

CHESS BARS

Preheat oven to 350 degrees F., rack in the middle position.

Ingredients:

1 package yellow cake mix *(I used Duncan Hines, 15.25 ounces)*

1 stick (½ cup) salted butter, softened

4 eggs

3 and ½ cups powdered sugar *(pack it down when you measure it)*

8-ounce block of cream cheese *(I used Philadelphia)*

½ teaspoon vanilla extract

⅛ teaspoon salt

Directions:

Line a 9-inch by 13-inch cake pan with aluminum foil.

Spray the foil-lined cake pan with Pam or another non-stick cooking spray.

In the bowl of a stand mixer, combine the cake mix, softened butter, and one of the eggs.

Pat this mixture in the bottom of your foil-lined baking pan, making sure it covers the entire bottom.

Rinse and dry the mixing bowl and return it to the stand mixer.

Place the powdered sugar, cream cheese, vanilla extract, salt, and the other three eggs in the mixer. Turn the mixer to LOW and combine those ingredients thoroughly.

Remove the bowl from the mixer and pour the resulting contents over the cake batter in your cake pan.

Place the cake pan in the oven for 35-45 minutes or until a toothpick inserted in the center comes out clean and the top is brown and puffy.

Hannah's 1st Note: If you're not sure if your Chess Bars are done, put on oven mitts and shake the cake pan to see if it jiggles in the middle. If it doesn't jiggle, your Chess Bars are done!

Place the pan with the Chess Bars on a cold stovetop burner or a wire rack and let them cool so they will firm up completely. (This should be for at least 15 minutes, or even more.)

Cut your Chess Bars into squares and serve them on a pretty platter.

According to rumor, these will taste even better with a little sweetened whipped cream, vanilla ice cream, or even a bit of jam and powdered sugar on top!

Hannah's 2nd Note: Doc loves these bars with all three on top!

Chapter
Thirty-five

"Hannah?" Hannah's eyes cracked open at the sound of Norman's voice. "Sorry, Hannah, but you asked me to wake you up at six."

"Six," Hannah repeated. "Six in the morning?"

Norman laughed at her. "Yes, six in the morning. I've got coffee made in the kitchen for you. That should help you wake up."

Hannah sat up in bed and blinked rapidly several times to clear her eyes. "Okay, I'm awake," she said, yawning widely.

"Well, I can't be sure about that, so I'm going to wait right here until you get out of bed and walk into the shower before I head downstairs. And if you're not downstairs in twenty minutes, don't think for a second that I'm not coming back up here to get you!"

Hannah groaned and glanced out of the bedroom window. It was true. The sun was up! She swung her legs over the side of the bed, really fighting the urge to let her head just fall back onto the very comfortable pillow. She gave a pitiful little moan as she placed her feet on the floor and began to pull on her slippers. "I'm up now."

"You'll forgive me if I don't blindly take your word for that," Norman said with a grin. "Nope. I'll just stand right here until I hear the shower running, first."

"I'm up, honestly, I'm awake," Hannah promised him. "You go ahead and head down to the kitchen. I'll be right there after my shower."

"And I am running out of ways to rephrase this. I'm not budging one inch until you are in the shower and I hear water running. Don't forget that you have Hank coming in for an interview this morning, and you promised him you would have a muffin and coffee waiting when he got there!"

"Right," Hannah agreed, shrugging into her robe and shuffling into the bathroom to turn on the shower. She called out over the noise of the running water, "Okay, shower's on and I'm awake now."

The shower helped her to wake up all the way, and Hannah made quick work of washing, brushing her teeth, and running a brush through her hair. She slipped into a clean pair of jeans and a dark green tee shirt. After pulling on her socks and shoes, Hannah headed downstairs guided by the enticing aroma of freshly brewed coffee.

"I made it," she said, sitting down in one of the chairs at the kitchen table. "Coffee?" she requested in a plaintive voice.

"Right here," Norman announced, setting a large cup of the life-sustaining elixir in front of her. "Drink up. I made it extra strong this morning. Do you want some coffee ice cubes in it, to cool it down a little?"

"Yes, please," Hannah stated, glad that she had taught Norman the trick of making coffee ice cubes out of leftover coffee. It was a great way of cooling your coffee when you were in a rush, and it wouldn't dilute the coffee the way that regular ice cubes made from water would.

Hannah picked up her coffee cup, drained her now-cooled coffee with several large gulps, and then held the empty cup out to Norman. "More please?"

"Right here," Norman told her, coming over with the coffeepot and refilling her cup to the brim. "Another couple of coffee cubes for this one, as well?"

"Thank you, but no. I am awake now, and I want to take time and enjoy this cup. So . . . you are sitting in on Hank's interview this morning, right?" Hannah asked him.

"As long as no one minds, yes. I thought, if I'm there in person, we can always talk about it later."

"Perfect," Hannah said, smiling at Norman. "That'll make things a lot easier and we can compare notes when Hank leaves."

Chapter
Thirty-six

Hannah was just taking muffins out of the industrial oven when there was a knock at the back door.

"Coming!" she called out, rushing over to the door. Just in time, she remembered to look through the peephole. Hannah smiled as she saw Hank standing there. Hannah opened the door and greeted him. "Hi, Hank! Welcome to The Cookie Jar."

"Hi, Hannah," Hank nervously stammered out, taking off his hat and wringing it in his hands.

"Come in, come in!" she said with a smile for her friend. "You're here early."

"I know. I just kept thinking about those muffins you promised to make for me."

"Then you're in luck, because they are almost cool enough to eat by now. Have a seat, Hank." She guided him over to a seat at the work station and sat him down there.

"I'm here, too," Andrea called out as she walked

through the door from the coffee shop. "Hi, Hank. Everything all right?"

"Hello, Andrea. I'm just a little nervous."

"It'll be fine, Hank. They just want to ask you a couple of questions." Andrea gave Hank a sympathetic smile, then turned to her sister. "Rick and Lonnie should be here soon."

True to Andrea's prediction, there was a knock at the back door. "That must be them now," Andrea said, rushing to the door to usher in Rick and Lonnie.

"Sit down, guys," Hannah said, gesturing over to the work station across from Hank. "I've got Orange Marmalade Muffins with Orange Honey Butter, if you're hungry."

"Is anyone else coming?" Hank asked, looking a bit shaky.

"Just Norman," Hannah replied, "but he wanted to make sure it was okay with you first if he sat in on the interview."

Hank laughed briefly. "Why not!? Everybody and his cousin is already here anyway! Besides, Norman is a friend."

Once Norman had arrived and everyone was all settled with muffins, butter, and coffee around the work station, Hannah looked over at Hank and said, "Shall we get started?"

Hank nodded. "What do you want to know?"

"Will you please tell everyone what you told me about Roman Ganz?"

"Yes," Hank agreed. "I really hated to say anything about it, but I knew I had to tell someone. Roman was acting really . . . strange."

"What do you mean . . . *strange*, Hank?" Rick asked.

"Well . . . It wasn't so much what he said, but how he acted. He ordered a whiskey, neat, rather than the beer he usually has. And when he gulped it down, I noticed that his hands were shaking. Then when he asked me for another one, I knew something was wrong."

Rick looked straight at Hank. "Did you ask him why he was so upset?"

"Of course I did. Part of my job as a bartender is to listen to people's troubles. They tell me things because everyone needs someone to talk to."

"What did Roman tell you?" Norman prompted.

"He told me he was still upset that his granddaughter, Emily, had sneaked out of the farmhouse to ride on the back of that convertible."

Hannah jumped in. "You're talking about the car that No-No was driving, right?"

"Yes," Hank replied. "He said he wanted to jump right into his truck when he realized she'd left, and drive to town to see what she was up to, but he hesitated because he wasn't quite sure."

"So Roman was worried about Emily?" Rick asked.

"Yes, he said the telephone rang, and a minute later, he heard the back door slam. He knew that Emily hadn't left with his wife, because she'd already gone to town much earlier to catch the best early bargains at the Summer Solstice Sale. So, when the back door slammed, he knew it had to be Emily."

"I'll bet he was more worried about Emily, than he was angry at her," Hannah stated.

"Maybe at first," Hank answered. "But the more he sat and thought about it, the angrier he became. He said Emily always told her grandparents where she was going and who she'd be with. Emily sneaking out, with no notice, really riled Roman up. Then the phone call came in . . ."

"Phone call?" Norman prodded Hank.

"The phone call from their neighbor, down the road."

Rick frowned, then spoke up slowly and deliberately. "Neighbor? What neighbor? And what did the neighbor say on the phone call to Roman, Hank?"

"Tony Barnett, that's Roman's neighbor a ways down the road, called to tell Roman that he'd seen Emily sitting up there on the back of that convertible and she was wearing nothing but a short skirt and a bikini top!"

"Yikes!" Lonnie cried out. "That must have put the cat among the pigeons. What did Mr. Ganz do next?"

Hank rubbed his chin and looked skyward for a second. Then he replied, "It lit a fire under him, Lonnie, that's for sure. He told me that he wanted to tear right out after them, but he slowed down just about long enough to put on his good pair of boots and a clean shirt, 'cause he'd been mucking out the stalls. Then he jumped in his truck, and chased off after her!"

"Anything else you have to tell us?" Hannah inquired.

"Well, I'm sure you already told them about Roman catching up with that big-headed fool, and giving No-No the what-for out there at Junction 15, right, Hannah?"

"Yes, I did tell them over the phone about the confrontation Roman had with No-No. At least, I think I did . . . Lonnie?"

"Yes, she let us know about it," Lonnie answered. "But it never came to blows being thrown or anything else physical happening, right, Hank?"

"Not really. At least, none of the four or five folks who told me the story never said anything like that! I just heard it got real loud with the yelling and all, that is," Hank stated.

"Is that it then?" Rick asked.

"Yes. Matter of fact, if it weren't for Roman looking so scared, and shaking so bad when he was in getting a drink of whiskey at my place, I wouldn't have said anything at all. Whiskey! When he'd only ever drank beer in my place for the last fifteen years! That, and the way he wouldn't let Doc Haggaman come out to help him with the calving, so he wasn't doing it all by his lonesome!" Hank said.

Rick shut his notebook with a snap. "Well, thanks, Hank. We appreciate you coming in and telling us about this. Be assured that we will follow up with Roman soon to see what he has to say."

Hannah leaned over and spoke in Hank's ear. "Thank you . . . you did a great job. I'll stop by your place soon to see you. And while I'm at it, I think I'll pick up another bottle or two of that champagne for Mother. It certainly calmed her right down!"

Chapter
Thirty-seven

Hannah stretched her back lazily as the kitchen timer went off, reminding her that the last batch of muffins needed to come out of her industrial oven. She had finished placing them on the bakers rack and was turning toward the coffeepot, when there was a knock on the back kitchen door. Hannah glanced over at the door. She didn't recognize the knocking pattern at all. Perhaps it was someone who didn't know if The Cookie Jar was still open or not, so they came around the back to see if anyone was there. The rapping came a bit louder now and Hannah shrugged as she moved over to check through the peephole, but didn't see anyone at first. Had they given up? Or was it all her imagination, and there was never anyone really there? Hannah looked through the peephole once again to make sure, her vision scanning left and right. Nope, no one there . . . Wait, what was that at the very bottom of her line of sight? It looked like a gray bundle of some sort . . .

"Hannah Louise Swensen, you open this door right now!" a voice said, sounding more than a bit cranky.

"Grandma Knudson, is that you?" Hannah questioned.

"Well, who else do you think it is, you ninny? Are you going to let me in, or just keep me out here on this stoop all day?"

Hannah hurried to open the door, then stepped back quickly, as a small gray-haired whirlwind (or so it seemed to her) blew by Hannah on its way to a stool. Hannah blinked twice. "I'm sorry, Grandma. I wasn't sure it was you at first. Can I get you a little something?"

"What is that I smell? Oh, ho! Yes, I'd love to have a muffin, Hannah," Grandma Knudson said.

"Sit down and relax, and I'll plate a couple for you."

"What kind do you have?"

"I have two different types. Orange and lemon."

"Well, that's a difficult choice to have to make."

"Not necessarily. Why don't you have one of each?"

Grandma Knudson laughed in delight. "I like the way you think, Hannah!" she said, obviously in a much better mood now that she was inside.

Hannah filled a basket with muffins and prepared a bowl with softened Honey Butter. "What brings you here?" Hannah asked her friend.

"Emily Ganz. I'm worried about her, Hannah."

"What's wrong with Emily?" Hannah asked, while taking a stool directly across from her guest.

"Emily is very upset, Hannah. Ever since her grandfather, Roman, caught her riding on the back ledge of that baseball player's convertible, he hasn't spoken a word to her and neither has her grandmother! Both of them accused Emily of ruining the family reputation."

"How old is Emily now?"

"Seventeen. She won't be eighteen until the end of next month. She told me she knew she'd been foolish, but she never thought they'd be this horribly disappointed in her!"

Hannah sighed. "I agree that it was foolish of Emily, but seventeen-year-olds occasionally do dumb things. She's young. I'm sure she's learned some sort of lesson from this experience."

"I tried to tell her grandmother the very same thing, but Ida is awfully mule-headed, once she's sure that she is right about something. And that's not even a patch on how stubborn Roman is when he's perched up there on his high horse!"

"You make her grandparents sound like they'll never let her forget what she did. How long do you think they'll keep on like this? Giving her the cold shoulder, I mean."

"I dare say, a good long time, Hannah . . . More's the pity. Perhaps it would do Roman and Ida some good to be reminded what it says in the Good Book. The part about forgiveness being a virtue. In the meantime, Emily is feeling lonely, without a friend in the world, and I'm worried about her." Grandma Knudson snapped out of her anger, and a smile broke out all over her face, as she took her first bite of Hannah's Orange Marmalade Muffin. "Say, these are wonderful, Hannah."

"Thank you," Hannah replied, as she buttered, then tasted, the one on her own plate. Grandma Knudson was right. The orange flavor worked perfectly with the Honey Butter.

They both ate for a while in silence, then Hannah spoke up. "Would you tell Emily for me, that I am sympathetic to her troubles, and that I would like to speak with her? I have to interview her anyway about where she was when No-No was killed, and we can talk about both things then."

"Of course I will." Grandma Knudson looked relieved at Hannah's words. "I was hoping that you might want to talk to her. What time are you free?"

"How about tomorrow afternoon?"

"That should be just fine," Grandma Knudson agreed. "Emily is supposed to play the organ for choir practice tomorrow, but I can always step in."

"I didn't know that you play the organ," Hannah remarked, looking surprised.

"I don't really, but Mabel Canfield does. If I ask her nicely, she'll fill in for Emily and she'll never say a word about doing it."

Hannah smiled. This wasn't the first time that Grandma Knudson had offered to be a co-conspirator. "That sounds great!"

"What time should Emily be here tomorrow?"

"How about noon? I should be done with the baking by then. Would you like to sit in on the interview?"

"I think I would, thank you. I'll ask her just to make sure, but I know that Emily trusts me and she would probably like to have me here."

After Grandma Knudson left, Hannah took out the shorthand notebook that she always referred to as her "murder book" and wrote down a list of questions that she wanted to ask Emily.

Chapter
Thirty-eight

It was a lovely day in Lake Eden with the temperature in the low eighties and the humidity under 70 percent for once. Of course, Hannah thought to herself, as she pulled into The Cookie Jar back parking lot, *it IS only 6:45 in the morning.* Hannah got out of the Suburban and walked to the back door of The Cookie Jar. She unlocked the door, took one step inside, and flipped the light switch located on the wall.

"Ah," she muttered to herself happily, "work, sweet work . . ."

Granted there were times when Hannah dreaded dragging herself out of bed and going into The Cookie Jar to start the baking early, but today wasn't one of those days. She had stayed in bed for an extra half hour, and Hannah had even taken the time for a third cup of coffee before she'd . . . Coffee! It was time to start brewing the coffee! Even as she rushed over to the coffeemaker to begin concocting the life-sustaining black elixir, she was filled with a sense of contentment. Once the coffee was burbling merrily in the pot, Hannah turned around with a joyful look on her face as her eyes wandered all about her kitchen. She peered over at her gleaming bakers rack, her trusty industrial oven, and finally at her stainless steel work station and sighed. *Yes, sometimes things really are . . .*

There was a series of sharp knocks at the back door and Hannah leapt about three feet off the ground in surprise. She wasn't expecting anyone this morning, was she? Heart pounding with adrenaline, she looked through the peephole to see two people standing there. One was a young woman Hannah did not recognize, and the other woman a small, gray-haired . . .

"Grandma Knudson?" Hannah yelped, before flinging open the back door. "I thought you were coming at noon today!"

A tiny, wizened, good-natured face peered up at Hannah from the doorway. "We decided to come early! Are you going to let us in, Hannah? Or would you prefer to interview Emily in the parking lot?"

"Come in, come in, both of you. Sorry about that. You took me by surprise. I was under the impression you were stopping by later on today," Hannah babbled. "Would you care for coffee, juice, or some milk? I'm sure I have some cookies made that I could get for you."

Emily looked over to Grandma Knudson for her approval, and at her nod, spoke up, "Yes, please, Ms. Swensen. I would really like some milk and a cookie or two, if it's not any trouble."

"It's not any trouble at all, and you can call me Hannah. Would you prefer I call you Ms. Ganz, or may I call you Emily?"

"Emily is great. If someone calls me Ms. Ganz, I figure I must be in some kind of trouble . . . I'm not, am I?"

Grandma Knudson chipped in. "Of course you're not in any trouble, dear! Hannah just wants to know more about you and No-No, to see if you have any information she hasn't heard yet that might help catch his killer. Right, Hannah?" Grandma paused for a second to catch her breath for a second, then went on. "I'm sorry, Hannah. I know I set up the interview for later this morning, but Emily slept over at my place last night. Neither one of us has been sleeping very well lately, so we decided to take an early-morning walk about town. Anyway, I noticed your truck in the parking lot, so we came over to see if you were free to chat now."

"Absolutely," Hannah said, going to get some milk and cookies for Emily. After placing them in front of the girl, she turned to her friend. "What can I get for you?"

"I'm sure you could talk me into a cup of coffee and another one of those muffins I had yesterday . . . if there's any left?" Grandma Knudson told her with a small, sly grin.

"Coming right up!" Hannah replied, as she bustled around the kitchen gathering muffins, honey butter, and strong, hot coffee for herself and her guest. Once they all were cheerfully chewing and sipping, Hannah looked over at Emily. "I hear you've been having a bit of a rough time at home lately, Emily. Tell me what's been happening with you since No-No came to town."

"Gosh, Ms. Swensen," Emily said, after swallowing the last bite of her cookie. "I'm not sure where to start! I guess it all began with a phone call from Desiree. She's a really popular varsity cheerleader at school, and I guess I always kind of looked up to her. Well, the morning No-No came to town, I was already really upset because it felt like my grandma and grandpa were picking on me something awful. They kept going on and on about me not trying hard enough in school, and hanging around with the bad crowd, or something like that. So after my grandma left to go to the Summer Solstice Sale, I decided I needed to get out of there! Just then, the phone rang and it was Desiree. She said an older guy friend of hers, with a really hot convertible, was coming to town, and if I wanted to get off the farm for a while, they'd pick me up on the main road in ten minutes."

"Then what happened?"

"Desiree said to dress a little sexy, 'cause No-No didn't want any girls in the convertible that weren't hot. I still wasn't really sure what to wear, so I got dressed and put on a bikini top that I borrowed from Desiree and hurried out the back door to the road."

"And they were waiting out there for you?" Hannah asked the girl.

"Yes. Desiree and I have a code. She rings once, hangs up, waits ten seconds, and then calls again. That means it's her. I snuck out the back door right away, and when I got out to the road and saw the car . . . Wow! Desiree was right. It was a really nice convertible. I got in and No-No looked over his sunglasses at me, nodded once, then we took off down the road to town. Desiree said we were picking one more girl up, then we'd have some fun. I was a little nervous about that, but it was so nice in the convertible, just sitting on those soft leather seats, with the top down on the car and the wind blowing in my hair, I started to relax a bit. Then, when we pulled up to a really nice neighborhood and I saw who we were picking up, I was shocked! Little Miss Goody Two-shoes herself, Susie Connor, got into the car! She was always looking down her nose at the farm kids at school, and was really cold to almost everyone, except maybe Tony Sloan. Anyway, there she was, and she was dressed just like us! She was being much nicer to me than she'd ever been before."

Emily paused for a moment, trying to decide what was next, so Hannah helped her out.

"We know about the ride through town on the back of the convertible already, Emily. Tell me what happened when your grandpa, Roman, caught up to you in No-No's car."

Emily took a deep breath, a big swig of milk, and replied, "Grandpa guessed wrong at the way we took into town all right, but he sure guessed right about how we'd leave town! When we got to the junction at the far side of Lake Eden, Grandpa peeled out from the side of the dirt road and stopped sideways, right in front of the convertible. He completely blocked off the road! He flew out of the pickup like his pants were on fire, and he screamed at No-No, telling him what a piece of trash he was for taking innocent young girls and making them look like hussies in front of everyone in town."

"How did No-No react to that?" Hannah asked.

"At first, he just sat there with a smirk on his face, like he was some kind of big shot, and Grandpa was just a hick that wasn't even worth his time. But then Grandpa got under his skin a little. He called No-No *a has-been who was lucky he'd ever made it out of the trailer park* and told No-No that *everyone in town had laughed at little No-No, who thought he was a big man now!* First No-No tried to climb out of the convertible, but Grandpa made him look stupid. He would climb partway out, but Grandpa kept shoving him back down like he was a little child. He tried to get out through the door, but Grandpa slammed the door shut on him every time he tried. Finally he gave up. Grandpa reached in the back seat and yanked me right out . . . He almost pulled me out of my sandals! Then Grandpa marched me over to the pickup, opened my door, and shoved me in. On the way home, he never said a word to me. He just kept muttering about himself and Grandma, saying *It was all our fault, maybe we just didn't raise her right, that's why she strayed so far from the path.* And *It's not the child's fault, maybe we were too lax with her,* and then he said, *I remember now, but it's too late . . . the Good Book says, spare the rod and spoil the child.* But he hasn't said a word to me since, Ms. Swensen. I don't know what to do! And Grandma . . . Grandma just keeps looking at me, shaking her head and calling me her *poor lost lamb.*" Emily burst into tears, and Hannah came around the work station to hug her.

"Emily, would you like me to talk to Roman and Ida for you?" Hannah asked. "I could remind them that wisdom comes with age, and we all make mistakes when we're young."

Grandma Knudson rose from the work station, her eyes flashing like heat lightning in the summertime, spelling trouble for Emily's grandparents. "No, Hannah! Let me take care of this for her. I think a few words from someone they know from church, someone who's the same age they are, will do wonders for their attitude. Maybe a little reminder of what the Good Book says about forgiveness, and family, will straighten them up. And if that doesn't work, I'll sic my grandson, Reverend Bob, on them!"

Hannah had just seen Emily and Grandma Knudson out and was walking back inside after waving to them, when the phone on the wall rang once, then stopped. Then, after about ten seconds, it rang again. Hannah hurried to answer it.

"The Cookie Jar. This is Hannah speaking. How may I help you?"

"Is this Hannah Swensen?" a small, somewhat hesitant, voice asked.

"This is Hannah. How may I help you? Is there an order you would like to place?"

"No, but I have some information I need to tell you!"

"Excuse me, who is this?" Hannah responded.

"My name is Desiree Morgan. I used to be a friend of Emily Ganz, until I saw what happened!"

"All right, Desiree. What do you want to tell me?"

"I saw Emily Ganz run out from under the bleachers, on the day No-No was murdered!" Desiree blurted out in one breath.

"I'm listening. Tell me about it," Hannah requested.

"Fine," Desiree said. "I was supposed to meet No-No under the stands, in between games. So I thought that I would show up a little early and surprise him, but it was me who got surprised instead, by that two-timing jerk! I got there a little before one, but when I turned into the parking lot, I saw Emily running out from under the canvas in the back of the bleachers, headed across the parking lot. She looked like she was crying and she was running really fast. So I stopped the car and I ducked down real quick so she couldn't see me. Sure, I knew Susan had a thing for No-No, but I never in a million years would have thought Emily did, too!"

Hannah was a little stunned by Desiree's story. *Was Emily not as sweet and pure as people thought?* She wondered . . . *Had she killed No-No after all? Why hadn't Emily told her any of this when Hannah had just interviewed her?* Then something else occurred to Hannah and she thought, *Or was Desiree lying because she'd killed No-No herself?*

"Desiree, why are you telling me this now? Did you meet No-No under the bleachers after Emily ran away from there?"

"No way!" Desiree stated emphatically. "After I saw Emily come running out crying from under the stands, I figured he was two-timing me. When Emily took off through the parking lot, I burned a U-turn and took off for home just as fast as I could. I stayed there in my room, feeling sorry for myself and crying-mad at how stupid I'd been. Seriously I don't know how I ever believed I was the only one

No-No wanted. I fell for that snake. He promised me I was the one for him! Boy, did that come back to bite me. I'm glad he's dead!"

"I'm so sorry, Desiree. I can only imagine how sad and how foolish you must feel right now. Thanks so much for coming forward with this. I'm sure someone will follow up if they need more information."

"**P**hone call for you, Hannah," Lisa announced, coming through the door leading from the coffee shop and bakery, with an empty display jar in her hands. "It's Norman."

"Hello, Norman," Hannah greeted him once she had walked over to the wall and picked up the receiver. "Do you have time to stop by for coffee?"

"That's exactly what I was about to ask you!" Norman replied. "In five minutes?"

"Perfect. I'll put on a fresh pot and dish up some of my new Lemon Muffins for you."

Hannah had no sooner hung up the phone when it rang again. "The Cookie Jar," she said, answering the call quickly. "This is Hannah."

"Good, I got you," the caller said. "Hannah, it's Stella."

"Stella?" Hannah was surprised, to say the least. "What's happening? Is everything okay?"

"Not really! Mike is driving me up the wall with questions about the investigation. He'll probably call you the second that I give him his phone back."

"What do you want me to say, Stella?"

"Just remind him that you've got it all covered there."

Hannah paused for a second. "Do you really think that he'll believe me?"

It got quiet on Stella's end of the line, then she answered Hannah with a little laugh in her voice. "Probably not, but it's worth a try. I'll tell you one thing that I know for sure, though."

"What's that?"

"Mike is going to pump you for information about the case!"

"You're probably right. That's exactly what I used to do to him."

"Yes . . . but it drove him a little nuts sometimes."

"I'm beginning to know how he felt. So, what do you want me to tell him about our progress on the case?"

Again the line went silent and then Stella spoke once more. "Just do your very best to assure him that everything there is firmly under control . . . I've got to go, Hannah."

There was a click in Hannah's ear. Stella had hung up. Hannah did the same, then hurried to the kitchen coffeepot to put on a fresh pot. She'd just finished, when there was a knock on the back door.

"Come on in, Norman," Hannah called out. "It's unlocked."

Norman walked in, came over to give her a hug, and took the stool situated across from the one Hannah usually used. "What's new?"

"A lot," Hannah answered, after she had set a cup of coffee in front of Norman. "Emily and Grandma Knudson stopped by for an interview, and I heard from Desiree Morgan, the third girl in the convertible with No-No. AND I just got off the phone with Stella, who told me that Mike is twitching for news on the investigation."

"Aha! And what does Stella want us to do, in the very likely event that Mike does call and ask?"

"Stick to our guns . . . and tell him that *we've got it covered.*"

"All right," Norman told her. "I understand. Stella guides us on all matters Mike-related, anyway."

"Well . . . she is the one who is staying right there at the lake cabin with him, after all! And she is the only one of us who's really qualified to make a judgment call on Mike's state of mind right now."

"Good point, Hannah."

Just then, the phone on the wall rang once and stopped. Norman and Hannah looked at each other briefly, and then turned their attention to the door leading through to the coffee shop. Within seconds, Lisa hesitantly poked her head through and, looking very nervous, said in a whispery sort of voice, "Hannah, it's for you . . . it's . . . it's *Mike!*"

"It's all right, Lisa," Hannah responded. "I've got it from here."

Lisa gave her a quick bob of the head and then ducked back into the coffee shop as though being chased by wolves.

Hannah walked over to the phone on the wall, picked up the receiver, and recited her usual greeting. "The Cookie Jar. This is Hannah. How may I help you?"

A voice came on the other end of the phone, sounding a bit growly and with a rough edge to it. "Hannah, it's Mike. How's the investigation going?"

Hannah laughed, her voice a little higher in pitch than usual. "Hello, Mike. Everything's just fine here! How's the fishing?"

"Nice deflection, Hannah. How's the investigation going?" Mike growled back.

"Well . . . all's quiet here, except for the big Winnetka County All-Star Baseball Tournament, of course. Everybody's very excited about that. Oh, and the Summer Solstice Sale is going great!" she replied brightly.

"Uh-huh," Mike said in a skeptical voice. "All's quiet, hmm? You mean, except for the ongoing investigation into the murder of an ex-big league baseball player who also happens to be a local celebrity?"

Hannah grew a little irritated at the sarcastic bite she heard in Mike's voice and in the way he seemed to be questioning her statements.

"Mike, what I meant was, it's all being handled here, we've got this, and you shouldn't concern yourself with this while you are on vacation."

"Hannah, in case you don't know . . . there's been a murder, a big murder, in *my little town,* and you are telling me not to concern myself with it?"

Norman shook his head sadly at the look in Hannah's eyes and in the angry set of her jaw. *Do you want me to take over for a while?* his eyes seemed to ask her. Hannah looked over at Norman and her own eyes flashed back to him, *No, but thank you. I'll take care of Mike!*

"Mike, I am aware of the murder which occurred, *in our little town*, because Bill has asked us to sit in on all of the suspect interviews. You should be aware by now *that we've got this*! And by saying *we*, I am referring to the Winnetka County Sheriff, the two deputy sheriffs who you, yourself, have trained for this type of a murder investigation, and two consultants, myself and Norman Rhodes, who have assisted on many murder cases closed by the Winnetka County Sheriff's Department!" Hannah ended her statement with a definite edge to her voice, and then listened for Mike's voice on the other end of the phone. . . . There was a long pause and then Mike came back on the line again.

"Okay, fine! If that's the way you want it." Hannah heard a click, followed by a dial tone.

"Norman . . . he hung up on me!" Hannah said in disbelief.

"It's all right, Hannah," Norman told her sympathetically. "You said just what Stella wanted you to say."

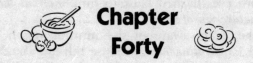

Chapter
Forty

Hannah almost had time enough to sit down, tell Norman what Emily and Desiree had to say, and recover a bit from her phone call with Mike, when there was a knock at the back door that she did not recognize. She looked through the peephole and saw . . . Was that Dick? Yes, it was Dick, her favorite bartender and bar owner from the Lake Eden Inn! Hannah's mind shot quickly to what Bill had told her. Bill said that he'd asked Dick to do some discreet spying on the two gentlemen in the bespoke suits Dick had overheard talking about No-No. The very same ones Dick had told her and Norman about while sitting at his bar . . . Perhaps Dick had news for the investigation?

Hannah flung the door open and laughed out loud. "Hey, what do you know, it's my favorite mixologist. What brings you to The Cookie Jar, Dick?"

Dick scuffed his shoe tip on the doorstep, looking like a little boy who'd been caught doing something that wasn't quite right. Then he said, with a slightly embarrassed look on his face, "Umm . . . Hello, Hannah. Is now an okay time to talk, or is this a bad time to show up here? Am I disturbing you while you have something in the oven?" he asked her, his words tumbling over themselves in a rush to exit his mouth.

Hannah shook her head no, but still looked a bit puzzled at Dick's words. "No, it's fine, Dick. Norman and I were just sitting here having a little coffee break. Would you like some coffee and a Curveball Cookie?"

Now it was Dick's turn to look confused. "Is that a new cookie on your menu?"

Norman joined the conversation to explain, breaking into an overly exaggerated baseball announcer's voice. "Not exactly, Dick. In fact, right now, it's another *Winnetka County All-Star Tournament exclusive*, brought to you by your *local hot spot to shop for fine baked goods*, The Cookie Jar, and served to order from your own Lake Eden Gulls Snack Shacks during this tournament!"

Dick looked over at Norman in disbelief, as if Norman had suddenly sprouted two heads from his neck. "Was that your attempt at impersonating Harry Caray or something? That may have been the worst impression I've heard since the time Sally tried to channel her inner Marilyn Monroe and sang 'Happy Birthday, Mr. President' to me!"

Hannah chuckled to herself as she walked over to the coffeepot, poured Dick a cup, and grabbed four Curveball Cookies for him on a plate. Bringing the snack and beverage over to Dick, who was by now seated at her work station, she attempted to steer the conversation back to her first question.

"Let's try this again, shall we? Dick, it's always a pleasure to see you, but is there some other reason for you stopping by today? Other than to have some of the new exclusive Curveball Cookies, which I'll bet you didn't know existed before now?"

"Actually," Dick said in a smaller voice, replying to Hannah's question at last, "I came in to apologize to you, Hannah. Well, to you both, I guess. Came in to say I'm sorry to you for jumping to certain conclusions in what I told you the other night."

"Certain conclusions, Dick? I'm afraid I don't understand." Norman turned back toward Dick as he spoke to his friend. "What part of whatever you told us was wrong?"

Dick let out a deep sigh. "All right," he finally said. "I guess that I'll just come straight out with it! It was what I told you about the two guys in those expensive bespoke suits and great shoes, the two who came into the Lake Eden Inn bar. You know, the two from out of town who I overheard talking about No-No? Remember that I thought, for a little while, anyway, that they *might have been* hit men, and that I may have thought, briefly, that they *may have been* here in town to collect on a contract on No-No? Well, I was totally wrong!"

"Really!" Norman said. "That's your way of *coming straight out with it*, Dick? You *may have thought* they were hit men, and you thought *briefly* they *may have been here* to collect on a contract on No-No? I'll say it once more. *Out with it!* Why *were* they here then, and *what* did you misunderstand in the words they used?"

"Let me tell you what happened after Bill called me and asked me to keep my distance, but discreetly try and get some more information about what the two men were doing in Lake Eden."

"Okay, Dick. Take your time and just tell it to us straight. Just remember that we are your friends and we understand that anyone can make a mistake," Hannah told him.

"I'm sure you've heard that I've never exactly been noted for my patience in anything. And well . . . I blew it!"

"Blew it?" Norman questioned.

"Yeah, I blew it. I was minding my own business, just bartending as usual, when those two well-dressed men, the ones that I told you about before . . . you know, the *hitters*? Well, they came back into my bar and, Hannah, they were staggering a bit. It was obvious they had stopped somewhere else first, and they'd caught more than a little buzz there, wherever it was. They sort of grunted at me, but I finally understood that they were ordering some nice Single Malt Glenmorangie twenty-year-old. You know, the one I had left over from my personal stock?"

"Please, Dick, I am far less interested in what they settled on drinking and a lot more interested in what they said!" Hannah told him.

"All right, all right, I'm almost there. Geez, guys, here I am admitting I made a mistake, and I can barely get a word in edgewise." Dick looked at them both expectantly, then he sighed at the silence that slowly filled the room as Norman and Hannah just stared at him. "Fine! I lost my temper! There, I said it! Does that make you guys happy?" There was still no response from Hannah and Norman, who were steadfastly ignoring Dick's histrionics, so Dick continued speaking. "Well, they weren't saying anything, okay? I got tired of coming over to the booth all the time, trying to overhear part of a conversation. I tried everything! I brought them bar snacks, not a word. I brought them glasses of fizzy water, and not a peep out of them. I even wiped down the tables in front of their booth. Zip, zilch, nada! I was at my wits' end when I decided I knew how to get them to talk!"

Once again, silence filled the kitchen, then Norman blurted out, "Well?"

"I'm trying to tell you!" Dick exclaimed. "You're the ones who keep interrupting me! I walked right up to their table, and asked them straight to their faces . . . *Did you two come to town to hit No-No?*"

In unison, Hannah and Norman both screeched, "WHAT?!"

"Dick, what the heck were you thinking?" Hannah asked him, worried that her friend had put himself in deadly danger by confronting two potential hit men!

"Really, Dick?" Norman huffed in disbelief. "Bill asked you to please keep an eye on those two potential murderers, yes, but to *keep an eye on them discreetly* . . . the word of the day being DISCREET, Dick! Confronting two murder suspects, and by the way, two murder suspects who probably killed No-No by whacking him in the head with a baseball bat, is hardly what I'd call *keeping an eye on them discreetly!* You could have easily gotten yourself kidnapped, beaten badly, or worse, been rubbed out by two professional hitters!"

Hannah nodded in full agreement with Norman at the end of each of his rather dramatic sentences.

"All I was doing was trying to help!" Dick bleated.

"Dick, Norman's right!" Hannah said to Dick, trying to be a little softer, while still stressing her concern over his actions. "You could have jumped right to the top of their hit list with that question. Letting them know that you suspected them of killing No-No? Why would you put yourself at risk like that?"

"But . . . I am trying to tell you what happened, Hannah. It's just that I'm trying not to leave anything out! What I found out *helps eliminate suspects.* Okay, it was a little dangerous, but I'm still here, aren't I?" Dick reminded them. Then he continued. "Hannah, they spit their drinks out laughing at me. They told me that they weren't sure what I'd heard but they were in town for the tournament, trying to get information that would give them an inside line on the baseball players for their sportsbook. Guys, they are bookies, not killers!"

"'Bookies,'" Norman repeated with a lost expression on his face. "But Dick, I don't get it . . . didn't you overhear them say that they were *hitters*? And talk about how they would *hit* No-No?"

"They explained to me that if I'd just listened a little longer, I would have realized that when they said *hitters*, they meant they were *hitters* in college baseball! And when they talked about how they'd *hit* No-No, they were talking about whether they'd *hit* his fastball or his curve!"

"Wait a minute, Dick," Hannah interjected. "You're telling me that you think we can cross them out of the murder book now?"

"Yes!" Dick replied, smiling happily at her, and throwing Norman a wink. "That's what I think, and Bill agrees! I found out what college they played ball at, up till two years ago, and found out they both hit well enough to turn pro, but neither one was very good at fielding. In fact, Darren, one of the guys, had a great nickname while he played college ball. He was so bad at fielding that, even when they stuck him out in right field, he would still boot the ball almost every single time it was hit to him. His hands were legendarily bad. In fact, they were so bad that his teammates called him *Clank.*"

"*Clank?*" Hannah asked Dick. "That's a strange thing to call him. How did he get that nickname?"

Dick rubbed his chin thoughtfully, his eyes looked skyward, and he prepared his story. "Well, now . . . I hear tell *Clank* came about because of the last game he played for the Winona State Warriors. A game in which he played his usual position in right field. I guess he must have been really bored, 'cause not even one ball was hit to him all game. All went well until the best slugger for Moorhead State, Jerry Easton, came up to hit in the top of the ninth inning, with a man on and his team down by one run. There were two outs, but since Jerry was Moorhead State's power-hitting lefty first baseman, he was always a threat! Jerry stood about six feet three inches tall and weighed in at around two hundred and thirty-five pounds. He was strong as an ox, and about as bright, but man, he could hit a ton!

"Well, the story was that Jerry pounced on a hanging curveball, and he laid into that pitch so hard that it looked like it was headed into outer space. It went so high into the air that a rocket booster should have kicked in, but all its momentum was up, not out, and the ball came down in right field, headed straight for Darren, aka *Clank*. Everyone said that all Darren would have had to do was stick his mitt directly over his head and the ball would have landed right in his mitt!

"Unfortunately, Darren was lost in his own little world, thinking of the home run he had hit in his last at-bat, and of the date which he had set up with one of the girls on the Moorhead State swim team after the game. He never heard the cries of panic from his teammates when the ball screamed down, or the roar of the crowd who'd tried to warn him. The ball whistled right at Darren, who stood there motionless, oblivious, and clueless with his mitt hanging down at his side. He'd no idea of the drama all around him, or of the ball which screamed down at him. That was the day which would make him a local, nay, a Minnesota legend, and earn Darren a nickname which endures to this very day. Those fans who had been there at the game, and even those fans who would later claim that *they were in the stands that day* (but weren't), swore that the sound that the ball finally made when it made contact was so loud that you could have heard it hit all the way in the parking lot! It was a hollow echoing *Clank*. That's what they all said. *Clank* went the baseball, which arrived first with stunning impact onto Darren's ball cap! From there, the fans claimed, the baseball abruptly changed course, ricocheting backward off of Darren's head, and flew clean over the right field fence for a home run! I'm glad to say, while it may be true that only the players remembered the final score, or even how the game ended, the legend of *Clank* lives on forever more!"

"Right!" Hannah said when she finally stopped laughing. "Well, if Bill is sure they didn't do it, and

if that story checks out, then who am I to argue?
The way I see it, anyone who's been involved in an
incident where a ball bounced off their baseball
cap and into the stands for a home run, couldn't
possibly be coordinated enough to have killed
No-No!"

After Dick left, Hannah and Norman sat back
down at the work station.

"What now, Hannah?" Norman asked.

"Well, first of all, we still haven't checked out
Tony Sloan's alibi," Hannah answered. "I'll ask Lisa
how to get out to the Sloan farm. If she doesn't
know how to get there, I'm sure Herb does!"

Chapter Forty-one

As Norman and Hannah were getting ready to walk out the door, the phone rang and Hannah picked up the receiver. "Hello, The Cookie Jar, this is Hannah."

"Hannah, I'm glad I caught you . . . Stella, here."

"Hi, Stella. What's up?"

"I just wanted to let you know that Mike is doing much better. I think he might be ready to come back to work."

"That's fantastic, Stella. We were just getting ready to check on Tony Sloan's alibi, and then two or three others after that!"

"Tony Sloan? Who is he?" Stella questioned.

"He's the basketball player who was planning to marry Susan Connor. She was one of the girls who rode on the back of No-No's convertible. He doesn't have an alibi worth a darn, and Norman and I want to check it out, so we can cross him off the suspect list. Then we're heading from there to the Ganzes' farm to check on Roman Ganz and his granddaughter, Emily, to see if they want to change their stories any. And finally we're off to check up on Little Miss Cheerleader, Desiree Morgan, who apparently was dating No-No on the sly!"

"Sounds like quite the day . . . but the Sloan farm, that's where you're headed first?"

"Yes. As soon as I get the directions to Tony's farm from Lisa, we're off. I'm not one hundred percent sure that one of these people is the killer, Stella, but something tells me they're all worth another look."

Norman drove for a bit, and out her side of the car Hannah noticed that the sky was rapidly turning into an ugly shade of gray with green streaks scattered throughout.

"I don't know about you, Norman, but I really don't like the way the sky is looking right now!"

Norman had both hands on the steering wheel now, as he fought off some wind gusts which were buffeting the car around. He craned his neck forward to peer through the windshield to try and catch a glimpse of the looming storm.

"I think you might be right, Hannah," Norman replied. "Keep a sharp lookout for the next gravel road coming up on the right. That's where we turn for the Sloan farm."

"Got it," Hannah told him, peering to her right. "Hold on, I think I see it. Yes, this is it . . . turn here."

They turned off onto a narrow gravel road and Hannah could see cornfields with tall stalks of corn growing on both sides.

Hannah spotted the Sloan farm a ways off, but getting closer and closer, and turned her head toward Norman, now speaking with much more confidence in her tone. "Let's keep going. I see a farmhouse right up there."

"You got it," Norman told her. They drove for a minute or two more, then pulled into the driveway which ran close by the side of the farmhouse. Norman put the car into park, then shut off the engine. "In which direction should we begin looking to find Tony? And should we stay together or split up?"

"You take the farmhouse to see if anyone is home. I think I just heard a tractor in the cornfield. I'll go check on that."

"Right!" Norman replied as he moved toward the farmhouse rapidly.

Hannah walked toward the sound she'd heard, the wind whipping her hair around her face and into her eyes. The sound of the motor grew louder as she drew closer to the cornfield. She stepped out into the field, walking carefully through the rows. She noticed that there was a large piece of farm equipment that looked like a picker, idling between the corn rows, but she couldn't see anyone there.

"Hello, Ms. Swensen, what are you doing here?" a voice asked, coming from somewhere behind her.

Hannah whirled around to find Tony standing about ten feet behind her. "Hello, Tony. I just had a few more questions for you. My, my, doesn't that corn look wonderful! It's grown so tall! Looks like you'll have a bumper crop this year."

"Let's hope so. What do you want to know?"

"You told us that you were at the lake when No-No was killed. Are you positive that nobody saw you there?"

"I don't think so, but why are you asking me again? We already went over this." Tony scowled at her.

"I know," Hannah said while edging farther away from Tony. "But I have to check into your alibi so that I can eliminate you as a suspect. Without anyone backing up what you told us . . . you see our problem, don't you?"

"You mean you *still* suspect me?" Tony asked her incredulously.

"Actually, without someone vouching for your alibi, you'll probably jump to the top of the suspect list."

"What do you mean, *top of the list*? There's no way you found my fingerprints on the bat!"

Hannah's eyes narrowed as she realized what Tony had just said. "Tony, how did *you* know the murder weapon was a *bat*? That information was never made public."

"Hannah, are you out there?" Norman's voice came from the near edge of the cornfield. He stood with his hand shading his eyes, looking for her. "Where are you?"

"I'm over here, by the picker!" Hannah called out, while inching away from the intimidating basketball player.

Tony was frozen with indecision, looking back and forth between Hannah and Norman. First where Hannah was attempting to turn invisible by vanishing into the corn, then to Norman, who was coming straight as an arrow through the field right toward him. "You had to stick your nose into my business, didn't you, Hannah? You just couldn't leave well enough alone!"

"Why did you kill No-No, Tony? Was it because of Susan?" Hannah asked, retreating even as she spoke.

Tony chuckled softly, shaking his head. "You just don't get it, do you, Hannah? Girls like Susan are a dime a dozen, but NOBODY embarrasses Tony Sloan in front of his friends! There's a price to pay for that, and No-No had to pay it. And now . . . you and your friend will have to pay, too!"

Hannah made a break for it, cutting through the cornfield and trying to keep out of Tony's line of sight. She ran as fast as she could through the field, dodging between the towering corn rows and trying to keep low so Tony couldn't see her. She heard the picker rev up as Tony climbed on and put it in gear.

"Hannah, hang on, I'm almost there." Hannah heard Norman's voice. It sounded much closer to her as he swiftly closed the distance between himself and Tony.

Hannah could hear grinding close behind her as Tony shifted gears and started to gain on her. She looked back and saw Norman leap onto the picker. She zigzagged closer to the steep ditch bordering the road, stumbling and almost losing her footing as she pushed her body to new limits in her frantic efforts to get away.

Hannah looked up from her headlong flight to see a car barreling down the access road toward her, raising a long plume of dust behind it. Gasping for air, buffered about by cornstalks and staggering from side to side, Hannah struggled toward the car. From behind her, and over the motor, she heard shouting and cursing. She scrambled her way down the ditch and up the embankment. She looked over her shoulder to see that Norman was desperately fighting for control of the picker that had headed down the ditch and was coming up the steep embankment behind her. She looked back at the road and saw the car veering off the road and straight at the picker. She realized someone was diving out the passenger door. Hannah felt something hit her and she went rolling head over heels down the embankment. She somersaulted, over and over, faster and faster, coming to an abrupt stop in the bottom of the ditch. There was a crash behind her, and she turned just in time to see Norman hurtling off the corn picker, keys in hand, falling down through the cornstalks on his way to a safe, if somewhat dusty, touchdown in the field. The picker, already way off-balance from its precipitous attempt to follow Hannah up the embankment, was not helped in the slightest by the addition of Stella's car, which had deliberately driven into the picker's tire closest to the road. There was a hiss of steam punctuated by a groan from the picker, which had tilted way off center and was leaning dangerously toward the cornfield.

Hannah watched as the picker's two closest tires rose completely off the ground, and it began tilting past the point of no return. Hannah thought she heard a yell of panic when the picker, with a screech of tortured metal, came crashing down on its side in the cornfield. She slumped over, face-down, into the soft, welcoming dirt, almost as if it were her favorite pillow.

The next thing Hannah knew, Stella was there to help her to her feet and Mike was passing by her with a big victory smile on his face, marching a much subdued, and now handcuffed, Tony up the embankment.

"It's okay, Hannah, it's over, and you're safe now," Stella said soothingly. "Norman managed to pull the key out of the ignition to stop the picker, I tipped it over with my car, and as you can see, Mike has cuffed Tony and placed him under arrest. All we have to do is wait for Bill to come out with a squad car to take Tony into custody. Congratulations, Hannah! You've done it again."

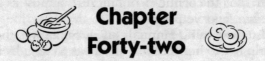

Chapter
Forty-two

Hannah and Norman drove fairly slowly, and quite carefully, back to the house. They'd agreed it might be wise, before doing anything else, to shower and perhaps change the ripped and dusty rags that used to be their clothing.

There was quiet and calm in Norman's car, broken only by softly playing music coming from the car radio. After a while, Norman spoke. "Well, Hannah, that was the best day ever! Thank you!"

Hannah looked over at Norman in shock, then burst into laughter at his statement. "Seriously, Norman? I run full tilt through a cornfield, almost breaking my ankles tripping between the furrows a bunch of times. I almost get turned into shredded Hannah by a picker that's driven by a killer, only to be saved at the last second by a hurtling human cannonball who knocks me you-know-what over teakettle. Then I just happen to look up in time to see you doing your best *Bruce-Willis-in-Die-Hard* impression, leaping off the picker while it crashes down into the cornfield, just missing you by inches I'm sure, and yet, here you are thanking me for the *best day ever*?!" Hannah's laughter rang out over the music playing. Shaking her head in disbelief at Norman's words, she gently reached over and plucked a piece of corn silk from his hair. "I think that we both may be a bit loopy, Norman," she said to him with a smile twisting her lips.

Norman was also laughing by now, although his was a bit rueful. "Yes, sorry about that, Hannah, but think about how it felt from my end. . . . First I had to run down the picker, and I'm sure that I haven't run that fast since high school. Next, I had to climb up the side of a moving picker and maneuver my way inside. Then I had to fight off a six-foot, four-inch behemoth named Tony while struggling for control of a steering wheel and forcing the picker toward a steep incline which might have flipped it over at any time. Finally I had to get away from this behemoth, by faking and dodging his steam-shovel hands long enough to be able to turn off the ignition, grab the keys from the vehicle, and still be calm enough to make a death-defying leap to safety in the cornfield! Hannah, that's a wall-climbing class, a Krav Maga lesson, a parkour workout, and some sprint training, too, all rolled into one day. Now that's what I call one heck of a good time! Yes, I'll stand by what I said, Hannah. . . . *Best day ever!*"

Chapter
Forty-three

Hannah had just finished taking her shower and was getting dressed when she heard a distant ringing coming from the kitchen area. *Oh, gosh,* she thought to herself sarcastically, *I wonder who that could be?* She looked over at Moishe, who, upon hearing her cell phone ring, had his ears laid back as far as they could go, and his eyes turned into steely slits in a fierce glare. Hannah struggled her way into her best black jeans and a pullover top, while the phone continued mocking her by ringing stridently the entire time. She rushed down into the kitchen, where she'd left her cell phone plugged in to charge before showering, and snagged it off the counter. Answering her cell in one swift movement and holding it up to her ear, she said, "Hello, Mother. What can I do for you?"

Her mother made a clicking noise with her tongue as if she were vexed that Hannah had guessed who was on the other end of the line before Delores could even get out a greeting. Finally her mother answered. "Hannah, I *do* wish you wouldn't do that. You know it disrupts my train of thought! I usually have something all ready to tell you, or to ask you when I call, but when you answer with *Hello, Mother* before I can speak, it just throws my mind into a tailspin. How do you always know it's me?"

Hannah glanced again at Moishe and began making a *shushing* gesture with her index finger against her lips. Moishe, who it appeared couldn't care a fig about any desire she might have held for his silence, had gone into the *I'm-a-poor-starving-kitty song*. He began singing even louder now that Hannah had verbally confirmed that it was Delores on the other end of the phone.

Now he was softly meowing to her, interspersed with loud burbles—composed of equal parts purrs and chuckling meows—and was amusing himself by winding his body in and out of the space between her ankles. Hannah was positive that Moishe was not opposed one little bit to working on his *Grandma Delores's* sympathy for some extra food, and he knew full well that Delores would tell Hannah to take care of Moishe immediately, if she heard him acting up.

While Hannah was musing over Moishe's possible new career as a *master human manipulator*, she saw a movement out of the corner of her eye. Norman came strolling into the kitchen, moving silently on bare feet, still toweling his hair dry from his own shower. He was followed closely by Cuddles who, warned via Moishe—by *kitty telepathy*—that there was a sucker on the phone line, started mirroring Moishe's in-and-out movements.

Now Cuddles was weaving in and out between Norman's feet, almost causing him to trip over her, all the while singing a sad song of hunger and disappointment in her human.

Hannah was about to say something to Norman, and in fact had covered the bottom of her phone with her hand, when Delores inquired in a rather loud tone, "Are those my *grandkitties* crying? Oh my goodness, Hannah. Are you starving them now? Don't worry, my darlings, Grandmother will save you! We'll have all the *kitty num-nums* you can eat, and your grandfather has more ladybugs in the garden for you to chase."

Hannah tried valiantly to get a word in edgewise. "Mother, I was just . . ."

As the cats sang even louder now in the background, striving for the right tone to garner maximum sympathy, Delores cut her off sharply. "Hannah? Hannah! Are you there? Just listen to my poor babies now! Hannah, I insist you and Norman come over here for cocktail hour, which I might add is beginning immediately, and bring my poor, starving little *grandkitties* with you! We'll celebrate your latest triumph over crime with a toast or two, then all of us will go to the Red Velvet Room for a celebration dinner. They have an absolutely fascinating special called *A Quartet of Quiches*, and it promises to be divine! Hannah? Why are you still on the phone? Chop-chop!"

All Hannah could do was mutter, "Yes, Mother, we'll be there shortly." Bemused by her mother's proclamations, and looking at Norman with a shrug, she heard a sharp click and the other line disconnected.

"You heard the lady? Then we'd better get a move on," Norman said, a whimsical grin.

Hannah sighed. "I suppose we'd better go, and we'd also better bring the cats with us, or Mother will sue us for kitty abandonment. I'll go get the kitty carriers, and you pack up the beverages and kitty snacks!"

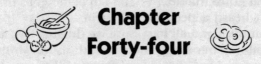

Chapter
Forty-four

It felt so soothing and cool in Norman's car. Just sitting there with the air-conditioning blowing out of the vents, Hannah could feel the flush leaving her face as the breeze generated by the AC cooled her down. When they'd first come out of the house and were walking toward the car, burdened down with the kitty carriers and various other things they were bringing for cocktail hour at Delores and Doc's, there had been so much humidity trapped in the outside air that they had both felt as though they were stepping into a sauna! Moishe and Cuddles had looked quite miserable when carried into the thick, damp outside air and had complained with a kitty duet of yowls. Hannah had been so uncomfortable herself, that even though she was wearing light cotton summer clothing, she'd thought seriously for a moment about calling her mother back to tell her that they just couldn't make it.

But now, everything was right with the world.

She was comfortable, the cats seemed calmer. She hadn't heard a peep out of them for more than ten minutes, and all had been made better by the car's air-conditioning. She glanced at the driver's seat and noticed that Norman, of course, was his usual stolid self, looking unflappable, calm and re-laxed in his dark blue jeans and his cream-colored, short-sleeved, button-down shirt. Hannah turned her head and peered into the back seat where Moishe and Cuddles had been placed with seat belts safely fastened around their carriers prior to leaving, and noticed that both cats were taking a little snooze.

A nap . . . What a lovely idea! She felt her eye-lids getting heavier and heavier until she just couldn't seem to keep them . . .

"Hannah? Hannah! Wake up, we're here!" A fa-miliar voice cut through her sleep like a pair of dressmaker shears biting through tissue paper, and Hannah realized it was Norman calling out her name.

"Just a second, hold on . . ." Hannah's voice trailed off as she fell back into her dreamlike state. That is, until an incredible burst of light seemed to burn its way straight through Hannah's closed eye-lids, then another flash came, shortly followed by a third! Hannah struggled to shake off her dream and wake up until she heard a series of thundering booms that threw her bolt upright in panic, hard up against her still-hooked seat belt. Opening her eyes as widely as she could, she saw brief flashes of things melded together like a collage. She saw glimpses of Norman, his usually calm face now look-ing distressed, as he stopped shaking her shoulder and leaned away from her quickly. She heard

Moishe and Cuddles caterwauling loudly, afraid and clawing away at the mesh of their cat carriers. She saw a white-hot bolt of lightning strike off in the distance, then heard a rumble of thunder which followed a mere ten seconds behind the lightning. And finally she saw, heard, and felt the impact of hailstones, which seemed to be as big as golf balls, slamming into the hood, windshield, and roof of Norman's car, stopping only when he finally pulled his car down the ramp and into the underground parking garage.

"I don't know about you, Hannah," Norman stated, with a note of relief creeping back into his voice, "but I am very, very happy that we're here instead of out there. I wouldn't have wanted to drive for even one minute more in that mess out there. It's been raining hard, and the wind has picked up a lot over the last fifteen minutes. There's a heck of a storm brewing up. On the way here, we passed a couple of phone poles knocked to the ground, and a downed power line!"

"Is this my friend Norman Rhodes I'm hearing?" Hannah teased him, while opening the door to the back seat and lifting out Moishe, still in his cat carrier. "Are you a Minnesotan?" she chided him. "You aren't so sweet that you'll melt."

"All right, you got me, Hannah. I guess it's just that . . . it got so darn quiet in the car. What with the radio out because our local station went down in the storm, with both cats napping, and you sleeping as hard as you were next to me, I got spooked a little," Norman told her, as Hannah unlocked the door to the lobby and pushed the button to call the elevator. After a minute, they heard a muted ding, the doors opened, and they climbed into the express elevator. Norman, who was deftly balancing a cat carrier in one hand, and holding the mini cooler he had brought from the house in the other hand, looked perplexed at first, until he laughed, shook his head, and then pushed the single button for the penthouse floor with the only option he could think of . . . his elbow.

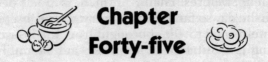

Chapter
Forty-five

"Hannah! Are you all right?" A slender body
with a long ponytail came hurtling at
Hannah so fast that she barely had time to put
Moishe's cat carrier down safely on the floor of the
penthouse. It was her youngest sister, Michelle,
and Hannah hugged her tightly for a moment.
They both stood there for a few seconds. Then another woman, this one a tad smaller than Michelle
and Hannah, and far blonder than either of her
sisters, came in to join them.

"All right, Hannah?" Andrea asked seriously.

"I'm great, Andrea, thanks," Hannah told her
cheekily. "Where's Mother?"

"Here I am, dear. It's good to see you," Delores
told her daughter.

"Hello, Norman. It's always a pleasure to have
you here, dear," the matriarch of the Swensens
said to him graciously.

"Hi, young man. How are you?" Doc appeared
from just behind Delores. "Everything all right?"

"Hello, Delores. Thanks for inviting us. It's been quite the day so far. Hi, Doc. Everything is just fine and we're glad to see you all tonight. Boy, it sure is getting nasty out there with the wind kicking up and all!"

"Well, at any rate, both of you are safe now." Delores looked at Norman, noticed that he was still holding the kitty carrier in one hand, and bending over to look at Cuddles, cried out, "My grandkitties are here! My babies! Don't you worry, little ones, your grandma and grandpa will take care of you right away." She straightened up and strode over to where Hannah had placed Moishe in his carrier on the floor, and cooed, "There's my handsome boy . . . you'll have so much fun tonight! You know we have lots of treats for you here, and everyone will be so pleased to see you."

Delores smiled at Hannah. "Let's take the kitties to the garden. Doc just bought a new batch of ladybugs he can release, and we can watch the kitties play while we have a cocktail."

"That sounds like a good idea!" Stephanie said, entering the room from the garden. "I was getting a little lonely out there by myself." She glanced over at Norman, who was beginning to move toward the garden with Cuddles. "Hi, Norman, I see you brought your little cooler with you. Are you making us another specialty drink for tonight's cocktail hour?"

Norman grinned back at her. "As a matter of fact, I did bring the makings for a new cocktail with me. I think you ladies will love it. Stephanie, I think it matches your sweater. I call it a *Pink Lemon Drop Martini*."

"And I have the proper glasses for it!" Delores

said. "They're in the garden bar. Follow me, everyone."

And they did . . . Hannah opened the kitty carriers and the cats charged out, headed straight for
the ladybugs that Doc had placed in the garden.

Norman headed to the bar with his cooler,
found the martini glasses Delores had mentioned,
and began to mix the drinks. Everyone watched
while Norman mixed the *Pink Lemon Drop Mar-
tinis,* his hands blurring as he added ingredients
and ice to the pitcher he found beneath the bar,
and then stirred it all carefully with a glass rod.
"This is a stirred martini, not shaken," Norman explained. "You don't want to bruise it, just mix it.
Mayor, you get to try the first one. Are you ready?"

Stephanie took the martini glass Norman
brought over to her, and smiled at him happily.
"Thank you, Norman! This looks fantastic."

Norman looked over at Delores and quickly
handed her a glass. "Here you are, Delores. You
didn't think I'd forget our hostess, did you?"

"I never had a doubt, Norman."

When everyone had a drink of some sort, Stephanie raised her glass high. "I know . . . Let's have a
toast. To all the business the Winnetka County All-
Star Baseball Tournament has brought to our local
economy. The Summer Solstice Sale is a huge suc-
cess! And I just learned that the final game of the
tournament will be shown on *national TV*! This
should really put Lake Eden on the map!"

The doorbell rang. "I'll get it, Mother," Hannah
said, hurrying to the door. She opened it to find
Mike and Stella standing there. "Hello, come on
in! I'm so glad you came. We're all in the garden

watching the cats stalk ladybugs, and trying out Norman's latest drink."

Mike and Stella followed Hannah into the garden. Everyone called out greetings to them as they made their way over to Norman at the bar.

"Hi, Mike. Hi, Stella," Norman said, from his position behind the bar. "Mike, I know what you want . . . Cold Spring Export, right? How about you, Stella? May I talk you into a Pink Lemon Drop Martini? It's my latest experiment in cocktails and it seems to be going over well."

Stella nodded in agreement, and Norman got their drinks for them quickly and efficiently.

"Mmm. This is really tasty, Norman," Stella said after her first sip. "Is there a hint of raspberry in there?"

"You're the first one to guess that, Stella, and you're right on target!"

"Enough with the small talk, Stella," Mike said loudly. "Tell everyone the good news!"

"Okay, Mike. Everyone, I've decided to move here to Lake Eden. I've rented the Hollenbeck sisters' condo. That's the one right across from you. Isn't it, Hannah?"

"Yes, it is. That's wonderful news, Stella," Hannah told her with a smile, as everyone came up to Stella and offered their congratulations.

"Okay, Hannah, we'd all like to know. How did you figure out Tony was the killer?" Bill asked.

"We didn't. Norman and I were just checking out his alibi. I knew Tony was the killer when he said that the murder weapon was a *baseball bat*! The only way he could have known that was if *he* had killed No-No. That information was never released to the public. Of course, there *was* one other suspect who knew the murder weapon was a baseball bat." Hannah turned to look at her mother.

"*Me?*" Delores squeaked. "You're not talking about *me*, are you, dear?"

Everyone laughed, and Hannah just smiled at Delores. "But, after all, Mother, you wanted to be the *prime suspect*, didn't you?"

There was a brilliant flash of white, which came from the clear dome above, and everyone's head swiveled up to look. That was quickly followed by two more flashes, each so bright that it left the viewers blinded for a moment, and a minute or so later a series of rumbling sounds shook the garden as the thunder caught up to the lightning.

"It's sure getting nasty out there," Mike proclaimed.

Delores raised her voice over the muted din of cocktail hour conversation and clapped her hands sharply once. "Attention, everyone. Finish your cocktails quickly. It's time to head down to the Red Velvet Room for dinner. I made a reservation for all of us, and that includes Mike and Stella, too!"

NORMAN'S PINK LEMON DROP MARTINI

Use either a cocktail shaker or a glass pitcher when mixing this recipe.

Norman's 1st Note: Whether you use a glass pitcher or a cocktail shaker for this recipe, you will stir this cocktail vigorously, rather than shake it. You will also need to mash the raspberries up in the bottom of the pitcher or shaker, before adding the ice, to achieve the correct color.

Ingredients:
   1 lemon wedge *(to moisten the rim of the glasses)*
   White *(granulated)* sugar *(to rim the glasses)*
   2 ounces of vodka
   ½ ounce Cointreau or Triple Sec
   1 ounce fresh squeezed lemon juice, or
      1 Tablespoon frozen lemonade concentrate
   1 ounce simple syrup
   7 or 8 fresh raspberries

Norman's 2nd Note: You should do the rimming of the glasses with sugar (see below)

before making any of the drinks. It will save time that way, plus it's hard to rim full glasses!

Directions:

Run a lemon wedge around the rim of a cocktail glass or margarita glass.

Dip the rim of the glass in the sugar to coat it for the drink.

Get a cocktail shaker and drop in the fresh raspberries.

Fill the cocktail shaker with ice cubes, ¾ of the way to the rim.

Place a lid on the shaker, or use another glass that will seal the top of the shaker.

Shake the raspberries and ice vigorously to bruise the raspberries and extract some of the color from them.

Add the vodka, Cointreau or Triple Sec, lemon juice, and simple syrup to the shaker.

If you find that the addition of these ingredients has dropped the ice level in the shaker sig-

nificantly, add more ice until it reaches ¾ of the way up the shaker.

Put the lid on the shaker and gently shake for 30 seconds.

Strain into the sugar-rimmed glass (this recipe may make 1, 2, or 3 cocktails' worth, depending on ice melt increasing the volume, or depending on the size of your glasses). Repeat for the rest of your guests or as needed.

Chapter Forty-six

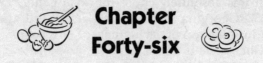

The Red Velvet Room was doing a brisk business and all the tables appeared to be full of guests, when their party walked in the door for dinner.

"Hello, Delores. Let's see now. Party of ten, right?" Georgina, their favorite waitress, came swooping up, effortlessly sliding her way between two tables overflowing with happy diners, and winding up in front of them.

"Sorry, Georgina, but it appears we're only nine tonight," Delores answered.

"That's okay. Mike's here. He'll eat enough for two."

After they were all seated at the largest table in the restaurant, and Georgina had taken their drink orders, Mike's phone rang.

"Excuse me," Mike said. "I have to take this." Mike stood up from the table and, speaking softly into his phone, quickly moved outside of the restaurant to better hear his caller.

Georgina came back to the table, rolling a cart

which was absolutely chock-full of quiche. "Let's see . . ." Georgina said, peering at the little signs stuck into the top of each quiche. "This is Spinach and Cheese. This one is Sausage and Cheese. This is Shrimp and Avocado. This is Traditional Quiche Lorraine. And this one just says MIKE. Speaking of Mike, where is he?"

"Here he comes now," Hannah said, looking toward the door. "Looks like he's done with his call."

Mike came back to the table, his features frozen into an emotionless mask. It was a look that Hannah knew well, and had always made her stomach clench. She called it the *I-Don't-Like-This* look, and it rarely heralded good news for anyone who saw it. "Norman . . . There's something I have to tell you," Mike said.

"What is it?"

"There is no easy way to say this . . . Lightning hit your house and caused a fire."

"The house is on fire? I have to get out there!" Norman began struggling to rise, but Mike put his hand on his shoulder, firmly holding him down in his chair.

"Calm down, Norman. It's going to be okay. The fire department has got everything under control there, and it looks like there's going to be very little structural damage. If you go out there, you'll just be in the way. They're the experts, let them do their jobs."

Norman visibly settled himself. "You're right, Mike. It's just . . . I want to do something, you know?"

"I understand, Norman. I'd feel the same way myself, but trust them to handle this."

Hannah shook her head in sympathy with Nor-

man, then a thought struck her. "Thank goodness
the cats are *here!*"

Norman looked at Hannah with a horrified look
on his face, then his face smoothed out as he
thought it all the way through. "You're right, Hannah. I'm so glad that the cats are here, with us!"

Mike sat down and noticed that there was a platter of quiche set directly in front of where he was
seated. It was topped with a sign sticking out, a sign
which read simply MIKE. Mike looked up quickly, his
eyes scanning the entire restaurant until he noticed Georgina looking straight at him, grinning,
and wiggling her fingers slowly in a wave.

Mike frowned at her and said in a low voice, "I
swear, someday I'll get even with that woman."

After several minutes, Mike's phone rang again.
"I have to take this," he said, standing up and moving away to take the call.

Mike returned to the table and sat down. His
face appeared to be set in stone as he methodically
began to eat his quiche. He did not say a word to
anyone, but Hannah noticed that his eyes were fo-
cused far, far off in the distance, as though he had
gotten lost in some deep, dark woods and was
searching desperately for a way back home.

"What is it, Mike?" Stella asked, recognizing the
disturbingly distant look in Mike's eyes.

"Norman, I'm so sorry. There is no easy way to
say this, but the fire out at your place apparently
hit a pocket of accelerant, and your house has
burned to the ground."

"My house!" Norman wailed, clearly distraught.
"Accelerant? What do you mean, Mike? I thought
it was all under control! Does that mean someone

set this fire deliberately? But why, Mike . . . ? Why would anyone want to burn down my house?"

There was a long silence following Norman's anguished question. Everyone looked stunned at the news. Even the happy diners talking in the background faded away. Mike's phone rang for a third time that evening, shattering the sudden silence. As Hannah hugged Norman in sympathy, the rest of the table watched Mike as the phone continued ringing. Mike remained calmly seated at the table, and after glancing briefly at the phone's screen, he answered.

"Okay . . . Okay . . . All right . . . Got it . . . thanks."

All heads turned first right and then left, as Bill's phone began to ring. Then a second or two later, so did Doc's.

As Doc and Bill answered their own phones, both of them rising from the table in a hurry as though they had to rush away to an emergency, Mike hung up his cell phone and turned to Hannah and Norman.

"Well, it looks like we know why, Norman," Mike growled, a grim expression twisting his handsome features. "The fire department just pulled a partially destroyed body out of the wreckage at the house. We won't know for certain until forensics examines the body, but it looks like the fire at your place was started to cover up a murder . . ."

INDEX OF RECIPES

Baking Conversion Chart

These conversions are approximate, but they'll work just fine for Hannah Swensen's recipes.

VOLUME

U.S.	Metric
½ teaspoon	2 milliliters
1 teaspoon	5 milliliters
1 Tablespoon	15 milliliters
¼ cup	50 milliliters
⅓ cup	75 milliliters
½ cup	125 milliliters
¾ cup	175 milliliters
1 cup	¼ liter

WEIGHT

U.S.	Metric
1 ounce	28 grams
1 pound	454 grams

OVEN TEMPERATURE

Degrees Fahrenheit	Degrees Centigrade	British (Regulo) Gas Mark
325 degrees F.	165 degrees C.	3
350 degrees F.	175 degrees C.	4
375 degrees F.	190 degrees C.	5

Note: Hannah's rectangular sheet cake pan, 9 inches by 13 inches, is approximately 23 centimeters by 32.5 centimeters.

A mild-mannered car salesman…a womanizing bartender . . . a beloved minister with a devoted family. Except for the fact that each of the murder victims is male, Minnesota police can't find a connection between the crimes. But that's because what links them can't be seen with the naked eye . . .

Losing everything can make a person do crazy things. No one knows that better than Connie Wilson. The shock of suddenly losing her fiancé, Alan, in a car accident, is almost too much bear . . . Until Connie comes up with a plan to stay close to Alan forever. And she's finally found just the man to help her. There's only one thing standing in her way: his wife. She's smart, beautiful, and has exactly what Connie desperately needs. Connie will just have to be smarter, more seductive—and stay one step ahead of a detective who's as determined to save her as Connie is to destroy her . . .

Please turn the page for an exciting sneak peek of Joanne Fluke's suspense thriller EYES available wherever print and e-books are sold!

PROLOGUE

Alan Stanford's smile disappeared with his last bite of turkey. It had been a pleasant Thanksgiving meal with his parents and his younger sister, but Alan's time was about up. He'd promised his girlfriend, Connie Wilson, he'd make the big announcement when dinner was over, and the traditional dessert was about to be served.

Alan's hands started to shake as the maid carried in the pumpkin pie. It was lightly browned on top and still warm from the oven, the way his father, the senior Mr. Stanford, preferred. When the maid presented it to his mother to slice, just as if she'd baked it herself, a wry smile flickered across Alan's face. It was doubtful that Mrs. Stanford had ever ventured as far as the kitchen, and the thought that his impeccably groomed, silver-haired mother might put on an apron and roll out a pie crust was patently ridiculous.

Rather than think about the words he'd soon have to utter, Alan considered the hypocrisy of etiquette. One praised the hostess for a delicious dinner, even if it had been catered. And one always called the daughter of a colleague a lady, whether she was one or not. The term "gentleman" referred to any man with enough money to make him socially desirable, and an estate was simply a home with enough land to house a condo complex. All the same, etiquette might save him some embarrassment tonight. There would be no scenes, no tears, no recriminations. After Alan had informed the family of his decision, his father would suggest he and Alan retire to the library where they'd discuss the matter in private.

"This is lovely, Mother." Beth, Alan's younger sister, was dutifully complimentary. "And I really do think it's much better warm, with chilled crème fraiche."

Alan's mother smiled. "Yes, dear. Your father prefers it this way. Another piece, Ralph?"

"Just a small one." Alan's father held out his plate. "You know I'm watching my cholesterol."

Alan waited while his mother cut another piece of pie. Nothing ever changed at the Stanford mansion. His father always said he was watching his cholesterol, and he always had a second serving of pie. Every Thanksgiving was exactly the same, but Alan was about to change the order of their lives. By next Thanksgiving, there would be two more guests at the oval table. The rules of etiquette were clear. They'd be obligated to invite his wife and his son.

There were three bites remaining on his father's plate, perhaps four if he ate all the crust. Alan knew how a condemned man felt as his father's fork cut and carried each bite, one by one, to his mouth. The white linen napkin came up, to dab at the corners of his father's lips, and Alan took a deep breath. He'd promised Connie. He couldn't delay any longer.

"I have an announcement to make." Alan's voice was a little too loud because of his effort not to sound tentative. "Connie and I are getting married."

There was complete silence around the table. It lasted for several seconds, and then Beth gave a hesitant smile. "That's wonderful, Alan. Isn't that wonderful, Mother?"

"Oh . . . yes." His mother's voice was strained, and Alan noticed that all the color had left her face. He could see the lines of her makeup, the exact spot where the edge of the blush met the foundation. "Yes, indeed. That's wonderful, dear."

Was it really going to be this easy? Alan turned to look at his father. The older man was frowning as he pushed back his chair. "Superb dinner, Marilyn. Alan, why don't you join me in the library for a cognac?"

It wasn't an invitation; it was an order. Alan slid his chair back and stood up. Then he walked to the end of the table to kiss his mother on the cheek. "Thank you, Mother. Dinner was excellent."

"Coming, Alan?"

His father looked impatient, so Alan followed him to the second-floor library. He accepted a snifter of cognac, even though he wasn't fond of its taste, then waited for all hell to break loose.

"Sit down." Alan's father motioned toward the two wing chairs in front of the fireplace. A fire had been laid. As it burned cheerfully, it gave off the scent of cherry wood. Naturally, the fire was real. The fireplace was made of solid river rock; no expense had been spared when his grandfather had built the Stanford mansion.

Alan's father took a sip of his cognac and set it down on the table. He then turned to Alan, frowning. "Now that we're away from the ladies, suppose you tell me what *that* was all about."

"Connie and I are getting married." It was difficult, but Alan met his father's eyes. "Don't worry, Father. I don't expect you to approve, or even understand, but I love Connie and I want to spend the rest of my life with her."

Ralph Stanford sighed and then shook his head. "Now, son, I'm sure she's a fine girl, but you can't be serious about actually bringing her into our family."

"I'm very serious." Alan managed not to drop his eyes. "We're getting married next week, Father. It's all arranged. Of course we'd be delighted if you'd come to the wedding, but Connie doesn't expect it and neither do I."

Alan's father sighed again. "All right, son. I'd hoped I wouldn't have to resort to this, but I see that I have no other choice."

Alan watched as his father walked to the antique desk and opened the center drawer. Ralph Stanford's mouth was set in a grim line as he handed Alan a typed report in a blue binding.

"Read this. There may be some facts about your intended that you don't know."

Alan's hands were steady as he opened the binder and started to read. Everything was here, from Connie's illegitimate birth to her mother's years on welfare. The investigator hadn't mentioned the name of Connie's father. That was too bad. Connie would have liked to know. But the report went into detail about the man Connie's mother had married, how he'd abused her and forced her into prostitution to support his drug habit, how she'd been an alcoholic.

It was a wonder that Connie was so kind and loving, coming from a background like hers. Alan sighed as he read about how her stepfather had repeatedly molested her, had even offered her to his friends.

Alan knew all about Connie's past, how she'd run away the night of her fifteenth birthday, lived with a series of men, worked in a topless club as a dancer, and finally saved enough money to finish a secretarial course. Alan had met Connie at work, when she'd come in as a temporary replacement for one of the secretaries. She'd agreed to move in with him only after she'd told him the story of her life.

When he'd finished the last page and closed the report, Alan handed it back to his father. Then he waited. The ball was in his father's court.

Ralph Stanford cleared his throat. "Well, son?"

"Don't pay him, Father." Alan managed not to grin.

"What?"

"Don't pay this detective. He left out the part about Pete Jones, the truck driver Connie lived with for almost a year. And he didn't find out about the job Connie took in a massage parlor on lower Hennepin."

"You knew about all this? Still you want to marry this woman?"

Alan smiled. His father looked utterly deflated,

the first time Alan had seen him like this. "It's not a question of *wanting* to marry Connie. I'm *going* to marry her. And nothing you can say will stop me!"

"But . . . why?"

"Because we love each other." His father seemed to have aged in the past few minutes, and that made Alan feel bad. But he'd promised Connie he'd tell him everything, so he had another blow to deliver. "Connie's pregnant. We didn't plan it, and she suggested abortion, but I wouldn't agree. She only did it to please me. She wants this baby just as much as I do."

Alan's father swallowed hard. A vein in his forehead was throbbing as he leaned forward to put a hand on Alan's arm. "Listen to me, son. You're falling into the oldest trap in the world!"

Alan shook his head. "It's not a trap. I'm the one who insisted that Connie marry me. She knew you wouldn't approve, and she didn't want to cause trouble in the family. She was willing to leave and raise the baby herself."

As Ralph Stanford remained silent, Alan's hopes rose. Was it possible he'd convinced his father? Would the family accept Connie and the baby?

The library was so quiet Alan could hear the individual flakes of snow as they blew against the windows. It was turning icy as the night approached; the temperature had fallen to single digits. Each gust of wind was followed by sounds like those of a snare drum as snow turned to sleet hit the glass panes.

At last Alan's father nodded. "All right. The two of you will continue to live in the condo, where she'll have every advantage. The family will support her, pay her medical bills, and provide any help she needs. When she gives birth, we'll do a paternity test; then you'll have our permission to marry."

"What!" Alan was so shocked, he stood up. "A paternity test would be an insult to Connie—and to me! I'm telling you, Father, this baby is mine!"

"Perhaps. But we can't take the chance that you're wrong. Just remember, son, it's a wise man who knows the father of his own child."

"You're crazy!" Alan was so upset, he found he was fumbling for words. "Listen to me, Connie would never . . . I can't believe that you'd actually . . ."

Alan's father rose and took his arm. "Calm down. I'm not accusing her of anything. I'm just saying that before you commit yourself, it's best to make certain. If it'll make you feel better, we won't even tell her about the paternity test. Our own doctor will do it in the hospital and will keep it strictly confidential."

"There won't be any paternity test." Alan's eyes were hard as he pulled away. "I'll give you until this time tomorrow to make a decision. You'll accept my wife and my child—welcome them into the family—or you'll never see me again!"

Alan's hands were shaking as he pulled out of the driveway. For the first time in his life, he'd taken a stand. He should feel proud that he hadn't let his father browbeat him into submission, but

he didn't, not yet. He was too furious about his father's accusation to experience any emotion but
rage.

How dare his father suspect Connie of tricking
him into marriage! What gall to say that the baby
might not be his! Alan was so upset he took the
curve a little too fast and his Porsche started to
skid on the slippery pavement.

He knew better than to stomp on the brakes.
He'd grown up in Minnesota and was accustomed
to winter driving. He steered in the direction of
the skid, gained control of the powerful car, and
touched the brakes lightly to slow. The Stanford
mansion was up in the hills, overlooking Lake
Minnetonka. The downhill road was steep and
curving, and the snow had turned to sleet. If he
didn't pay attention to his driving, he could skid
through the guardrail on his way home.

Connie would be waiting for him at the condo.
Thinking about her made Alan's anger begin to
subside. He wouldn't tell her about his father's reaction. He'd just say he'd given the family until tomorrow to work things out. And he certainly
wouldn't mention the accusations his father had
made; Connie would be crushed. It was up to him
to protect her from his family.

Alan switched on the car's stereo. Connie's favorite CD started to play, and he smiled. That was
when he noticed the lights in his rearview mirror.

A truck was bearing down on him, following
much too closely. The driver honked his air horn,
several rapid blasts to signify that he wanted to
pass, but there was no place to pull over on the
narrow, two-lane road.

The truck driver hit his air horn again, one long

blast that shattered the stillness of the night. His emergency lights were blinking on and off, and Alan knew what that meant. The driver had lost his brakes and was heading for the escape lane about a mile ahead.

Alan pressed down on the gas pedal. He had no other choice. If the driver had lost control of the truck, he'd be rear-ended.

The next few moments were tense. Alan screeched around the curves, hoping he could out distance the runaway truck. He came out of the curves much too fast for a road partially covered with icy snow, but the exit for the escape lane was just ahead.

Alan watched in his rearview mirror as the truck barreled onto the escape lane. This stretch of roadway climbed gradually uphill, with sand traps to slow the truck. At the end was an absorbent barrier, especially designed to stop a runaway truck with minimal damage.

"Thank God!" Alan reached up to wipe his forehead. Sweat was streaming into his eyes, and he was almost weak with relief. If the truck had rear-ended him, they'd both be dead. But he'd made it through the curves. Now everything was just fine.

There was a sound like a gunshot, and Alan's Porsche swerved sharply, almost wrenching the wheel from his hands.

His right front tire had blown. He was heading straight for the ditch!

He fought the wheel with all his strength, struggling to control the skid. It worked, and he was just thanking his lucky stars, when the unexpected happened again. There was another explosion, and his left front tire blew out.

Alan wore an expression of shocked disbelief as his Porsche swerved in the opposite direction. Then he was crashing through the guardrail, hurtling out into space, rolling end over end to the bottom of the hill.

When the Porsche hit the rocks at the bottom of the ravine, it flipped over several times, coming to rest on its roof, its racing tires spinning uselessly in the air. Alan was trapped in the expensive shell of his luxury car. He didn't hear a passing motorist call out to him, didn't smell the stench of gasoline or experience the salty, slightly metallic taste of his own blood. He didn't see the paramedics flip open his wallet to discover his organ donor card, didn't feel careful hands pull him from the wreck. The quick action of the well-trained emergency team kept his heart pumping blood and his lungs taking in oxygen, but the brain of the man who had been Alan Stanford showed when checked at the hospital, a flat, unending line on the graph—death.

Chapter One

Connie Wilson frowned as she stared out at the snow-covered courtyard. The condo association had decorated for Christmas, and this was the night they'd turned on the lights. She had watched them from her third-floor windows, draping the tall, stately pines with strings of multicolored bulbs. Now that the lights were on, the gently falling snow reflected all the colors, but Connie was too worried to appreciate the lovely sight. She didn't even smile as she spotted the life-size sleigh nestled under the trees with the illuminated figures of Santa and his elves. It was almost ten, and Alan still wasn't home.

He'd never stayed at his parents this late before. The Thanksgiving dinner had begun at three, and meals at the Stanford mansion were always served on time. Even with all the courses associated with the traditional Thanksgiving feast, they must have been finished by four or four-thirty.

Alan had promised to make his announcement

right after dessert. Perhaps that had been as late as five, but there was no way the obligatory snifter of cognac, sipped with his father in the library, could have taken more than an hour. Even if Ralph Stanford had objected to the marriage, as Connie was sure he had, father and son wouldn't have argued this long.

So what was keeping Alan? She paced back and forth across the white carpet, doing her best to think positive thoughts. Alan loved her. She was sure of that. And he was determined to marry her, with or without his parents' permission. He had been ready to slay dragons for her when she'd kissed him good-bye; nothing Alan's parents could say or do would sway him.

And he wasn't the type to stop off for a drink. He always called her when he knew he'd be late. Even if there'd been a terrible family fight, he would come straight home to her. But what if his parents hadn't objected? What if he had convinced them that marriage to her was acceptable? Was it even remotely possible that he was with his family right now, planning the wedding?

Connie thought about that for a moment, then shook her head. Alan had told her all about his family, and she was sure the Stanfords would never approve of her as a prospective daughter-in-law. They were probably laying down the law right now, telling Alan that if he went ahead with this unsuitable marriage, they would disown him.

She pictured Alan coming in the door, his face lined with worry. She'd put on coffee, so it would be ready when he got home. He loved a good cup of coffee. One was bound to make him feel better.

Connie measured out the espresso beans, put

them in the electric grinder. She loved coffee, too, and she adored the espresso Alan had taught her to make in his machine. But the doctor had told her that too much caffeine during a pregnancy could cause problems, so she had decided to give up coffee until after the baby was born.

There were so many things to remember. Connie frowned slightly as she glanced at the list she'd tacked up on the kitchen bulletin board. No caffeine, no alcohol, a high-fiber diet, moderate daily exercise, and plenty of rest. She was doing everything her doctor had recommended. Her friends from the past would never believe the fun-loving exotic dancer had stopped drinking, toned down her makeup, and let her bleached blond hair grow out to its natural color. Connie now looked like the girl next door, wholesome, sweet, and totally natural.

When the coffee was ready to brew, she went into the huge living room. She glanced at the clock and sighed again. It was almost ten-thirty. Should she call Alan at his parents' house to make sure everything was all right? She debated for a moment, even going so far as to pick up the phone, but she replaced the receiver in its cradle without punching in the number for the Stanford mansion. A call from her might rock the boat, and that was the last thing she wanted to do.

She sat down on the couch and stared at the snow falling outside. She was just thinking how pretty it was when the telephone rang. She reached out to it, crossing her fingers for luck. It just had to be Alan!

"Mrs. Stanford?"

The voice sounded official, and Connie could

hear other voices in the background. "No. I'm not Mrs. Stanford. Is this a sales call?"

"No, this is Central Dispatch, Minneapolis Police. Do you know an Alan Stanford?"

"Yes." Connie swallowed hard. "Alan's my fiancé. Is something wrong?"

"Two officers are on their way to talk to you. They should be there any minute."

"But . . . why? What's happened?"

"Just relax, Miss . . . ?"

Connie clutched the phone so hard, her knuckles were white. "Connie Wilson. But can't you tell me—"

"I'm sorry." The voice interrupted. "I'm just a dispatcher, and I don't know. They just told me to call this number to confirm that someone was home."

Connie's head was spinning. Had Alan been arrested? She was about to ask, even though the dispatcher probably wouldn't know, when she heard a sharp knocking. "Someone's at the door. It must be your officers."

"Please let them in. And thank you, Miss Wilson."

There was a click, and Connie dropped the phone back into its cradle. Her legs were shaking as she rushed across the carpet to answer the door.

"Miss Wilson?" The older officer flashed his badge. "May we come in, please?"

"Yes. Of course." Connie stood to the side so both men could enter. "But . . . how do you know my name?"

"The dispatcher told us. We were in radio contact. Please sit down, Miss Wilson."

Connie had a wild urge to refuse. If she didn't

sit down, perhaps they would leave. And then Alan would come in the door, and—

"Miss Wilson? Please."

The older officer gestured toward the couch. Connie sat. "What is it? What's wrong?"

"There's been an accident, Miss Wilson."

The blood rushed from Connie's face, and she swallowed hard. "But . . . Alan's all right, isn't he?"

"I'm afraid not." The older officer shook his head. "Do you have anyone who can come to stay with you, Miss Wilson?"

"No. There's no one. But I don't need anyone to stay here. I have to go to the hospital to see Alan!"

"There's no need for that, Miss Wilson."

"Alan's dead?" Connie's eyes widened. "No! That can't be true!"

"I'm afraid it is. Why don't you let us call someone for you. A friend? Family? You shouldn't be alone at a time like this."

"No!" Connie shook her head so hard, she became dizzy. "You've got the wrong person, that's all. It was someone else. You just thought it was Alan. Alan's alive! I know he is!"

"Calm down, Miss Wilson."

The older officer tried to put an arm around her shoulders, but Connie shrugged it off. "You'll see. It's a mistake, that's all. Alan'll be coming through that door any second, and we'll all have a good laugh."

"Miss Wilson . . . I know how hard this is to accept, but we made positive identification at the scene."

"Nooooo!" Connie started to sob, and tears

poured down her face. Alan couldn't be dead! Not Alan! Then she was hit by a terrible cramping. She screamed in pain.

"Miss Wilson . . . Connie. Please." The older officer looked terribly concerned. "Are you ill?"

She opened her mouth to tell him, but nothing came out. She felt so weak she could barely move, and dark spots swirled in front of her eyes. Another cramp struck, as if it were trying to split her in two, and she looked down to see that the couch was wet with blood.

"The . . . the baby! Save the baby!" Connie forced herself to choke out the words. She heard the younger officer radio for an ambulance, but just as he was giving the address, everything went black.

Visit our website at
KensingtonBooks.com
to sign up for our newsletters, read
more from your favorite authors, see
books by series, view reading group
guides, and more!

BOOK CLUB

BETWEEN THE CHAPTERS

Become a Part of Our
Between the Chapters Book Club
Community and Join the Conversation

Betweenthechapters.net

Submit your book review for a chance to win exclusive
Between the Chapters swag you can't get anywhere else!
https://www.kensingtonbooks.com/pages/review/